WILD MAN'S CURSE

ALSO BY SUSANNAH SANDLIN

Storm Force

The Penton Legacy series

Redemption
Absolution
Omega
Allegiance

The Collectors series

Lovely, Dark, and Deep
Deadly, Calm, and Cold

WRITTEN AS SUZANNE JOHNSON

Christmas in Dogtown
Pirateship Down

The Sentinels of New Orleans series

Royal Street
River Road
Elysian Fields
Pirate's Alley

WILD MAN'S CURSE

A Wilds of the Bayou Novel

SUSANNAH SANDLIN

Montlake
Romance

Published by Montlake Romance, Seattle.

www.apub.com

Amazon, the Amazon logo, and Montlake Romance are trademarks of Amazon.com, Inc., or its affiliates.

ISBN-13: 9781503934740
ISBN-10: 1503934748

Cover design by Michael Rehder

Printed in the United States of America

PROLOGUE

The bones said death was comin', and the bones never lied.

Eva Savoie leaned back in the rocking chair and pushed it into motion on the uneven wide-plank floor of the one-room cabin. Her *grand-père* Julien had built the place more than a century ago, pulling heavy cypress logs from the bayou and sawing them, one by one, into the thick planks she still walked across every day.

She had never known Julien Savoie, but she knew of him. The curse that had stalked her family for three generations had started with her grandfather and what he'd done all those years ago.

What he'd brought with him to Whiskey Bayou with blood on his hands.

What had driven her daddy to shoot her mama, and then himself, before either turned forty-five.

What had led Eva's brother, Antoine, to drown in the bayou only a half mile from this cabin, leaving a wife and infant son behind.

What stalked Eva now.

The bones said death was coming and, once Eva was gone, the curse should go with her. No one else knew the secrets of Julien Savoie and this cabin and that box full of sin he'd dug out of the bayou mud back in Isle de Jean Charles.

Might take a while, but sin catches up with you. Always had. Always would. And the curse had driven Eva to sin. Oh yes, she had sinned.

She'd known her reckoning would catch up with her, although it had taken a good, long time. She'd turned seventy-eight yesterday, or was it eighty? She couldn't remember for sure, and the bones said it didn't matter now.

On the scarred wooden table before Eva sat three burning candles that filled the room with the soft, soothing glow of melting tallow. She'd made them herself, infusing them with the oil of the fragrant lilies that every spring spread a bright-green carpet over the lazy, brown water of the bayou. The tools of her ritual sat on an ancient square of tanned hide passed down through generations of holy ones, of those blessed by the gods with the ability to throw the bones.

A small mound of delicate chicken bones, yellowed and fragile from age, lay inside the circle of light cast by the candles. Daylight would come in an hour or so, but Eva didn't expect to last that long. Death was even now making his way toward her.

She leaned forward, wincing at the stab of pain in her lower back. Since the first throw of the bones had whispered her fate two days ago, she'd been cleaning. Scrubbed the floor, worn smooth by decades of bare feet. Washed the linens, folding them in neat piles in a drawer at the bottom of the old pie safe. Discarded most of the food in the little refrigerator that sat in the corner. Dragged the bag of trash down the long, overgrown drive past LeRoy's old 1970 Chevy pickup that she still drove up to Houma for groceries and such once a month. Left the white bag at the side of the parish road for the weekly trash collection.

She'd spit on LeRoy's truck as she passed it because she couldn't spit on the man who'd bought it. He was long gone.

Now the cleaning had been finished. Whoever discovered her raggedy old body wouldn't find a mess, not in Eva Savoie's house.

A few minutes ago, with the old cabin as clean as she was capable of making it, she'd thrown the bones one last time. Part of her hoped they'd read different, hoped she'd be granted a few more days of grace.

But the bones still whispered death. Eva accepted it, and she sat, and she waited. At least the girl, Celestine, would inherit a cleaned-up house. The girl, Antoine's granddaughter, knew nothing of the secrets, nothing of the curse. Eva had made sure of that.

Eva figured it would be a game warden who found her. Since the thirty-day gator season had started a week ago they'd passed back and forth on Whiskey Bayou at least once or twice a day, their sharp eyes scanning the waters for anybody up to no good, their boats moving steadily through the still, dark bayou. If years past were any sign, every few days one of the wardens would knock on her door all polite, askin' if she needed anything. She always said no.

LeRoy used to say the game wardens kept honest folks from eating, kept them from earning a living because of all their rules and laws about what you could hunt and how much fish you could catch. Eva figured while there was an argument to be made for that, they also helped protect the old ways of life. Couldn't tell LeRoy that, though. Couldn't tell old LeRoy nothing. She'd wasted too many breaths trying.

If the game wardens came round this time, she wouldn't be alive to answer. Whoever drew that unlucky straw, well, he'd find her where she sat.

Eva waited for her heart to fail—that seemed to be her most likely way to go. As she rocked, she noted each steady beat, biding her time for the instant when the *thump-thump-thump* would falter and her breath would catch, then stop. She reckoned it would hurt a little, but what if it did? The curse had doled out worse ends to those who came before her.

She'd doled out worse herself.

The buzz of a boat's motor sounded from outside the cabin, faint but growing louder. Wardens on patrol already, most likely.

The boat's engine increased to a deafening buzz, finally coming to an abrupt stop so near it had to be right outside her door. Silence filled the room once again until, through her bones, she felt the thud of someone jumping onto the porch that wrapped around the cabin. The porch formed the platform on which the house sat, linking it to the spit of land behind it when the water was normal. When storms blew through, it provided an island on which the cabin could sit or, if need be, float.

As heavy footfalls crossed the porch, Eva struggled to her feet. Every pop and crackle of her joints knifed streaks of pain through her limbs as they protested the cleaning they'd done, followed by the sitting.

Too bad the game warden hadn't stopped a little later, after she was gone. She didn't like to think of her body having to bake in the hot cabin for days before anyone found her.

But the curse was what it was, and the bones said what they said.

The knock, when it came, was soft, and Eva reached the door with the help of a sturdy cane she'd carved herself. Opening the door, she squinted into the glare of a flashlight that was almost blinding after the soft light of the candles. She peered up at a young man with eyes that gleamed from beneath the hood of a jacket. He was not a game warden, and it was too hot for a jacket.

"Who are you?" Her voice cracked. She knew who he was. He was Death.

"The devil come to pay you a visit, Eva." The man's voice was smooth as silk, smooth as a lie, smooth as death itself. "And you know what the devil wants."

She knew what he wanted, and she knew the only way to end the curse was to deny him.

She'd been granted no easy passing by the Savoie curse after all, but she *would* die today to end it.

The bones never lied.

CHAPTER 1

A pair of dark, reptilian eyes and a gray, bony snout rose above the waterline two feet from the bow of the grayish-brown mud boat, the smallest, most nimble of the Louisiana Department of Wildlife and Fisheries' fleet. From the boat's hiding spot deep in the shadows, below a stand of trees overhanging Whiskey Bayou, Senior Enforcement Agent Gentry Broussard tracked the alligator's movement.

A lively little six-footer, judging by the length of the head, and the third alligator Gentry had spotted since having eased the boat into its spot an hour before sunrise, within sight of two traplines laid the night before. With any luck, he'd have a poacher in custody before the day heated up enough to make hell look like the Arctic. Mosquitoes the size of B-52s had already begun the process of eating him alive as they frolicked on the exposed skin of his arms.

Since the nearest line was pulled taut this morning with the bait end underwater, a gator likely sat on the bayou's muddy bottom with that pronged hook lodged in its gullet. It was going to be one pissed-off reptile.

Gentry pitied the animals, but he understood why the state let hunters trap and kill gators for thirty days at the end of each summer.

It kept the gator population from growing out of control, true enough, but mostly, the valuable meat and hides made up a big chunk of local hunters' annual income. It was good for the economy, and the gators were more than plentiful.

So Gentry had no problem with the licensed hunter who'd set the lines the night before under his supervision—the guy had been here in Terrebonne Parish his whole life, worked hard, followed the rules. But the poacher was another matter. If he showed up this morning, Gentry would take him down. In this world of living close to the land, there was no place for thieves trying to steal what others spent grueling, dirty hours to earn.

Nothing came easy here at the bottom of one of the biggest wetlands and swamps in the United States, a truth woven into the twisting, isolated tangle of the lower Atchafalaya Basin and the marsh and wetlands stretching like fragile bits of lace into the Gulf of Mexico. Places like Terrebonne Parish. Places like Whiskey Bayou.

Places where a bored, sleep-deprived agent like Gentry Broussard might work off some energy. All he needed was one dumb jackass to show up and claim his illegal prize.

Gentry settled back in the shallow boat behind its curtain of hackberry limbs, raised his binoculars, and followed the gator's progress. It glided in a graceful arc across the narrow bayou, leaving a V-shaped wake. Before reaching the opposite bank, the reptile dropped into deeper water and out of sight.

For the past three days, Gentry and the bulk of Louisiana's Wildlife and Fisheries agents, including his enforcement unit, had been doing water-safety checks because of the Labor Day weekend. Now that things were settling back toward normal, it should be a slow day, even for a Friday.

Normally, slow would be fine with Gentry, but with three days off looming ahead of him, the more energy he could work off during this shift, the better—even if it meant chasing a wild boar or a wilder human who'd drunk too much before taking his boat on a joyride down the bayou south of Montegut. He needed to wear himself out before ending his shift and coming face-to-face with a different kind of chase—his own demons, hot on his heels.

Every day off provided a distinct chance the demons might win.

As the day dawned, the veil of gray shadows thinned into light. Gentry glanced up and down the bayou. His gaze ticked across a downed tree. A white ibis stretched its graceful neck out of the tall, dense sawgrass. A narrow path of beaten-down foliage revealed where a gator had slid into or slithered out of the water. A few hundred yards to Gentry's left sat old Eva Savoie's cabin, its wood weathered and grayed from age and humidity and storms. She made a little money each year by leasing out her corner of the bayou to one or two hunters for gator season, and thinning out the gators kept her safer as well.

Some said that the old Cajun woman was a voodoo priestess, others that she was a witch. All agreed she chose to speak little distinguishable English, only the thick Cajun French patois that the old-timers here clung to with an almost religious fervor. Most could understand and speak English perfectly well.

She had company this morning, though; the small boat tied up at the corner of her porch looked like something that got dragged in by the last hurricane.

A muffled thump from the cabin sent an itch of unease up the back of Gentry's neck, and he scratched at it absentmindedly as he focused his binoculars for a better look at that boat. It bobbed in the water, empty. Whoever was visiting old Eva hadn't planned to fish or hunt. No ice chest. No life jacket. Not even an empty candy wrapper, judging by what he could see from across the bayou.

Gentry didn't like it. His gut didn't like it.

However, everyone agreed Eva Savoie was a woman who would as soon take a knife to you as welcome you into her home, if she didn't like your looks. He was probably just starting to feel the exhaustion he'd been seeking.

Gentry's lieutenant, Warren Doucet, always told his agents to check on Eva if they were working the area, and Gentry had stopped in a few times in the past. She was physically frail but mentally sharp. She'd won him over when she said she remembered his daddy as *un bon garde-chasse*, a fine game warden, even though it had been two decades since agent Hank Broussard had died of a heart attack in their home in Dulac, twenty miles west of here.

Hank's youngest son, Gentry, had just turned twelve. He'd idolized his dad and didn't remember a day of his life when he hadn't wanted to be a wildlife agent.

Gentry didn't believe in voodoo, and he didn't believe in witches. Crazy old Cajun women with knives and guns were another matter. None of the licensed local hunters—a wary lot regardless of their outlook on voodoo or witchcraft—underestimated the power of a pissed-off woman with a shotgun. Not a one of them would dare set a gator line within sight of Eva Savoie's front door without a license, much less steal someone else's gator.

That meant Gentry's poacher was either one of the hunters who came in from North Louisiana or Texas for the season and hadn't figured out the system yet, or it was some greedy dumb-ass amateur. If the poacher hadn't shown up by seven, the licensed hunter would claim his gators and Gentry could check on old Eva before finishing out his shift farther down the bayou.

Or maybe not. He cocked his head as the faint buzz of an outboard motor echoed over the still water, then closed his eyes to focus on the sound. It was coming in fast from the west, off Bayou Terrebonne.

The seconds it took the boat to appear seemed like an hour, but Gentry finally spotted it rounding a turn from the juncture of Terrebonne and Whiskey Bayous.

He raised the binoculars again, moving slowly to avoid detection. The newcomer killed his engine and stood up, using a pole to propel his boat in silence toward the gator line. The guy looked up and down the bayou, pausing to stare at the Savoie cabin. The poacher was alone, didn't have a flotation device anywhere Gentry could see, and wore an old, long-barreled pistol in a holster on his hip like he was freaking John Wayne.

Looked like Gentry had found his dumb-ass amateur.

September had begun like August had ended, hot enough for Gentry to be sweating inside his summer uniform: dark olive-green shirt with "LDWF Enforcement Division" patches on the sleeves, and uniform pants in the same color. Easy to move around in, but guaranteed to induce a sweat in places one didn't discuss in polite company. And that was before you took into account the twenty pounds of gear hanging off his belt.

Gentry squelched the urge to stop the guy immediately and forced his gaze to stay with the binoculars. No serious law had been broken yet, and that itch at the back of his neck over Eva Savoie's visitor hadn't given him a reason to ignore his original mission.

Gentry settled into an easy crouch and watched as the vessel, a beat-up waste of aluminum with a torn tarp stretched on poles above it for shade, glided toward the gator line. The potential poacher leaned over the line and appeared to be wrestling his prize to the surface. Patient, Gentry eased out his cell phone and snapped a few shots of the poacher at work, then texted the nearest fellow enforcement agents patrolling the parish this morning: *GOT 1. STAND BY.* If they didn't get another text in two or three minutes, they'd know either Gentry had made an arrest or things had gone south. Either way, they'd come in for backup.

When everybody and his dog in the parish had a firearm of some kind and the temperature was hot enough to fry brains before noon, it didn't take much to send things south.

After a few minutes, the guy finally pulled the pistol from its holster and maneuvered to get a good shot at the only place one could kill a gator with a bullet—a small, vulnerable area at the back of the thick, bony plate across the animal's head. He took two shots. For a moment, Gentry feared the gator was going to pull John Wayne off the side of the boat, which meant he'd have to rush over there and save the idiot. Finally, despite such violent thrashing from the angry gator that torrents of water sprayed over the boat's ragged canopy, the poacher delivered the kill shot.

All he needed was to wrestle the dead alligator into the boat, and Gentry would have him.

As soon as the poacher tugged the gator's massive head over the side and appeared to be winning the fight to haul the heavy reptile the rest of the way in, Gentry used an oar to push the mud boat from its hiding spot, then pressed the switch to start the quiet trolling motor he'd used to get here from the little boat launch off Montegut Road. With an outboard, it was hard to sneak up on anybody.

The poacher was so intent on pulling at the gator that Gentry's approach didn't register until he'd gotten within a few yards. Last thing you wanted to do was surprise a guy with a pistol, even if the gun was back in its holster, so Gentry settled his shotgun into an easy carry in the crook of his left arm. It was a hold he could quickly turn to shoot if needed, and most people didn't want to argue with a shotgun.

He cupped his right hand around his mouth. "State wildlife agent. Need some help?"

The poacher stopped, turned, got a gator-in-headlights look on his face, and promptly sat on the reptile still hanging half in and half out of the boat. As if his scrawny ass could hide what looked like a well-fed nine-footer.

"Hellfire and damnation!" was the guy's first reaction, then he reconsidered. "Yessir, can ya help me pull dis big boy into da boat? Looks like I got a good'un to start da day."

Gentry put on his thickest South Louisiana drawl to match the poacher's. Having grown up across a few miles of bayou in Dulac usually won him a little trust and sometimes kept things from getting ugly. "That'll bring some money, for sure. This your first time huntin' round here?" The poacher paused to consider his answer while Gentry set his shotgun on the floor of the mud boat and stepped into the rust bucket. He moved his right hand toward the .45 in his own holster and flipped open the snap, just to remind John Wayne that he wasn't the only badass in the boat. Gentry might not have the shotgun, but he still had plenty of firepower within easy reach.

Moving slowly, he gave the poacher time to devise a strategy while he helped the man pull the gator from the water. It landed on its back with a thud, long claws still flexing. Gentry watched it a second to make sure the movement was a postmortem reflex. It wouldn't be the first time a stunned gator awoke and made breakfast out of a careless hunter's arm or leg.

The poacher strapped tape around the gator's jaws, moving with an exaggerated slowness that told Gentry he was hiding something. "Usually, I hunt down on Lac Chien," he finally said. "But thought I'd try me a new spot this year."

Gentry nodded. "Sure, I understand. Would you mind if I took a look at your hunting license? No worries; just standard procedure."

John Wayne cleared his throat again as he tapped on the pockets of his jeans. "Why, you know, I ain't got it with me. Left it on da table back at home, way down da bayou near Cocodrie. Want me to call my old lady, have her bring it out here? Take her a while."

Gentry nodded. "Sure, I got time. Go ahead and call her."

The poacher patted his pocket again. "Don't seem to have my phone."

"You can use mine." Gentry held out his phone.

"Forgot—she ain't home dis morning. Guess you'll have to write me a ticket fer not havin' no license."

Gentry pulled his ticket book from his pocket. "Yes, sir, and I also will have to take possession of that alligator." He paused. "Sir, have you been drinking this morning?"

The poacher looked at the huge alligator and pondered this unhappy turn of events for a moment. When he looked back at Gentry, his eyes had turned ugly. "You damned possum cop. Ain't got nothing to do but try and keep an honest man from making a living."

Gentry nodded. This guy was typical of what he'd come to expect from a certain breed of South Louisiana swamp hunter: short and wiry, dark-haired, leathery tanned skin, heavy on the ink that covered both biceps, the sleeves ripped off his faded, button-front red shirt, certain that The Man was out to rob him of his livelihood.

Most of the local folks' families had eked out a living from this muddy swampland for generations. They worked hard, earned honest pay, and possessed big hearts and generous natures.

Except the ones who didn't.

Gentry gave the man a steady look. "Sir, I know for a fact that you aren't licensed to hunt on these lands, and that you didn't set the line for this gator. Do you want to know how I know that?"

The poacher quit sputtering and watched Gentry with a dull, sullen expression.

"I know that because I helped the licensed hunter set this line myself after somebody cut his yesterday. So you're also facing a charge of poaching. Would you open the cooler sitting at the end of the boat, please?"

Cursing under his breath, the poacher stumbled en route to the cooler and opened it to reveal a couple of six-packs. Actually, the one nearest Gentry was now a four-pack. He leaned over and spotted an open can beneath the seat.

"I'll be testing you for operating a vehicle under the influence, sir. Do you have any other weapons with you? Do you have a flotation device anywhere on the boat?" He wanted the poacher to understand that Gentry could make this as long and complicated and expensive as he wanted it to be.

The man didn't answer, but didn't reach for his gun, either. He crossed his arms and pouted.

"Please turn around and put your hands on your head, sir. You got a name?" He couldn't keep calling him John Wayne.

"Joe Marks." As soon as the guy turned and slapped his hands on top of his head, Gentry reached over and removed the man's pistol from its holster. Old Joe seemed to have lost most of his fight.

"Do you have any more weapons in your boat, Mr. Marks?"

"No."

"You got any identification on you at all?"

Joe reached toward his pocket, but halted when Gentry pulled out his own pistol. "Move slowly, please."

Joe retrieved a wallet from his pocket, opened it, closed it, and threw the whole thing at Gentry. "Git whatever you want, possum cop."

"I've been called worse things, sir. Possums are fine animals." And Joe Marks would probably call him worse when he found out how much this adventure was going to cost him.

By the time another LDWF boat approached from the west, Gentry had administered a field sobriety test and determined that, while Joe had been drinking, his alcohol level wasn't above the legal limit. The guy had lucked out on that one.

Leaving his partner, Mac Griffin, behind the wheel, Senior Agent Paul Billiot boarded the poacher's boat as Gentry read the man his rights. Joe Marks seemed surprised to learn that possum cops were, duh, cops. He was more surprised when Gentry informed him that he'd be facing a litany of fines that would lighten his wallet by a few thousand dollars unless he opted for a few months of jail time.

The poacher also didn't appear happy to see Paul Billiot.

"You know this guy?" Gentry asked.

"We've met." Paul gave the man a grim smile. "Want us to take this fine specimen of humanity off your hands? Mac and I are off duty as of ten minutes ago, so we're headed back to Houma."

"You can take the gator back to Houma too, since you're going anyway. I want to check on old Eva Savoie before I leave, and then I'll go in and file the paperwork."

"You got it." Paul looked at the old cabin. "Looks like Miss Eva's got company."

"Yeah, gonna check on that too." Gentry couldn't shake the feeling that something was wrong about that boat.

Mac leapt onto Joe Marks's rust bucket and pulled a wet tarp over the reptile to protect it from the heat. "We can leave the gator where it is. I'll take it and this sad excuse for a boat back to impound." The gator skin would be sold, the money donated to a benevolence fund. The meat would be delivered to a local shelter. Nothing went to waste.

Except maybe Joe Marks of Bossier City, who'd revealed an impressive vocabulary of curse words that he used in abundance when he finally realized his gun and boat and gator would be going to Houma without him.

All Joe's tirade accomplished was getting him handcuffed. Paul Billiot didn't put up with much shit from anybody.

"Gonna find you again sometime, possum cop," Joe shouted as Paul's boat powered up and moved back toward Bayou Terrebonne.

As he followed in the poacher's boat, Mac waved at Gentry. "Bye-bye, possum cop!"

Gentry considered treating his colleague to a one-fingered salute, but he was supposed to be setting a good example for the younger agent. Instead, he sat down and finished a quick list of the charges against Joe Marks he'd need to file once he got to his home office. Then he'd be writing reports all afternoon. At least he could do it from home, since the region had only one office and it wasn't in this parish.

Behind him, another motor rumbled to life, one that sputtered and skipped before catching. He swiveled to see Eva Savoie's visitor sitting in the back of his boat, leaning over to fiddle with something around his feet. Finally, the guy glanced up, and from across the bayou, Gentry got a good glimpse at the face revealed when the hood fell back.

It was almost like looking in a mirror.

CHAPTER 2

Gentry's heart froze at the sight of the man's face.

His thoughts froze.

The world froze.

Finally, he took a breath and his brain reengaged. "State agent! Shut down that engine!"

He reached over, switched on his outboard motor, and jerked the wheel of his boat toward the cabin, never taking his eyes off the man who'd frozen into a locked gaze with him. A man with dark-brown eyes and curly hair a lot like his own. Tall, like Gentry, maybe a little taller. They'd always argued about who was taller. Same bone structure, but with fuller lips and a softness around the mouth and jaw. A lot skinnier.

The world shrank to the two of them as Gentry drew closer, until the man suddenly jerked his hood back in place and reached for his tiller. He accelerated, racing around the Savoie cabin so fast and hard the ripples skewed Gentry's boat and almost knocked him off the seat. By the time he regained his balance and turned again, the guy was already out of sight, around the bend toward Bayou Terrebonne. He could be halfway to the Gulf of Mexico—or farther north into the serpentine

Atchafalaya Basin—in no time. That boat might be shabby, but it had been moving fast.

Gentry paused, torn. His duty told him to check on Eva Savoie; his gut told him to chase down a ghost.

Get your shit together, Broussard. You don't even know what you're dealing with here. Might be nothing. Check on Miss Eva. He drew a deep breath and let it out. Then another and another, until his heart rate returned to normal. He'd let his imagination get the best of him, that's all. So what if the guy in the hoodie looked like Lang? The guy had broken the law by not stopping when ordered by a law-enforcement officer, but there was no proof he'd done anything else.

Still, the unease that had crawled up his back and coiled itself around his neck at the first sight of the man continued to tighten.

Gentry maneuvered the mud boat the rest of the way across the narrow bayou, tying up in a different spot from the other boat's in case evidence needed to be preserved. Or maybe he was just being paranoid.

"Miss Eva?" His voice echoed in the early-morning quiet of the bayou, now that the buzz of the outboard had faded. "Agent Gentry Broussard, Louisiana Wildlife and Fisheries. I'm coming onto your porch. That okay?"

A gator bellowed somewhere behind the cabin, followed by a splash, then silence.

He climbed onto the porch, noting the sag of the wood beneath his heavy boots, spots in the weathered planks so broken in places that glints of water shone through. He also noted an unmistakable odor that cinched his throat as if someone were tightening a vise.

Blood. Lots of it.

The door stood ajar, but he didn't have to push it open farther to see the blood pooling beneath it. He grasped his pistol—the standard department-issued .45 SIG Sauer—in his right hand as a precaution, reached out his left foot, and gave the door a gentle shove.

It opened a couple of feet before encountering resistance.

"Miss Eva, it's Agent Broussard again. I'm coming inside. Can you answer me?"

Quiet. Gentry looked back at his boat. His pack lay under the seat, filled with gloves and evidence bags, among other paraphernalia. He didn't want to waste the time retrieving it, even though he knew in his gut that he stood at a crime scene. His instincts told him that nothing—nobody—was alive in this cabin.

Careful to avoid brushing against the door facing, he leaned in and peered around the door into a riot of disrepair, poverty, and chaos. He noted details quickly as he scanned for movement: overturned chair with a broken leg lying a couple of feet away, drawers pulled out and contents strewn in the kitchen, a small table in front of the window with candles burning and what looked like sticks strewn across it, some paper money lying on the counter of the kitchenette, blood. Some kind of long-handled knife with a serrated blade.

On the floor at the edge of the blocked door lay a small, wrinkled hand curled into a claw, a thin brown arm protruding from a blood-soaked sleeve of blue-and-white cotton. He leaned in farther and closed his eyes briefly at the sight of a woman who looked at least eighty and would never see eighty-one. Eva Savoie.

Damn it. He edged into the room, moving nothing, each step choreographed to avoid the blood still pooling beneath the woman's body. He didn't see how she had any left; she was drenched in crimson.

He knelt and pulled out his radio even as he placed two fingers on Eva's already-cool skin to confirm the lack of a pulse. She'd been dead a little while, so the guy had hung around, maybe looking for something. Yet there was money on the counter.

First things first; get help on the way. He tugged his radio out of its holder. "This is WL-817, requesting a parish homicide team on Whiskey Bayou one-eighth mile east of Highway 55. Coroner too. There's been a murder."

The radio squawked with Stella Walker's shocked voice. "Doing it now." She abruptly cut him off.

A few seconds later, his phone rang. "Gentry Broussard, what have you gotten yourself into?" Stella knew better than to put personal chatter on the radio. Half the people in the parish monitored the whereabouts of local law enforcement, especially the people who wanted to avoid them. They did most of their communicating by phone these days.

"Just what I said, Stella." Gentry took another quick look around the cabin. "I'm at the cabin now. Where's the lieutenant?"

Stella's voice rose an octave and several decibels, forcing Gentry to wince and hold the phone away from his ear. "He's on his way. You stay outta that shack, Gentry. You know the stories about that woman. There's hexes all over that place. Wait outside in your boat."

Gentry knew that Stella wore her Catholicism on both sleeves, so she wasn't exactly a believer in voodoo. Like a lot of locals, however, she paid it a healthy dose of respect, just in case.

Gentry was already halfway back to his boat, but he had no intention of waiting.

"Tell Warren the details so he can get with the sheriff." Gentry described the boat, the killer, the faded jeans, the brown hoodie. But not the familiarity of the face, the same one that had haunted his dreams every night for the past three years.

He got in his boat but paused before starting it; the phone would be hard to hear over the motor. "We got other agents in this area? Billiot and Griffin are on their way to Houma with a poacher; see if they can come back."

Gentry wasn't a believer in voodoo either, but this scene was creeping him out all the same, for reasons he didn't want to think about. The killer couldn't possibly have been Lang. Gentry had let a resemblance and three years of pent-up guilt and sadness set his imagination on a wild ride.

Stella muttered a moment before answering. "Agent Sinclair's a few miles east. I'll make sure she heard the call."

Good. His night-patrol partner, Jena Sinclair, had a background in forensics. She might see something he'd missed.

"I'm heading south down Bayou Terrebonne to see if I can find the guy," Gentry told Stella. "Let me know when the sheriff gets here and I'll come back to give a statement. If I make a sighting, I'll call it in."

He bypassed the trolling motor and went for the outboard this time. He needed speed and he needed to stay busy so he could stall the questions roiling around in his mind.

Wondering what this old woman could own that was worth stealing, when there had been money left on the counter.

Wondering what she could know that was important enough to be killed for.

Wondering about the man's face he'd seen so briefly in that boat, the face of his older brother, Lang.

After all, Langston Broussard had died three years ago.

Gentry knew that for a fact. He'd been the one to pull the trigger.

CHAPTER 3

"Hey, babycakes! Whatcha doin' later tonight?"

A middle-aged drunk, poured into a snug camo sweater-vest and sporting a black cowboy hat, draped himself over the edge of the stage. He'd been bellowing at Ceelie Savoie for almost twenty minutes, since she'd begun her set. This was the first time he'd staggered away from his table, however.

Ceelie considered kicking him, but her rent was past due and planting a boot on a customer's expensive cowboy hat would probably get her fired.

She shifted the neck of her guitar to the other side of the mic stand and finished an admittedly half-baked version of Hank Williams's "Jambalaya" to a smattering of applause. The few claps were barely audible through the crowd chatter, the clink of glassware, and the drunk, who had contorted himself into a camo-clad pretzel in his attempt to throw a meaty leg over the edge of the stage.

Where the hell was Harvey, the manager? Surely even the lounge at the Opry Shed Motel, a fleabag operation on the outskirts of downtown Nashville, had a few standards. Although the fact that Harvey had insisted she wear a short skirt ("The customers like seeing some leg") and play only well-known songs ("The customers don't like that hippie Cajun crap") should've erased any expectations of quality. The fact he considered "hippie Cajun crap" a musical genre should've told her a lot.

Seeing no sign of Harvey, Ceelie broke into a favorite moldy oldie, one of the classics she didn't mind singing. "Walkin' After Midnight" fit her contralto voice and her mood most days. She'd done her share of late-night walking, lonesome and searching for something. She'd thought it was stardom; now, she'd settle for a little respect.

She'd left Houma, Louisiana, ten years ago with a half-empty suitcase, a guitar, a head filled with dreams and unwritten songs, and a promise to her late father. She'd sworn on his deathbed that she'd follow his greatest wish: as soon as he died she'd shake off the mud of Terrebonne Parish and never, ever look back.

She hadn't expected to meet others just like her on every Nashville street corner, all competing to see whose dreams would get crushed first. To see how long it would take for each of them to crawl back to his or her respective backwoods town, grateful for a job at Walmart or the Piggly Wiggly. To see which ones would stick it out here and keep beating their heads against closed doors.

She'd beat her head against so many doors she should have brain damage. Maybe she did. It would explain a lot.

By the time Ceelie reached the last chord of "Midnight," the drunk guy had managed to roll onto the stage and attract more enthusiasm from the audience than her music had. In fact, every eye was on him except those of her friend Sonia, who'd gotten her this gig out of pity. A part-time bartender, Sonia met Ceelie's gaze and shrugged as if to say, *What do you expect from a dump like this?*

Well, by God, if nobody was listening anyway, she'd try out her new song and screw the old country favorites. It was the first thing that had come to her after a creative drought that had lasted six months, maybe longer. Deep inside, she'd feared something so awful she hadn't wanted to verbalize it: that her ability to write had left her.

A few soft strums in an A-minor chord led her into the tune that had awakened her in the middle of the night last week, propelled her from a deep sleep to work on it until time for her to make the morning waitressing shift at Music City Pancakes. She couldn't get it out of her head and didn't want to—it marked the return of her muse. At least, she hoped so. It wasn't finished, but she could try out a part of it.

> *Its dying call is weak but clear*
> *Yet it's a plaintive voice I don't want to hear.*
> *I won't go back,*
> *I won't go home,*
> *'Cause next time, Whiskey Bayou won't let me go.*

Ceelie's voice, rich and strong and smoky, was the thing she'd always thought would set her apart. It cut through the bar noise, and first one woman, then a trickle of faces, turned away from the drunk guy sitting on the edge of the stage and riveted onto her. She sang to them, poured her heart into words she believed about a place she'd abandoned at the first opportunity and yet couldn't seem to forget.

The adrenaline shot through her as more people turned to listen. This was it. This was what she'd dreamed about. Not that the Opry Shed Motel lounge was the kind of place where talent agents or record producers hung out, but it was a start. People were actually listening.

Someone at a front table broke into a smile, and soon everyone began laughing.

"Whiskey Bayou" was not a happy song. What was she doing wrong?

From the corner of her eye, Ceelie registered movement a split second before the drunk guy reached her. He'd done a turtle crawl across the stage while she'd been wrapped up in her daydreams and now stood on his knees, holding out his arms to her.

Enough. Before she could talk herself out of it, Ceelie planted a solid boot to his shoulder and shoved.

The world flipped as the man fell backward, pulling her with him by one beefy hand wrapped around her knee. She screamed but no one could hear; the place had erupted into a thunder of laughter and applause.

Her guitar. Where had it gone? That vintage Gibson was the one thing of value she owned, and Ceelie scrambled to her feet in search of it, pushing the drooling letch away from her and expelling a breath of relief when she spotted it, intact, a few feet away on the stage.

She and the Gibson were getting the heck out of here.

The crowd continued to applaud as her unwanted co-entertainer climbed to his feet and took drunken bows at center stage. *Good for him.* His antics allowed her to exit without anyone taking notice.

Or so she thought. She spotted the missing manager before she'd cleared the backstage stairs and made it into the hallway to the dressing room, which was a fancy name for a converted closet. The only things crammed in it were a small table, a peeling mirror, and a gunmetal-gray folding chair.

"Honey, that was genius!" Harvey threw an arm around her shoulders and gave her a hug. He might have reached five-five in his shiny black platform shoes, which gave him a couple of inches' height advantage over Ceelie. Plus he smelled as if he'd fallen into a vat of cheap aftershave. "If you'd told me you were willing to do comedy, I coulda pulled in a bigger crowd. Who's your partner?"

Ceelie wrested herself from his grasp and gawked. *What an idiot.* "Seriously? You think that was planned? I should sue you for letting that letch onstage."

The glee drained from Harvey's expression, replaced by dead brown eyes and a downturn of thin lips topped by a wisp of hair he probably considered a moustache. "You mean that crap you were singing was supposed to be music?"

Ceelie thinned her own lips in response.

"Let's put it this way, sweetheart. If you and your buddy out there want to make this a regular act, I'll sign you on for a two-week run. You want to go onstage and sing that depressing shit, you're fired."

Ceelie considered the offer for a few seconds, then chided herself for being so desperate. She'd take an extra shift serving waffles to tourists in shiny snakeskin cowboy boots before stooping that low. After all, she'd practically been raised by the most independent woman in Terrebonne Parish, Louisiana, who always told her she was strong enough to follow her own mind and deal with the consequences.

"Pay me for tonight and you'll never see me again."

Harvey pointed toward the dressing-room closet. "Get your stuff and take a hike. You didn't finish a set. No set, no pay. I ain't running no charity here."

"Fine." She clutched the Gibson closer and stalked toward the dressing room. "And by the way, screw you and the pig you rode in on." Pity the pig.

"You wish, sweetheart."

It took Ceelie mere seconds to snatch up her makeup bag, purse, and jacket. When she stomped back out, intending to stop by the bar and let Sonia know what happened, Harvey stood blocking the hallway.

"I been thinking. You ain't half–bad looking with that dark skin and funny eyes—like a blue-eyed Injun. You want to get paid for tonight, I know another way you could make up for not finishing your set."

Ceelie ground her teeth but held her tongue long enough to give Harvey a slow, sexy-eyed once-over, from the grease in his dyed-black hair to the silver neck bling visible beneath the half-buttoned shirt; from the tight pants that promised way too little all the way to the pointy tips of his shiny platform shoes.

She looked him in the eye. "Eh, no thanks. I'd die first."

Turning on her heel, she headed for the back door at a fast clip, unsure if she'd slapped at a gnat or poked a grizzly and not wanting to find out which one old Harvey would turn out to be. He called her a few choice names but didn't follow.

Definitely a gnat.

The night air in Nashville had fallen into the low seventies with a promise of autumn, so Ceelie decided to forego the cab she'd have taken had it been either hotter or later. The neighborhood between here and her domino-sized studio apartment was well lit, and people tended to be mobile on Friday nights in Nashville. Plus, she needed fresh air and time to think.

She'd hit rock bottom. That's all there was to it. She didn't make enough money off tips at the pancake house to pay the rent and utilities, but that early waitressing shift left her afternoons and evenings free to write songs, knock on doors, and pick up a stray performing gig. Not that she had anything new in the songwriting department except a half-finished tune that was, as Harvey had pointed out, depressing shit. Cajun hippie depressing shit at that.

She'd been fooling herself; tonight had rubbed in that message loud and clear. Nashville thrived off the hard work and substandard wages of idiots like Ceelie Savoie, willing to do anything for the privilege of sustaining their dreams.

Her phone vibrated in the bag she'd slung over her shoulder, but she ignored it. Ceelie wasn't ready to talk to Sonia, who'd probably figured out by now that she was gone. The smartphone had been the one luxury she'd allowed herself, based on the conviction that any day now, the dream agent could call, or the guy who'd been in the back of fill-in-the-blank lounge had been touched by her music and wanted to talk contracts.

The acknowledgment that those dreams had begun to die brought with it other hard truths. She was bone tired, for one thing. Weary of the constant swim against the current, the struggle for money, the worry about when she'd catch a break, or if she'd break first. Her feet hurt, and not just because the soles of her boots had worn thin. Her heart hurt. When she'd left Louisiana with what little she had left from the sale of her dad's house, she'd never dreamed that a decade later she might be worse off.

Feeling more like sixty-eight than twenty-eight, Ceelie huffed to the third-floor studio apartment with her usual prayer—that the locks hadn't been changed while she was out. She'd already gotten the eviction notice. The key clicked home, however, and the deadbolt turned.

Inside, slid underneath the door, she found a note in the tall, looping handwriting of the building manager:

Sorry doll, but you gotta be out by Monday morning. You can store stuff with me if you need to. —J

Juanita was a good soul, even if her building was a firetrap and the absentee landlord made her do his dirty work. Like evicting deadbeat tenants.

Ceelie collapsed onto the only real piece of furniture in the place besides the futon she used as a bed, an overstuffed brown armchair she and Sonia had found at a yard sale for ten bucks and hauled up the steps themselves. Forty-eight hours and she'd officially be homeless.

Rock. Bottom.

Her options were limited. Sonia would put her up, but Ceelie's friend had a studio apartment not much bigger than this one, plus her own set of dreams. She tended bar at the Opry Shed, did odd jobs around town to help pay her way through the local community college, and hoped to earn a transfer scholarship to study art at Vanderbilt.

They'd joked about their futures: Sonia would buy her own art gallery, and Ceelie would take time off her third world tour to play at its grand opening.

Sonia would make it, but Ceelie's gut told her it was time for a do-over on her part. She could write songs, sing, and cook. Period. Since she'd proven incapable of supporting herself with the first two, maybe she could find a job in a restaurant kitchen and work her way up. Music would become a hobby, not a vocation. If she could accept that once and for all, the rest might work itself out.

Accepting that the thing she loved most was going to fail her, or that she had failed it? Gut-wrenching.

The phone vibrated again, and Ceelie dug it out of her bag with a sigh. Might as well break the news to Sonia that she would have an uninvited visitor, at least for a few days. She had nowhere else to live until she could find another job or go full time at the pancake house.

Ceelie frowned at the number on the screen, recognizing the 985 area code all too well. She'd used it her whole life, at least until she'd left Louisiana behind. Her mom had taken off when she was a kid, and her dad died from cancer at age forty-six after too many years working shifts at the gas plant. That was a fact of life and death in South Louisiana, which is why he'd practically ordered her to leave the first chance she got, before she got trapped there like he had been.

Bottom line: she had nobody in Houma anymore. Her "hello" was more than a little hesitant.

The caller, speaking in the heavy accent that sent an unexpected wave of homesickness across Ceelie's chest, identified himself as a deputy with the Terrebonne Parish Sheriff's Office. "We been tryin' to reach Celestine Savoie, formerly of Houma."

Ceelie had shaken off her full first name along with the bayou mud, and the sound of it pulled her into a time warp. "I don't go by Celestine anymore, but I guess that's me."

"I got some news about one of your family members, Ms. Savoie, and I'm afraid it's bad."

Ceelie shifted the phone to her left hand and rubbed her temple with her right. "Sorry, but you must have the wrong person after all. I don't have any family left in Houma."

The deputy paused, and the rustle of papers sounded through the phone. "We have you down as being the great-niece of Eva Savoie, who lived out on Whiskey Bayou south of Montegut. Is that correct?"

Tante Eva. The name brought back a rush of memories, good and bad, but mostly good. Ceelie had spent a lot of time with her great-aunt as a kid. "What do you mean *lived*?"

Past tense.

Twenty minutes later, after a long series of questions and answers with the deputy, Ceelie's mind spun with horrifying facts and half-remembered snatches of detail from visiting Whiskey Bayou throughout her childhood and early teens. He'd finally convinced her that she was, indeed, the old woman's next of kin, although only after confirming the death dates of every other possible relative Ceelie could remember.

"Other than the real old-timers, not many folks round here knew Miss Eva or knew anything about her other than some, uh, unusual stories." The deputy sounded as if he found the whole conversation more awkward than Ceelie, which might not be possible.

"You must not have been in the parish that long, or you'd know the unusual stories weren't that far off base." Ceelie's voice held dry humor. "Anytime a boy came near me in school, the mean girls would tell him to be careful because I'd hex him the same way my Tante Eva the voodoo queen taught me. I knew she was a practitioner."

Throw the bones, ma petite fille. *Let them tell you what's to come. The bones, they never lie.*

The deputy cleared his throat and rustled more papers, pulling Ceelie out of her memories. He clearly had no answer for voodoo confessions. "You'll need to contact Carreux Funeral Home up in Houma; once the autopsy is concluded, that's where she'll be taken. The parish can help with burial costs if you're unable to afford them."

God, what did a funeral cost these days? "What happens with her cabin?"

"I'm not really qualified to talk about that, Ms. Savoie. As her next of kin, you should be able to claim any possible inheritance, but you'll need to talk to a succession attorney or the probate office."

Right. Because Ceelie was loaded with cash for lawyers as well as funerals and travel.

She did have enough for a bus ticket, but . . . Wait. "Inheritance? I can't imagine Eva had anything of value other than the cabin itself."

In fact, the deputy had told her the biggest mystery surrounding her great-aunt's murder was what the killer could possibly have wanted. No one could figure it out. "Wouldn't the killer have stolen anything worth stealing?"

"Not really." The deputy waited half a heartbeat before continuing. "He seemed to be looking for something specific. There was a small amount of cash left in the cabin."

Earlier, the man had said there were no clues as to the murderer's identity. "You say 'he'—that means you do have some information about who the killer might be?"

"Ah . . ." The deputy's voice grew muffled as he spoke to someone in the background, then returned. "We can fill you in when you get here. As for what your aunt had, I couldn't really tell you that. There's the cabin and its contents. There's an old pickup truck. Some land. Again, I'm not the one to assess that, however, and you'll have to talk to someone else about what your aunt owned, and any encumbrances on her property."

She might suddenly be a Terrebonne Parish landowner? Ceelie almost laughed at the irony. But land meant she had a place to go and regroup, didn't it? Selling it to a developer for fishing camps—the Louisiana term for a rustic waterfront spot for weekend anglers—could bring in enough money for her to return to Nashville or even go on to Los Angeles or New York or Chicago.

In the meantime, she could stay in the cabin, although for the life of her she couldn't remember if it had plumbing. "Is the house habitable?"

The deputy's pause spoke volumes. "It's, uh, rustic. And what the killer didn't mess up, the forensics team did. You'll want to stay somewhere else."

Yeah, well, she had nowhere else to stay, and cleaning up a mess would keep her from drowning in self-pity.

Then she remembered something. "Wait—what about Eva's husband, LeRoy? I realize he's gone, and I doubt he's still alive since he was older than my aunt. He ran out on her about twenty years ago. But he had a son or a nephew or something." What was that boy's name who'd spent part of one summer out there when she was a kid?

The crackle of turning pages sounded through the phone. "No, I'm pretty sure . . . Wait." More page-turning. "Yep, here we go. Some of the older folks mentioned a man named LeRoy Breaux who used to live with Ms. Savoie, but your great-aunt was never married to him, so even if he has survivors they'd have no claim on her estate unless there's a will somewhere—again, you'll need to talk to probate."

Tante Eva and Nonc LeRoy weren't married? That gave a whole new meaning to *shacked up*, given what she recalled about that cabin. It beat sleeping under a Nashville overpass, however.

"I'll be there by Monday."

CHAPTER 4

LDWF Agent Jena Sinclair tugged at the collar of her department-issued shirt, long sleeves cuffed at the wrist despite the suffocating heat of the bayou even at seven in the morning.

It was her favorite time of day out here on the water, as the things of the night fell silent and the creatures of the day awakened. The humidity was thick and viscous, but the oppressive heat hadn't caught up with it yet. The waters stirred with splashes and croaks, and the slight breeze caused the heavy Spanish moss dripping from the trees to sway like the skirt of a dancing woman. Birds competed to see which species could out-call the other. The smell of wild things and the ever-present odor of DEET blended with the scents of mud and lilies.

Even after a long, hard night of work, the bayou made Jena feel alive.

The long sleeves had been her choice—they were the only surefire protection against the mosquitoes. As bad as the parasitic monsters were in the daytime, they were worse at dusk and at dawn. Just her luck that she seemed especially tasty to them, judging by the number of bites she collected during evening shifts.

"Don't you get bit?" She scratched at a welt on her neck and glared at her partner. If he'd been gnawed on during the all-nighter they'd just spent cruising in the waters off Bayou Terrebonne, he hadn't let on. Of course, they'd been too busy to think about it until now.

"Guess I'm just not as sweet as you, Red."

"Obviously." Jena pulled at her collar again and slapped the green LDWF baseball cap on her head backward, matching her partner's. Gentry Broussard was too damned cool ever to admit he was as miserable as she was. "And stop calling me Red."

Gentry shrugged. "Dye your hair. Or I could call you Sally."

"What the heck is that supposed to mean?"

"You know that old song, 'Long Tall Sally'?"

Great. Lieutenant Doucet already called her Stringbean half the time. Lanky redheads were destined for bad nicknames, especially when they worked with a gang of alpha males.

"So, Broussard, does that mean you want me to call you Curly in honor of those pretty brown locks?" Or sexy as sin, more like, although she'd never admit her opinions to him. Besides, he was way too moody to get involved with, even if she were interested in anything else, which she wasn't.

"Hey, Curly was my favorite of the Three Stooges." Gentry gave her enough smile to flash a quick sight of rarely glimpsed dimples, but it seemed halfhearted. He'd had a couple of long days. After coming up empty on his initial search for the killer, he'd gone out on a couple of extra shifts. Personnel from all law-enforcement agencies were on the lookout for that boat.

"Figures," Jena said. "I'll just call you Stooge."

She didn't push the banter this morning. Gentry had been quieter than usual all night, even before they'd been pulled into the search-and-rescue operation for a kid who'd fallen off a dock. The dock stretched into a lake behind his family's house, in a rural area near the road that cut off to Isle de Jean Charles, southeast of Montegut.

After a couple of hours of searching, a neighboring parish LDWF agent had found the little boy's body washed up on a spit of land a half mile from the dock. That kid should've been asleep at midnight, not wandering around outside. Whether any kind of negligence was involved would be the business of the sheriff's office.

In Louisiana it was the wildlife agents, not the Coast Guard or sheriff's deputies, who served as the primary search-and-rescue first responders on waterways. They'd been among the first on the scene after Hurricane Katrina hit New Orleans in 2005, and they were the first ones called out whenever someone went missing on the water.

This kind of outcome was the worst part of the job, especially when a child was involved. The absolute worst. No competition.

She didn't think that was the only reason Gentry had been so quiet, though. He'd been distant and distracted even before the search got called in.

"Eva Savoie was buried yesterday." Jena pulled her sunglasses out and settled them on the bridge of her nose. Daylight had come up fast, and bright glints already reflected off the water. Gentry had pulled out his shades ten minutes earlier.

His expression didn't change; he gave good blank face. "Yeah, so I heard."

"I went." She looked out over the bayou, still and peaceful, the hunters not yet out in this spot. "Thought you might be there."

"I spent the day in Dulac." Gentry took off his sunglasses and gave her an intense look. "Why'd you go? You hadn't even met Eva Savoie."

Jena wasn't sure why she'd felt compelled to go to the woman's funeral, but the impulse had been strong and she'd followed it. At the heart of things, she'd been afraid no one would be there except the woman's great-niece. Being so old, dying so badly, and then having no one to mourn you—it was sad. "I think I just went out of respect, you know? She was so alone, and her death was . . ."

No need to say the words. It had been the worst crime scene she'd ever encountered, and Jena had seen some bad stuff in her three years as a street cop with the New Orleans Police Department.

It wasn't that she didn't have the stomach for blood; her degree was in forensic biology. She spent a lot of time looking at dead things—gators, birds, snakes, even nutria, the gross, orange-toothed rodents the size of a healthy housecat. She'd seen her share of death.

What she didn't have the stomach for was the violence one human could willfully inflict on another. That was why she'd left NOPD nine months ago after hearing LDWF had a couple of openings. The six-month training academy had been pure hell, but she'd learned why these agents had the reputation as the state's best-trained—they had to know how to work in all kinds of conditions on land and in water, and almost every person they encountered carried multiple firearms.

She'd wanted to work in the outdoors, away from the city, and it had been eye-opening to find out how much the problems of drugs and crime had stretched into the rural areas. But at least their violent cases were rare here in Terrebonne, broken up by long stretches of blue sky and fresh air.

For three months, it had been the best job in the world. Until she walked into that cabin full of blood and found Gentry looking like he'd seen a ghost.

"Lieutenant Doucet was at the funeral, and a couple of the sheriff's guys came," she said. "I think the parish paid for the burial."

He didn't respond, so she asked the question that had been nagging at her since he mentioned his hometown. "Were you looking for the suspect in Dulac? Was it somebody you recognized?"

Something had felt off-kilter about the way Gentry had reacted to the Eva Savoie murder, almost like it was personal.

Gentry had been staring into space but looked back at her now—sharply, she thought. "Why would you think that? I was just tending to family business." He paused, then shifted gears. "Any of the old-timers from down the bayou come to the funeral? Anybody who looked out of place?"

She frowned. "Out of place like maybe her murderer?" Gentry's description could fit half the guys in Louisiana: tall, thin, dark-brown hair of medium length, brown eyes, short beard. "There were a few people there. Other than law enforcement, there wasn't anybody under seventy except Miss Eva's niece—well, great-niece."

"Hmph." Gentry steered the boat around the curve into Wonder Lake and headed northwest toward their launch on Bayou Terrebonne. "Heard the niece was some kind of entertainer up in Nashville."

Jena stifled a grin. He'd stretched out *en-ter-tain-er*, stressing each syllable, as if it were a criminal activity he needed to put a stop to. "You got something against entertainers, Broussard?"

"Just not an occupation that appeals to me." He relaxed and sped up the boat now that they were on open water. "I can't see some fancy, high-maintenance woman hanging round Montegut or Chauvin."

She smiled. "Or Dulac?"

"Got dat right."

Jena had seen him turn on the Cajun charm before. He'd settle into a heavy South Louisiana patois to fit in and make the people he dealt with feel comfortable talking to him like he was a regular guy. In reality, he'd gone to LSU, same as her, and had worked several years in LDWF's Region 8, including metro New Orleans, before transferring back to his home parish.

She still hadn't quite figured out what made her partner tick. He was single and uninvolved—or so said Stella, the dispatcher and resident busybody, who'd supplied the rest of the biography. Including the fact that Gentry had transferred in three years ago after a case went wrong in New Orleans. Jena had looked up the case and understood a lot more about her partner's moods once she saw that he'd killed his brother during a drug bust.

Jena could see other things for herself. Gentry was too ruggedly handsome for his own good and had the potential for trouble written on every muscle, of which he appeared to have many. The man even looked sexy in the LDWF uniform, and their uniforms were about as sexy as a dead swamp rat. Yet he was a loner, and there was an undercurrent of sadness to him sometimes when he had his guard down. Maybe because of what had happened with his brother.

Still, out of the five-agent LDWF unit assigned to Terrebonne Parish, Jena had to admit the lieutenant had paired her with the right person for her first months of field duty. They'd become friendly, maybe almost friends, without an ounce of real sexual chemistry—exactly how they needed to be as work partners. She was woman enough to admire his looks without wanting to do anything about it. LSU and New Orleans were their common ground, and he didn't treat her like a rookie.

Besides, her other potential partner had been Senior Agent Paul Billiot, a solemn-faced, quiet man from Isle de Jean Charles and an active member of the area's tribe of Biloxi-Chitimacha-Choctaw Native Americans. Paul Billiot had a way of looking straight through her as if he could see her soul.

"Have you heard how Mac Griffin's doing as Paul Billiot's partner?" She and Mac, a transplanted rookie agent from Maine, of all places, had started in Region 6 the same week.

This time, Gentry's dimples caught and stayed. "Let's just say I'd love to be a fly on their boat one night. I think we need to start a pool to see which one breaks first."

Jena laughed. "That's what I thought." Mac was talkative and gregarious and fancied himself a ladies' man ready to conquer the females of South Louisiana. A full one-eighty from her impression of Paul Billiot, in other words.

"I wonder—" Whatever Gentry wondered was cut short by his sudden look down at his shirt pocket, from which he fished his phone. He turned off the engine so he could hear and glanced at the screen before answering. "It's Lieutenant Doucet."

Gentry listened a few moments, looked at Jena's upraised eyebrows, and shrugged. "We're almost across Wonder Lake headed for Bayou Terrebonne and the boat launch."

Jena groaned inwardly. It had been a long, stressful night, and the lieutenant wouldn't be calling if there wasn't something he needed them to do before going off duty. Gentry put the phone on speaker.

"Eva Savoie's great-niece wants to talk to you," the lieutenant was saying. "Mostly you, Broussard, since you found her aunt, but you were there too, Sinclair. So as a courtesy, I told the sheriff I'd have you drop by."

Well, at least they were headed back toward Houma anyhow. Jena had a small apartment in a generic complex on the outskirts of town, and Gentry had a house somewhere around Montegut. She wasn't sure of the location; they might be partners but they didn't socialize. As far as she knew, Gentry Broussard didn't socialize with anyone, although Stella said he had some kind of big, macho dog.

"No problem." Gentry's mouth spoke the words but his expression looked anything but agreeable. "What's her name? Where's she staying?"

"Celestine Savoie." Warren paused. "She goes by 'Ceelie' or something like that."

Gentry rolled his eyes. "Sounds high-maintenance."

Jena stifled a chuckle.

"She'll meet you down the bayou." Like the other locals, including Gentry when he was in Cajun mode, Warren's *bayou* came out sounding more like *buy-ya*.

"At her aunt's cabin?"

Ugh. Jena put a hand over her mouth. God, that place had been a disaster when they left, blood from one end to the other, belongings in disarray. It was probably worse now that the investigators had gone through everything a few times. Had they warned the woman what she'd face when she showed up?

"When do we need to be there?" Gentry's deep, smooth voice cut through Jena's thoughts.

"Told 'em you'd be there by eight. And Broussard?" Warren paused. "I also told the sheriff you'd be polite no matter how big a pain this woman might be. She's apparently got a temper, and you've apparently got a reputation for being a smart-ass."

Gentry grinned, a wicked slice of white teeth above his tanned jawline. Those dimples were deep enough to dive into, his expression that of a man who'd been issued a challenge. "I'm always polite, Lieutenant."

"No, you aren't." Warren said. "So play nice."

"He's got your number—hey!" The rest of Jena's comment was cut short as Gentry took a curve too fast and she had to grab hold of the seat. She should ticket the jerk—he'd done that on purpose. It wouldn't be the first time he'd taken her by surprise and dumped her on the floor of the boat.

At seven thirty, they reached Bayou Terrebonne, and Gentry let the boat idle a moment, looking north and south.

"You want to go in by boat or drive down?"

Well, that was a no-brainer. "Drive. I have a yearning for air-conditioning."

He throttled up and headed north. "My thoughts exactly."

The trip up Bayou Terrebonne to the boat launch near the fire station took no longer than ten minutes, and, after some discussion, they left the LDWF boat with Gentry's truck and took Jena's identical department-issued black pickup.

She stifled a yawn as she pulled onto Montegut Road, aka Highway 55, headed south. Bayou Terrebonne hugged the road on the right. "Reckon anybody got that cabin cleaned up so she doesn't see it the way it looked after her aunt died?"

Gentry leaned over and turned the fan on the air-conditioning as high as it would go. "Hope so, but I doubt it. Seems like a bad idea to meet her there. Gotta say, I don't look forward to going back in there myself."

It struck Jena again that Gentry seemed to have taken Eva Savoie's murder personally. When he'd returned from his futile search for the killer that morning, his face had been downright waxen, but it wasn't because of the brutality of the scene. He'd watched everything the sheriff's deputies had done, without a flinch. Without any expression at all. In fact, he hadn't made any attempt to leave until the parish guys ordered them to get out of their way, even though Jena had offered a couple of times to take him home and pick up his boat the next day.

Then again, one didn't often find eighty-year-old women dead of blunt-force trauma that the coroner said had been preceded by more than a dozen nonlethal stab wounds. Torture; there was nothing else to call it. The woman had been tortured.

Stella called just before they rounded the last curve and entered Whiskey Bayou area. Jena turned down the AC fan so she could hear the phone.

"Y'all out there yet?" Stella wanted details on the cabin; she'd pinned Jena down earlier, wanting to know about voodoo trinkets, and had been disappointed no skulls or crossed chicken bones had been in evidence. They were in evidence, of course, but it wasn't her place to tell Stella those kinds of details. If the woman wanted to read the reports, she probably could.

"Not yet, but almost." Jena jammed her baseball cap back on her head. "What's up?"

"Deputy ain't gonna make it out there, so Warren says y'all need to go ahead and talk to the niece, Celestine. Use your own judgment in how many details to give her. No point in upsetting her more than she already is."

40

Jena frowned as they rounded the last curve before the highway straightened out for a long run and eventually fizzled into unstable wetlands. She slowed down and began scanning left for the turnoff to the Savoie cabin. "How's she getting out here, then? She got a rental car?"

"I asked that very thing." Stella tsked her disapproval. "She's living out there, I guess. You'll have to tell me what it looks like since she moved in."

Uh, that would be no. Jena had never been a gossip and didn't plan to start now. "Almost there. We'll report in when we leave. Gotta go now—Broussard needs help." She ended the call before the woman could ask any more questions.

Gentry raised an eyebrow. "And what exactly do you think I need help with?"

"Getting me off the phone with Stella." Jena leaned over the steering wheel and finally spotted the unpaved, rutted dirt drive onto the Savoie property.

When Jena came to a stop in the drive and killed the engine, Gentry rolled down his window and cocked his head, closing his eyes.

"What's wr—"

"Shhhhh." He held a finger over his pursed lips, and Jena opened her senses to whatever had caught his attention. The truck wheels had made no noise on the hard-packed dirt of the drive.

Finally a sound reached her: a voice.

And what a voice. Deep, throaty, but not in a sexy way. In a haunted way. A voice full of heartbreak and ghosts.

> I won't go back, I won't go home,
> 'Cause in this place, the dead still roam,
> 'Cause this time, Whiskey Bayou won't let me go.

"Is that her? The singer?" Jena looked back when her fellow agent didn't answer.

His eyes were open, but his expression had changed to match the words and the tone of voice that had captured him.

Gentry Broussard didn't wear the face of the cocky guy who kept his emotions close to the vest and often couldn't find his manners with a map.

He wore the face of a man both heartbroken and haunted.

CHAPTER 5

No one would ever mistake Gentry for a music connoisseur, but he knew what moved him. Those stark words in a voice that conveyed a firsthand knowledge of loss and heartbreak? They stabbed his heart like the blood-covered knife he'd seen near Eva Savoie's body.

The words summed up the state of his mind: the dead were still roaming.

Only, what if Lang wasn't dead? Could that even be possible? There had been a funeral. He'd sat stoically beside his weeping mother at a graveside service in Dulac that no one had attended other than his step-father, two stepsisters whom he barely knew and who had never even met Langston Broussard, and the guys from his Region 8 enforcement team from Orleans Parish. His real brothers. The ones he hadn't been forced to put down with two bullets.

Lang's body had never been found, the search called off after dragging the uncooperative Mississippi River for days. He couldn't have survived those shots, the water, that dark night of torrential rain and wind.

But the face Gentry had seen under that hood had been so like his brother's.

"You okay, Broussard?"

Gentry jolted back to awareness at the touch of Jena's hand on his arm. He had to pull his shit together or he'd be enjoying some more forced time off courtesy of the state of Louisiana. Only this time, no old friend of his father's would come to pull him out of the quicksand, as Warren Doucet had done—the lieutenant had started his career as Hank Broussard's partner.

This time, there would be no coming back.

"Yeah, sorry," he mumbled, opening the truck door and climbing out. God, but he was exhausted. The dreams had become worse since Eva's murder, but he'd be damned if he would turn to a bottle of pills or alcohol to subdue them. He'd soldier through it, as his dad used to say when things got tough. Of course, soldiering through had cost his dad a heart attack when he was only forty-three years old, eleven years older than Gentry was now.

"Any particular tactic you want to use in talking to Celestine Savoie?" Jena slammed the truck door, and the haunting music ended abruptly. Gentry found himself longing for it to continue. Maybe he could find out what the recording was, listen to the whole song, and spend the night wallowing in self-pity to his heart's content.

"What do you mean by tactic?" He glanced at Jena as they approached the back of the house, skirting around an ancient turquoise-and-white pickup. Not ancient enough to have reached a second life as a cool novelty, but just ancient enough to be ugly and outdated. "You mean like good cop–bad cop? This ain't an interrogation, Red."

Jena rolled her eyes and strode ahead of him. The touch of light banter took the edge off Gentry's nerves, and he said a silent thanks for his lanky, red-haired partner. She was so earnest and eager to do her job well that it made her an easy mark for teasing. Which meant Gentry didn't have to do anything unpleasant like talk about his feelings—his initial fear when he'd found out he was being assigned a female LDWF rookie for a partner.

So sue him. He could be a sexist pig.

They stepped onto the part of the porch that wrapped around to the back of the house, and Gentry called out, "Ms. Savoie? Agents Broussard and Sinclair, Wildlife and Fisheries."

"Front porch." The voice that answered was what Gentry thought of as a bedroom voice—a woman with a natural whiskey-and-cigarette rasp. At least, he guessed it was natural. Nashville entertainers might suck down Jack Daniel's and puff on unfiltered cigarettes every dusk until dawn. Probably did, now that he thought about it.

They rounded the corner of the wraparound porch, and Gentry fought off a wave of déjà vu at the sight of the weathered cypress planks. What looked like a scrubbed bloody shoeprint lay near one of the rotted-through patches. Might have even been his; the soles of his shoes had been coated in crimson despite his best efforts to stay out of it. They'd cost a fortune, but he'd thrown them away.

"Ms. Savoie?" Jena held out a hand for a shake. "I'm Agent Jena Sinclair, and this is Senior Agent Gentry Broussard. The parish sheriff's office said you wanted to talk to us?"

Standing behind Jena, Gentry didn't get a look at Celestine Savoie until she stepped around his partner and offered him a hand to shake. "Ceelie Savoie," she said in that bedroom voice. "Thanks for coming."

Yeah, he was definitely a sexist pig, because he was here to answer dark questions about a horrific death and yet this woman took his breath away. It wasn't just the voice, which he realized had been *her* singing and not a recording; a beat-up guitar stood propped against the side of a rocking chair. She looked way too wholesome and sexy to have spent much time smoking and drinking.

In other words, whatever mental image he'd had of a Nashville singer, Ceelie Savoie was not it. "You're the entertainer?" He purposely avoided looking at his partner.

"Well, I was a singer-songwriter. I guess I still am. 'Entertainer' is a matter of opinion." She turned toward the door. "You guys mind coming inside?"

He and Jena exchanged glances. Hell no, he didn't want to go inside, but Ceelie had already grabbed her guitar and disappeared through the doorway.

"You okay?" Jena had assumed a mother-hen expression, so he clenched his jaw and strode into the cabin following Ceelie, failing to avoid noting her petite-but-curvy figure in her black tank top and worn jeans. Why had he expected the woman to be wearing sequins and have enormous, teased-out platinum hair?

Red kept telling him he needed sensitivity training, whatever the hell that meant. Maybe she was right.

Eva Savoie's great-niece defied show-business stereotypes. She had the olive-tan skin so common in this corner of the country, home of the true American melting pot. Almost three centuries ago, French-speaking Acadians exiled from Canada had begun hooking up with members of two different Native American tribes and French-speaking free people of color. The result was today's distinctive gumbo of locals, where race was rarely either clear-cut or relevant.

Ceelie's jet-black hair was woven into a thick braid pulled to the left side, giving her the look of a warrior princess, yet her eyes were the dark blue-gray of a summer day when a storm was moving in from the Gulf.

"You got a problem?" Ceelie propped her hands on her hips and speared him with a look that brought the storm clouds closer to the surface. Yep, the woman had a temper.

Had he been staring that hard? From his peripheral vision, he saw Jena mimicking Ceelie's stance, giving him a perplexed look.

He cleared his throat. "No, sorry, I just expected you to be . . ." Damn, how was he going to get his foot out of his mouth? *Flashier? Better dressed?* "Taller."

Jena made a rude noise and shook her head. "Sorry, Ms. Savoie. Agent Broussard heard you were a singer from Nashville, so I think he was expecting cowboy boots and big hair."

Gentry frowned at Jena, who ignored him.

"Ah, gotcha. Well, I never quite figured out how to fit in in Nashville. Maybe I should have tried that." Ceelie propped her guitar against the wall and sat cross-legged on the bed in the corner. "Anyway, thanks for coming. Have a seat. You can pull over those dining chairs if you want. I needed to ask you some questions about my Tante Eva."

Gentry gave himself a mental slap upside the head. He'd gotten tongue-tied around a sexy woman and forgotten why they were here. This was far from a lighthearted visit.

He pulled two chairs away from the small round table near the kitchenette and carried them into the middle of the room. This whole place was about the size of his living room, and his house in Montegut was small.

"We'll answer whatever we can, but I'm not sure there's anything we can add to what the sheriff's office told you. They're in charge of the investigation." He sat on one of the chairs, wincing at a stain on one rung of the ladder-back. Looked like blood, although the place smelled like Pine-Sol. "Did the parish clean this place up for you?"

"Hell no. I've been on my hands and knees scrubbing since I got here three days ago." Ceelie looked around, and Gentry noted where her gaze stopped—wherever dark spots remained visible. Blood had soaked into the old wood. He wasn't sure she could ever get rid of the stains.

"To be fair, the sheriff's office offered to find someone to clean it for me, but I felt it was something I needed to do for my aunt." She tugged on her braid. Scraped a palm across her thigh. Moving. Restless. "I hadn't seen her in a long time, and that's on me. But I remember coming here a lot as a kid, and even though it was old and rundown, she kept this place immaculate. She'd be horrified to know what it looked like when . . . when you found her."

Gentry recognized regret and guilt woven into that amazing voice. He knew both emotions intimately.

"Are you planning to stay here long?" Jena asked. "Do you need anything?"

Ceelie shook her head. "I was surprised to find that Tante Eva had a little money tucked away in a jar on the kitchen counter, and that ramblin' wreck of a truck in the backyard still runs. I've been able to pick up what I need. As for how long I'll be here?" She shrugged. "Depends on how long it takes to settle the estate. It's giving me a chance to evaluate whether I want to go back to Nashville or make a change."

Gentry remembered seeing several hundred dollars, maybe more, scattered around on the counter when he'd found the body, and it had been one of the oddest parts of the scene to him. Even if robbery wasn't the motive, it took a certain kind of obsession—or a personal kind of rage—to leave money behind. Human instinct would always be to take the cash.

At least it had given Eva's niece something to live on, and if Ceelie needed her great-aunt's money, it told him her career in Nashville hadn't been going well. Which made him feel even guiltier for making assumptions about her.

He swatted at a mosquito on his arm, ignoring his partner's raised eyebrow. "Well, what can we tell you, Ms. Savoie?"

"Call me Ceelie." She got up and walked to the small table in front of the window, the one that still held the voodoo-ritual items he'd spotted the morning he'd found the body. Opening a drawer, she pulled out a tall, textured candle and a box of matches. "Citronella," she said, striking the match and setting the candle on the table. "For the mosquitoes. Agent Broussard, would you start at the beginning and tell me everything you saw the morning you found my aunt?"

He huffed out a breath. "Ms. Savoie—Ceelie—are you sure you want to hear it? I'm sure the sheriff's deputies—"

"Humor me." Ceelie's tone was friendly, but firm. "It makes no sense to me that someone would murder an eighty-year-old woman who lived in a glorified fish camp in the middle of nowhere. No sense whatsoever. You might remember a detail that sparks a memory or means something to me that didn't mean anything to the deputies."

She paused, and when she spoke again, her voice cracked. "Please."

So he told her, beginning with when he noticed the boat and, later, heard the thud. "Maybe if I'd checked here straightaway instead of stopping the poacher . . ." He didn't finish the sentence. Didn't need to. He'd been saying that sentence to himself ever since that morning.

"Don't," Ceelie said. "If you hadn't taken the time to stop by, no telling when anyone would've found her."

She peppered them with questions for more than a half hour. She wiped away tears a couple of times, but never lost control. Her demeanor was forthright and plainspoken, but never aggressive. She reminded Gentry of her great-aunt, at least in the few conversations he'd had with Eva. Ceelie's forthrightness must not have set well with the TPSO detectives if they'd labeled her as temperamental—or maybe she'd just had time to calm down.

"I have one more thing to ask," she said, fingering the patched spread on the bed. "Tell me about the table and what it looked like that morning—the small one beneath the window."

Gentry blinked. After the money on the counter, that table had been the next-oddest thing about the crime scene. Funny that she would home in on that.

He shifted to look at it, remembering how it had looked about this time five days ago. "The main thing I remember about the table was that it didn't appear to have been touched. It was one of the few places that hadn't been disturbed. Everything else was . . ." Hell, she knew what it was.

"A bloody mess, I know." Ceelie's storm-cloud eyes seemed to almost glow from the darkened corner where the bed sat. Gentry wasn't sure he'd ever seen anyone quite so striking. He'd like to just sit and look at her, which was . . . pathetic. "What was on the table?"

Gentry glanced again at the small piece of furniture. "The two wide candles were on there, although they were farther apart, at opposite corners of the table. They were both lit."

"And there was a pile of sticks on the table," Jena added.

Ceelie nodded. "Not sticks. Bones."

Gentry jerked his gaze from the table back to Ceelie. "What kind of bones? So your aunt really was a, uh, practitioner?"

Ceelie smiled, but Gentry thought it was more ironic than amused. "Chicken bones. And do you mean was Tante Eva really a voodoo queen? Or did she follow the ways of the native mystics? Don't worry—I've heard the stories. Maybe so. I don't know what a voodoo queen is, really. Do you?"

Gentry opened his mouth to answer, then snapped it shut and shook his head. He didn't know a damned thing about voodoo or mysticism except that it was creepy and there was more of it out here in the dark corners of the parish than most people thought. His were a superstitious people. And their superstitions and beliefs weren't the type of "spells" and paraphernalia tourists bought at shops in New Orleans.

"I do know she believed in some of it," Ceelie said. "Maybe more than some. Anyway, do you remember anything else about the table?"

Gentry walked over to it and looked down. It was a small wooden rectangle with simple, straight legs attached by what looked like hand-cut dovetail joints. Which meant it was old and probably twice as strong as most of the pressboard crap being made today.

He studied the items on the table. "This piece of leather or hide was underneath the candles and bones that morning, placed just like it is now. The bones were in the middle, and the candles at two corners. There was no blood on the table, which is what struck me as odd. I don't remember anything else." He looked at Jena. "You?"

"No. Why is the table important, Ms. Savoie—Ceelie?"

She shook her head. "I just thought it was weird that the table hadn't been disturbed when everything else in the room had been dumped out or torn apart. Seemed like my aunt's murderer was afraid of it, maybe, which means he knew what it was and had enough respect for it—or fear—not to touch it."

Gentry looked back at Ceelie. Smart woman. He hadn't thought about it, but she was right. It was the only thing to explain that table being undisturbed. All it really meant, though, was that the killer knew the local culture, which didn't narrow things down much.

Would Lang have been afraid to disturb the table? Could he have committed the awful crime that had taken place here? God forgive him, but Gentry hoped not. He'd rather his brother stay dead and at peace than be alive and capable of such cruelty.

Ceelie caught his gaze and smiled, a sight that jerked his thoughts away from the crime and sent them toward places they didn't need to go. Then her expression turned thoughtful. "You look familiar, Agent Broussard. Have we met somewhere?"

"Call me Gentry." Hell no, he would never have forgotten that voice, those eyes. "I don't think so, but I grew up in Dulac. Maybe you've seen me around."

"Maybe, but I haven't been back in the parish in a decade." She kept staring and it made him twitchy. "It'll come to me. Anyway, don't guess you knew LeRoy Breaux when you were growing up in Dulac, did you?"

Probably a quarter of the people in Terrebonne Parish were named Breaux; another quarter were Broussards. "No, sorry. Is he important to the case?"

Ceelie shrugged. "He lived with my aunt for a while when I was a kid, and I just wondered what happened to him—not that he'd have killed her. I mean, he was older than her, as near as I can remember. I always thought they were married, since I grew up calling him Nonc LeRoy."

Gentry hadn't heard anything about a man in Eva Savoie's life. "So this LeRoy Breaux lived with your aunt? What happened to him?"

Ceelie walked to the window, blew out the citronella candle, and squeezed the wick between her fingers to make sure it was out. "He ditched Tante Eva when I was a kid. I think it runs in the family; my mom did the same thing to my dad."

Gentry blinked and gave Jena a helpless look. What did one say to that?

"Is there anything else you wanted to ask us about your aunt?" Jena gave him a *you're-hopeless* head shake. "I got here later than Gentry, but if there's anything else . . ."

Ceelie turned and squared her shoulders. "No, I just needed to hear all that. Thank you."

She followed them to the door and onto the porch. The air outside was hot and sticky, but unlike the air inside the cabin, at least it was moving.

Gentry turned back, leaving Jena to continue to the truck. "By the way, I know a guy over in Chauvin who rehabs used AC units. We've still got at least six weeks of hot weather. Want me to see if he's got something that would work for you?"

"Thanks, but unless he's giving them away, I'll just sweat it out." Ceelie smiled again, and it looked good on her. Too good. "I'm calling it my swamp diet. Every step's a sweaty workout."

Gentry bit his tongue before he could offer up his opinion that there wasn't a thing on her that needed work. Instead, he slid his sunglasses out of their resting place—hanging by one arm out of his shirt pocket—and stuck them on his face. Better put them on now in case his pupils had dilated with lust or something else humiliating that she didn't need to see. She was a short-timer, a woman who'd rejected this place he'd loved his whole life. She'd made it clear she was leaving Terrebonne behind as soon as she got Eva's estate settled. Plus, agents didn't ogle crime victims.

"You got a card?" Ceelie asked. "You know, in case I have any other questions. Would it be okay to call you? Agent Sinclair gave me her card when you got here."

Yeah, and if he hadn't had his head so far up his backside, he'd have done the same. It was standard protocol. He obviously needed sleep. Preferably without the nightmares.

"Let me know if you change your mind about the air conditioner." He fished a business card out of his wallet and handed it to her. "And call me anytime. My cell number's on the card."

He found Jena waiting around the corner, obviously eavesdropping. She wore a smirk but kept her mouth shut until they climbed in the truck and got back on the highway.

"Call me Gentry," she purred. "Call me anytime. My cell number's on the card."

He turned the AC fan on high and tugged down the bill of his cap, slumping in the seat and closing his eyes. "Shut the hell up, Red."

CHAPTER 6

Ceelie stuck her head around the corner, watching Gentry Broussard follow his partner to a dusty black monster of a pickup truck. *Nice ass.*

Then again, there was something about a guy in a uniform most women found irresistible. Ceelie and Sonia had pondered this peculiar phenomenon over late-night glasses of moscato back in Nashville. They'd decided it had to be the belt and all the equipment that dangled from it when the guys walked, which not only was phallic but probably released extra sex pheromones into the air and turned women into nectar-seeking honeybees.

Which was exactly why it was dangerous for her to stay too long in Terrebonne Parish. It felt too comfortable. In fact, it felt damned good. It felt like home in a way Nashville never had. Staying would be too easy, and one day she'd wake up and realize she hadn't left Terrebonne Parish in ten years, or twenty.

Plus, the men here were one of two types: either total losers or sexy and overburdened with testosterone. Too many of them, like Gentry Broussard, had a confident, unconscious sexuality that would bulldoze a woman into a single-wide with a half-dozen kids before she knew what hit her.

And a dog. A guy like that probably had at least one or two hunting dogs, and not cute little beagles, either. Big dogs.

Ceelie preferred cats and small dogs, although they tended to be eaten by alligators around here, as she recalled. Munchability wasn't a desirable trait in a pet. She also didn't like trailers, and she was pretty sure she didn't want kids. Between having been abandoned by her mom and bullied by small-town mean girls, her own childhood had sucked; she wouldn't have her own child subjected to it.

So yeah, a guy like Gentry Broussard left her feeling restless and needy and defiant, all at the same time. She was annoyed that she'd checked out his left hand for the wedding ring and had been pleased there hadn't been one.

Weapon-belt pheromones. Had to be.

He did look familiar, but she couldn't figure out why. She'd been gone ten years, so if she'd seen him before, they'd both been a lot younger. If she'd recently seen that curly hair, those melted-dark-chocolate eyes and for-God's-sake dimples, she would remember.

Other than awakening her libido, which she'd now have to beat back into submission, the visit hadn't accomplished much. She wasn't sure what she expected the game wardens to tell her that she didn't already know, but it had been worth a try. And Gentry had confirmed her suspicion that nothing on Tante Eva's throwing table had been touched.

Ceelie hadn't touched it either, and she wasn't sure she was ready. So first, she filled another bucket with water, mixed in some bleach, and got on her hands and knees with a sponge, scrubbing at bloodstains for at least the sixth or seventh time. The light coming through the open windows and door at different hours of the day kept revealing blotches she'd missed earlier.

After the bleach, she retraced her steps using the pine cleaner until the place reeked. At least it reeked of clean things and not death.

Finally, she couldn't stand it any longer; that shrine beneath the window whispered to her like some kind of dark siren. She stashed the cleaning supplies in the cramped cabinet under the sink, then approached the throwing table. Tante Eva had called it that when Ceelie came out on weekends and, during the summer, for whole weeks or two at a time. That had been in the years after her mom left, until she'd turned sixteen and her dad forbade her to visit anymore.

Forbade her because of what she'd learned at this table and had been stupid enough to let him catch her doing.

Those had been bittersweet years. At the time, she'd thought her dad sent her here so often because she loved Tante Eva so much. Looking back as an adult, she thought maybe Dad had simply been overwhelmed that the woman he loved had packed her bags and taken a bus out of town in the middle of his afternoon shift at the gas plant. All while their eight-year-old daughter was trying to learn multiplication tables in her third-grade class.

Now? She thought he'd sent Ceelie to stay with his Tante Eva not only to give his daughter a mother figure but to give himself private time to mourn the life he'd lost. He'd have struggled to make sense of it, would have wanted to figure out how he'd misjudged the character of his wife so badly. Would have needed to vent his anger where his daughter wouldn't see him.

The day her mom ran off to Texas or California or wherever she'd ended up—not running *toward* anything but simply away from them—Ceelie had come home from school to find a silent house and, on the kitchen counter, a white sealed envelope she'd instinctively known was not hers to read. Unsure of what else to do, she had taken her favorite teddy bear and crawled in her parents' bed to wait for Daddy to come home. Afraid he wouldn't. Afraid she'd be alone.

Dad had been trapped in a dead-end, dangerous job that eventually served up a cancer cocktail, and he had gotten stuck with a confused, lost daughter to raise by himself. No wonder he'd made her promise to leave Houma the first chance she got.

Now, here she was, back on Whiskey Bayou, which made Houma look like New York City.

Humming that damned song she couldn't finish but couldn't get out of her head, Ceelie dragged over one of the kitchenette chairs and sat in front of the throwing table. The memories in this cabin were visceral, palpable things, and maybe seeing this table explained why they were pummeling her with such force. She rarely thought of her mom's cut-and-run anymore, but the ghosts had paraded past her like Mardi Gras floats since she'd gotten off the bus in Houma and found a driver willing to bring her down here—*down da baya*, as the old-timers said.

Ceelie moved the candles to the northeast and southwest positions before realizing what she'd done. Even through the *eau de Pine-Sol*, they smelled sweet, like the water lilies she remembered from being here as a kid. Most likely, Tante Eva had poured these candles herself. Ceelie remembered rows of new candles hanging at the end of the side porch, waiting for Tante Eva to bless them before she'd bring them into the house and light them.

A fine lot of good those blessings had done. Ceelie wrapped the candles in a paper towel and placed them in the middle of the drawer, then took the fragile, yellowed chicken bones and settled them one by one into the satin-lined carved wooden box Tante Eva kept for them.

"Bones gotta have a special place of respect," she'd told Ceelie more times than she could count. "You treat them right and they'll always speak true."

"The bones never lie," Ceelie whispered, placing the last one—a tiny skull—into the box and closing the lid.

She settled the box in the drawer along with the rolled-up square of leather that Tante Eva had told her was a gift from the greatest mystic in the parish. Ceelie didn't remember his name, only that he'd lived even farther down the bayou.

Ceelie splashed some water on her face and neck before picking up her guitar and going back to the porch. She'd forgotten how quiet it could be out here during the heat of the day, even with the occasional buzz of an outboard wafting across the water as the gator hunters did their thing.

At night, as she had relearned, the bayou came to noisy life, filled with croaks, growls, hisses, and splashes. The first night, still surrounded by blood and chaos, she'd jolted awake at each noise. Now, the sounds were comforting proof of nature's resilience no matter how hard humans tried to destroy it.

She strummed the notes of the song, picking it out in different keys until she hit the one that felt right today. Tomorrow, it might be different. Until a song told you it was done, it remained a moving, growing thing.

> *I won't go back, I won't go home,*
> *'Cause in this place, the dead still roam.*
> *In this old house lies a pile of bones.*
> *Throw them down once,*
> *Throw them easy,*
> *Throw them slow.*
> *'Cause Whiskey Bayou, she won't let me go . . .*

A distinctive, guttural hiss interrupted Ceelie's song, and she watched, mesmerized, as a dark-brown bird with at least a five-foot wingspan made a wobbly circle overhead before coming to rest on a cypress knee rising from the water a few feet from the front of the cabin. It hissed again and turned its bright-red head, a black glittering eye, and its sharply hooked beak toward Ceelie.

"*Carencro,*" she whispered. "*Mauvaises choses.*"

A vulture, Tante Eva always said, was a sign of impending danger and sorrow. Despite temperatures in the midnineties and a hundred percent humidity, a line of chill bumps rose on Ceelie's arms and shoulders as she and the turkey vulture, the ugliest of the *carencro*, stared at each other.

She set her guitar aside and went in the house to hunt down the salt, finding an almost-empty box on the kitchen counter. The bird watched as if in disdain as she sprinkled a line of white granules around the perimeter of the porch, with a double line at the threshold of the door and the bottoms of the window casings.

With a final hiss as if to tell her the low regard in which it held her rudimentary ritual to ward off evil, the vulture flapped its enormous wings and took off with a clumsy leap. For a moment, she thought it might fall in the water—hoped it would—but it rose, circling over the cabin a couple of times before disappearing. It wasn't completely gone, though; it had left behind the stench of its latest rotten-meat meal and fine particles of something foul that wafted behind in its wake.

Now there was only silence, ominous where earlier it had sounded clean and pure. The buzzard might be gone, but something else watched her. She felt it.

Forget the heat. Ceelie took her guitar inside, closed and locked the door and the two front windows. She crawled onto the bed, wedged into an alcove beneath the small side window, and closed and locked that one, too. She coated the door threshold and all the windowsills with what was left of the salt.

You're being an idiot, Celestine. And she was going to have heatstroke in this house with no air moving, but between the memories and the buzzard, she was too jittery to open things up again. Tomorrow, if she hadn't been baked alive overnight, she'd call Gentry Broussard and ask about the guy with the cheap air conditioners.

CHAPTER 7

Saturday nights always kept LDWF enforcement agents busy, so nothing about the evening had surprised Gentry. People drank and hunted, drank and fished, or drank and steered boats around the parish waterways like they were nautical bumper cars. Sometimes they smoked crystal meth, argued, and shot each other, but that was the sheriff's problem—unless it happened while they also were hunting, fishing, or boating.

Gentry and Jena had already hauled out of Lake Gero two guys who'd run their boat onto the bank and were still sitting in the half-submerged hull arguing about who was at fault. The agents had issued four other DUIs and had impounded two boats no one was sober enough to drive. They'd fished a poodle out of Bayou Dulac. They'd caught a boater with enough marijuana to make him a Colorado millionaire, and turned him and his stash over to the sheriff, along with a semiautomatic and high-capacity magazine.

Now, at midnight, they were headed back to the boat launch to get in their respective trucks and spend a few hours doing paperwork.

Except Gentry had something on his mind, and he'd put it off as long as he could. They'd exchanged their usual banter tonight, neither of them mentioning Eva Savoie or the murder case. Gentry had no intention of discussing how much he'd been thinking about Ceelie Savoie and her sexy voice. He did have an agenda related to the case, though.

"Hold up, Red," he said after they'd gotten the boat hitched to the back of his truck and stashed their gear. "You still got some contacts at NOPD?"

Jena leaned against her truck, her face shadowed in the dark parking lot lit by a single streetlight. "Depends on why you're asking. What's up?"

"I want to look at the paperwork on a closed case from a few years back."

Jena crossed her arms. "You worked in Orleans Parish long enough to know they'd let you look at a closed case file if you asked. You were Wildlife and Fisheries, but you worked with the police force a lot. What are you not telling me?"

"I need it to be under the radar." Gentry tried to read her expression for any sign of suspicion, but couldn't see well enough. Plus, she was good at keeping a blank expression; he bet the NOPD had hated to lose her.

"Gentry, I won't do it unless you tell me what you're up to." Yep, she was definitely suspicious. "Does this have anything to do with Eva Savoie?"

He needed to trust her, but could he? He trusted her with his life on the job every night they partnered together, but could he trust her with his secrets? Especially this secret?

"You can talk to me, you know. Partner-partner privilege."

He chuckled. "You mean like doctor-patient or attorney-client privilege?"

"Something like that." She wasn't laughing.

He took a deep breath and plunged into the bayou of trust. It was deep, and its waters swift and dangerous. "I want to look at the files of the last case I worked in Orleans Parish. An interagency drug-smuggling case."

"The one where your brother was involved?"

They'd never discussed it, but he should've realized she'd know about his background, about why he'd eventually decided to transfer out of Region 8. He'd done his research on her, so she would've done the same, especially with her NOPD resources. He'd lay odds his file was a lot thicker than hers, and it wasn't just that he'd been an agent longer.

"You mean the case that involved my brother because I shot him? Yeah, that one."

"Okay." She paused. A long pause. "Can I ask why you want to revisit the files?"

Oh hell, maybe it would help to talk about it. "I caught a glimpse of Eva Savoie's killer, right?"

"Your description was pretty generic. Not a lot to go on."

True enough. "Yeah, well, the Broussard men aren't very distinctive, I guess."

Jena came to stand in front of him. He was six-two and she could almost look him in the eye, which was unsettling. Her expression had edged out of the shadows, and her brows contracted in a frown. "What are you saying, Gentry? What are you *not* saying?"

Deep breath; just get it out. "The killer was a dead ringer for my brother Lang, no pun intended." He looked past her into the darkness of Bayou Terrebonne. A shrimp boat rocked gently in the water, its white nets illuminated by the streetlight like misshapen spiderwebs. "I know it sounds nuts. Lang's dead. We buried him."

Jena shook her head. "No, you had a funeral. You didn't bury him, though, did you? His body wasn't found."

She'd definitely done her homework, and the fact they'd worked together for three months without her even hinting at what she knew upped his respect for her.

He huffed and ran his fingers along his jawline. He hadn't talked about that night in almost three years. For six months before that, he'd done nothing *but* talk about it—to the department psychiatrist, to his mom, and then to Warren Doucet and the region's captain up in Thibodaux, who wanted to make sure Gentry's head was screwed on straight before he offered him the position in Region 6 that let Gentry come home. Until then, he hadn't realized how badly he wanted to come back to the parish.

"Lang was strung out that night." Gentry spoke softly. "Really strung out. He'd been screwed up for a long time, but the drug use had gotten worse. That night, he had a gun and a nothing-to-lose attitude."

He and his LDWF partner had been doing what started as a routine boat check in bad weather, not expecting to find a haul of drugs in the small trawler. Lang had been on the aft deck, on guard over the fishing tanks full of drugs.

"What went wrong?"

"He tried to bluff me. He took aim at my partner, thinking I wouldn't call his bluff. Lang was sure his baby brother wouldn't shoot him." In his nightmares, Gentry always saw the defiance on his brother's face turn to shock when he saw the kid he'd always called Gent raise his weapon and fire without hesitation. "I put two bullets in him. I didn't miss."

Jena nodded. "And he went over the back end of the boat?"

The ship had been tossing like a kid's toy in that maelstrom. "I don't see how he could've survived with those wounds in those conditions. We were at the tail end of a tropical storm and the river was as rough as I've ever seen it."

Rough and wide and deep. The Mighty Mississippi had earned its nickname that night.

"Well, you weren't that close to Eva's killer and he was wearing a hood. It's probably just somebody who looks like your brother." Jena fished her truck keys out of her pocket. "But yeah, I'll get the digital files sent to me and send them to you on the down-low. But there are two things I want in return."

"Name them." He appreciated not only her not being judgmental, but also the way she'd nudged him through his story without pushing.

"Keep me in the loop, Gentry—no going rogue. Talk to the lieutenant. Tell Warren what you just told me. It's probably got nothing to do with your brother, but on the off chance that it does, Warren needs to know. Let him make the call as to whether or not it goes to the region's captain or the sheriff, but don't let him get blindsided."

Damn it, she was right and he knew it. Warren deserved that consideration and more for taking a chance on the youngest son of his first partner, "Big Hank" Broussard. Warren was only in his midforties, but he had his shit together. He was no-nonsense but fair and, in his way, kind.

Gentry took a deep breath of the heavy night air and watched the shrimp boat for a few moments. "Agreed. Let me look at the files, and I'll talk to Warren."

He didn't look forward to either one.

Before heading back to Montegut and a pile of paperwork, Gentry decided to take a short jaunt west to Dulac. If somehow, by some miracle, Lang had survived that night, he would come back here, return to his old stomping grounds. It was possible that, even if he were alive and laying low around Dulac, he wouldn't know Gentry was back in Terrebonne Parish. They had never run in the same circles. Just after Gentry graduated high school, Mom had moved to Shreveport with her second husband—Louis the accountant—and Gentry's two stepsisters; he had few ties in Dulac from the old days. Four years older, Lang by then had been deeply immersed in his small-town gang, picking up day jobs on the shrimp boats to make ends meet.

More than anything, though, when a person was hurt and needed to lick his wounds, he went home, or whatever passed for home. It was why Gentry had wanted the job in Terrebonne so badly. Lang would have the same instincts. He'd fallen in with a loser crowd here in Dulac. He'd gotten his first taste of alcohol and drugs here. It was home. It was where he'd go if he needed to hide out and regroup.

For the next hour, Gentry cruised up and down streets and alleyways along Bayou Dulac, looking for the beat-up shitpile of a boat that had been at Eva's house last Saturday morning. He drove to Lang's old haunts, or at least the ones he knew about that were still there. Many had been washed away by the steady procession of hurricanes that had flooded the parish over the last decade: Lili, Katrina, Rita, Gustav, Ike, Isaac.

He pulled the truck into a convenience-store lot and went inside to buy a soft drink; the sight of a skinny kid with buzzed white-blond hair and an armful of tats reminded Gentry of a name he hadn't thought about in years. Tommy Mason had been Lang's best buddy back in the days after high school. Gentry would be sweating on the football practice field with the Terrebonne Tigers as a sophomore running back and see Lang and Tommy through the fence, hanging out in the parking lot, smoking Marlboros and who knows what else. Even then, they'd been on different life tracks, and Gentry's idolatry of his older brother had long faded.

Using the computerized unit mounted to his truck's center console, Gentry ran a simple Internet search for a Thomas Mason in the parish and got three hits—one with a Dulac address.

He had a lot of reports to write, but Gentry couldn't resist tracking down the current home of Tommy Mason, if it was even the same guy. The house was a raised modular rectangle on Shrimpers Row, about a mile south of town and west of the bayou. Like the rest of the parish, Dulac had been dealt a hard blow by Hurricane Ike in 2008. The whole parish had been underwater, and, as was usual in hurricane flooding situations, LDWF agents were all-in with search-and-rescue efforts.

Those who stayed rebuilt higher, and it looked like Tommy Mason had been one of them. Gentry's place in Montegut was a little bigger and a little higher, but not by much. The house was dark, and no vehicles were home. Also no boat. It might be a long shot, but Gentry's gut told him that if Lang were somehow alive and back in the parish, Tommy would know.

Gentry wanted the element of surprise, though, so he wouldn't leave a business card as he'd do if his visit were any kind of official matter. Instead, he'd try again tomorrow before going on shift. This highly unofficial call needed to be done on his own time, and if he got even a whiff that Tommy was lying or covering for Lang, he wouldn't promise to follow the rules.

CHAPTER 8

Ceelie woke up with her cheek resting on an ax handle and a handle-shaped indentation on her face that took a lot of scrubbing to erase. She'd slept with the rusty ax and two knives—a fish-cleaning blade under her pillow and a butcher knife beneath the mattress, handle out.

Near the top of her to-do list today, following visits to the health department to pick up Tante Eva's death certificate and the parish probate office to talk about the estate: buy a gun, or at least a new ax.

She knew how to shoot. Her dad had never been a hunter, but he'd indulged his daughter's desire to learn and signed her up for a gun-safety class offered by the sheriff's office when she was fourteen or fifteen. She was rusty, but figured she could practice on any buzzards that happened to show up outside her door.

Because if the appearance of a *carencro* had freaked her out enough to make her sleep with an ax, she figured her subconscious was not-so-subtly telling her to find an adequate means of self-protection. She might be Eva Savoie's great-niece, but she was also Gary Savoie's daughter, which meant she was practical enough to understand that salt would only protect her so far.

The probate office didn't open until ten, so Ceelie had a couple of hours to kill before leaving; she'd always been an early riser. First on the agenda was convincing herself to reopen the doors and windows and let in some fresh air. The sun was already bright, but the morning held a touch of coolness that caressed her skin when she finally worked up the nerve to step onto the porch. Nothing looked out of place, but she tensed at the sound of an outboard motor.

After an agonizing ten or twenty seconds that felt more like an hour, a boat came into view and Ceelie let out a whoosh of relief. She could tell by the gear and the two guys throwing casual, disinterested waves as they passed that they were fishing. Maybe they were fishing for gators, maybe for gar, maybe for catfish. But not for Eva Savoie's heir.

She needed to stop being a paranoid idiot. Other than the appearance of a common predatory bird and her own rampaging imagination, there was no reason to think Tante Eva's killer would have any interest in her. He had been looking for something specific, or such was the consensus of the authorities, since money had been left lying around and the cabin had been turned inside out.

The killer had probably gotten what he wanted. After all, he'd been leaving when Gentry Broussard had spotted him. Otherwise, the sexy warden would've caught him in the act, still on the prowl for whatever he sought.

Even if the killer hadn't found what he'd been looking for, the murderous SOB should have done his homework. So he'd know Celestine Savoie hadn't set foot in Louisiana in ten years. If he had half the brain God gave him, he'd realize that she couldn't have any useful information.

Last night, she had let superstition get the best of her, plain and simple. Her days back in Terrebonne had been filled with charity-funeral arrangements, legal matters, cleaning up bloodstains, and running from memories. Time to get real and decide what to do with the rest of her life. She sure didn't plan to spend it around Whiskey Bayou, sleeping with an ax.

After a tepid shower, Ceelie downed two cups of Eva's nasty instant coffee made with water boiled on the ancient white GE stove. She'd kept her clothes in her suitcase since arriving, not wanting either to stain them with blood and bleach or, maybe, to admit to herself that she might be here a while. Now she admitted it. She doubted that people were lined up to buy a spit of land in a place that turned into an island practically as soon as the skies turned dark.

Until she sold the land, she couldn't afford to leave.

Now, she dumped out her pathetic excuse for a wardrobe on the bed and surveyed her options. What hadn't fit in the suitcase, she'd bagged up before leaving Nashville and set in the hallway for Goodwill to pick up. Only the two pieces of furniture remained in the apartment.

Which meant, on some level, she'd known this move was permanent, at least as far as Tennessee was concerned. She didn't know where she'd go next, but without rent to worry about and with the money she'd found scattered around Tante Eva's cabin—*her* cabin—she could survive long enough to decide. Austin had a healthy music scene, and Texas might look more kindly on Cajun hippie music than Nashville.

Her best jeans were clean, so she pulled those on, along with one of her few tops that weren't long-sleeved, T-shirts, or tanks. The scoop-necked knit was black with three-quarter sleeves, which meant it would hold every bit of heat and she'd be sweating like a wild boar by the time she coaxed the dinosaur of a pickup all the way to Houma. Shopping was on her to-do list, but for food, not clothes. Clothes were a luxury.

At a quarter of ten, she grabbed her purse and the set of keys she'd found in Tante Eva's tattered black handbag that the woman must've been carrying around since the 1960s. In a nod to her paranoia of the previous night, Ceelie closed and locked all the windows and tried odd keys on the key ring until she found one that fit the front door. In her earlier outings, she hadn't felt the need to lock the place.

Maybe she'd really splurge with the paranoia and buy a new deadbolt while she was in Houma.

It occurred to her, as she rounded the porch to reach the driveway and the old pickup, that Tante Eva had once owned a boat. Anyone living out here with a lick of sense would have a boat, since the roads went underwater so easily. Maybe when Nonc LeRoy had decided to put on his walking shoes, he'd taken off in the boat and that's how Tante Eva ended up with the pickup. Had they worked out who'd keep what, or had LeRoy just left, or had Eva thrown him out?

Those answers, Ceelie figured she'd never know.

She did get some answers at the probate office, however. Since Tante Eva had died without a will, and Celestine Savoie was listed as the only surviving next of kin on the sheriff's paperwork and the death certificate, Ceelie only had to fill out a pile of forms and wait for ownership of the cabin and its contents to officially transfer to her. That was the smaller portion of her inheritance; the most valuable was the title to ten acres of land in Terrebonne Parish. The transfer process would take about a month, if no one showed up to contest it after the notice ran in the Houma paper.

Just like that, she was a property owner. Never mind that most of her ten acres was swamp. If she decided to keep it, she could lease hunting rights in different seasons and make a steady little income, or at least that's what the woman in the probate office had told her. She'd also said Ceelie would have to check with one of the local game wardens to find out the exact regulations.

For better or worse, she knew a couple of local game wardens.

Ceelie had spotted a Walmart on the way into Houma, so she stopped and picked up a deadbolt lock, a few groceries, and the largest container of unrefined salt she could find, just in case another flying bag of feathers gave her the willies and she felt the need to cast some more serious juju.

Ceelie would try to be mature about the whole bad-vibe thing, but at the end of the day, she was Eva Savoie's great-niece and had learned at a young age about the protective powers of a handful of Morton Salt, preferably without iodine.

Speaking of protection, Ceelie sat in the Walmart parking lot and reconsidered the wisdom of buying a gun, although she'd noticed a couple of sporting-goods stores and a gun shop on the way into Houma. It had been so long since she'd fired one, however, that she stood a good chance of ending up as one of those idiots brought into the emergency room after having shot off her own toes. Plus she had no medical insurance.

No gun, then. She climbed out of the truck and went back inside the Walmart, this time heading for the sporting-goods department. It took less than a minute for her to admit she knew nothing about knives and throw herself on the mercy of a bored store employee with a nametag that read "Dave."

"What you need depends on what you want to use it for," Dave said, settling his focus on her chest. Dickhead. "You wantin' to skin a boar or peel a tater?"

Ceelie narrowed her eyes. "I want it to use on an intruder in my house out on Whiskey Bayou, seeing as how my Tante Eva Savoie the voodoo queen has been murdered," she said, giving him a sweet smile in response to his widening eyes. "You know, as a fail-safe to cut out his heart with in case my own spell doesn't work."

Five minutes later, she was back in the truck with a brutal-looking tactical knife that would make a much better bed-buddy than the rusty old ax. She also had a scrap of paper on which Dave the Walmart salesman had scribbled his phone number. Turned out he was fascinated by voodoo rather than fearful of it, was turned on by a woman with enough confidence to cut out a beating heart, and thought they could have some fun together.

Ceelie thought so too. When hell froze over. She wadded up Dave's phone number and threw it in a Dumpster on her way out of the parking lot.

The twenty-mile drive south from Houma led her toward a blackening sky, with cloud-to-ground lightning already streaking in the distance.

A prickly sensation crossed her shoulder blades when she finally pulled into the long drive leading to the cabin. Nothing appeared out of place at the back of the house, so her unsettled feeling could probably be blamed on the weather. The sky had turned an ugly charcoal gray; even ordinary thunderstorms could be fierce here at the bottom of the world.

At least it would cool things down for a few hours. Ceelie had spent her cheap-AC-unit money on the overpriced knife.

She gathered her bags and papers, pushed the truck door shut with her hip, and made it to the protective overhang of the wraparound porch in time to escape the first raindrops. They fell in big, fat plops, slowly at first and, within seconds, so hard that visibility dropped to two feet, max.

A faint odor of cigarette smoke hung in the thick, humid air. Intent on looking for any signs of movement in the swamp or the sign of a smoker in a boat, Ceelie rounded the corner of the porch to the front of the house and didn't stop until something wispy brushed past her nose and cheek.

She let out an *eep* and froze a breathless second before backing up. A human skull hung from a frayed rope tied onto a hook in the porch ceiling, the dirty, worn strands of fiber woven through the eye sockets. It hung low enough for her to look the thing right in the eyes, or could if it had eyes. About half of its yellow teeth had been broken off. It swung toward her, propelled by the wind from the storm.

A tingle of adrenaline raced up her back and across her scalp. She did a slow one-eighty, looking for anything else out of place, and dropped her bags with a clatter when her gaze came to rest on the front door.

GO HOME, BITCH.

The words had been scrawled in red. Paint or blood, Ceelie wasn't sure. Through the heavy curtain of rain, she scanned the bayou again. Her breath hitched at . . . something. A dark shadow moved through the water close to the opposite bank.

Ceelie had no intention of hanging around to see if it was an alligator or a murderer. She kicked the probate papers and groceries out of the way, grabbed her purse and the plastic bag containing the knife, and raced back to the truck, digging the keys out of her pocket along the way. Once inside, she jammed down the door locks and backed out into the highway, barely missing a tanker truck racing northbound from one of the refineries.

She had to squint to see through the rain that blew in heavy sheets against the windows. People. She needed to find people, which meant going north toward Montegut. She stopped at the first public place she reached—a convenience store and gas station.

Through the Jiffy Stop's front windows, she could see people moving around the aisles, doing business as usual, talking, laughing. A couple of kids chased each other back and forth under the awning that stretched across the front of the store, holding their arms out into the rain and squealing when they got splashed. Around her, a few other folks sat in their cars, probably waiting for the rain to slacken.

Ceelie's heart rate slowed, although it was still far beyond normal, a trot instead of a full-on gallop. When she pulled her phone from her purse, her hands shook so badly that she dropped it on the floorboard. A card from her wallet landed beside it: Gentry Broussard's business card.

"Call me anytime," he'd said.

She didn't give herself a chance to rationalize her fear or talk herself out of asking for help. Seeking assistance wasn't her way, but she wasn't dealing with a drunk bar patron or a skeezy club owner.

"Broussard." Gentry Broussard's deep voice stroked her panic like a reassuring hand, calming her with his casual greeting. When she didn't answer immediately, his tone grew more clipped. "Is someone there?"

"Yes. I mean, no. Yes. It's Ceelie Savoie." God, her voice sounded like that of a frog, and now that she had him on the line, she didn't know where to start. "Somebody was at the cabin."

Lame. So lame.

"First, are you in immediate danger?"

Ceelie looked around her. "No, I don't think so."

His voice was solid, warm, and dead calm. Her trembling slowed and the tension in her shoulders eased. "Okay, tell me what happened, Ceelie. Someone showed up at the cabin? You're not there now, are you?"

"No, not there now." She took a deep breath. "Somebody was at the cabin. He hung a skull, wrote on the door in blood. Maybe paint. There was cigarette smoke." God, she was making no sense. She took another deep breath. For a woman who prided herself on her independence, she was coming across like a helpless victim. That thought was enough to help center her.

"Where are you now?" Over the phone, she heard a crunch of gravel, then the slam of a heavy door and an engine roaring to life. "I'll come to you."

She looked up at the sign on the front of the convenience store. "I'm at the Jiffy Stop on Highway 55 about a mile north of the cabin."

"I'm on my way from Montegut. Sit tight." He paused and it sounded like he took a curve fast. "Don't go back to that cabin until I get there."

"I'll wait on you. And Gentry, be careful." These roads were awful in this weather, and she was beginning to feel silly.

It didn't even occur to her until she'd ended the call that she probably should've called the sheriff's office rather than a game warden. But her heart knew what it knew, and it instinctively trusted Gentry

Broussard. She'd have a long talk with her heart later, because those kinds of instincts could easily get her in a different kind of trouble.

Unfortunately, her heart now also admitted that whoever had tried to scare her away from the cabin—and had succeeded, at least temporarily—would try again. Whatever had happened to Tante Eva, it wasn't over.

CHAPTER 9

Gentry had been tempted to stay on the line with Ceelie to reassure himself that she was really safe, but she seemed to have calmed down, and he needed to make a couple of other calls. She'd been smart to go to a place where there were a lot of people around.

First, he called Stella, gave her a brief update, and asked her to find out who the sheriff's office had in the area. To his relief, the closest deputy was Adam Meizel, a veteran officer who'd worked Eva's murder scene, so he knew the case. He and Gentry had worked together several times over the past few years and were on friendly terms. Gentry even had his number programmed into the phone.

"Why're you in the middle of this, Broussard?" Adam asked after getting the few details Gentry could provide. Ceelie hadn't been quite coherent. "How come Ms. Savoie didn't call us?"

"We're . . ." What were he and Ceelie Savoie, really? After one meeting, he couldn't even say they were friends. He was way out of practice, so he could've misinterpreted their simple exchange as a spark of chemistry. However attractive he found her, Gentry wasn't even sure he liked the woman. She planned to sell that piece of heaven that had dropped into her lap, for God's sake.

No, what he felt was guilt. "I was out there a couple of days ago answering questions about her aunt, so I was probably just the first person she thought of. This is your call; I'm just going as an acquaintance."

Sort of a friendly acquaintance. Maybe.

The fact she'd called him first, though, and called him by his first name and not "Agent Broussard" when she cautioned him to be careful, sent a ridiculous surge of heat through his body. This was in no way, shape, or form a case in which he needed to be involved.

First, he had mistaken the killer for his dead brother, which put his mental state in question.

Second, he found Ceelie Savoie sexy as hell and it pushed every protective, macho button in his caveman brain. That was just inappropriate: he was a law-enforcement officer and she was a victim.

Third, and probably most important, this case was not his jurisdiction, and the sheriff's office wouldn't tolerate him getting in the middle of it. Neither would his own lieutenant. Warren would stick him on permanent paperwork duty, or worse. Rumor had it, after Mac Griffin had mouthed off in a meeting one day, Warren had made him sharpen a hundred pencils with a manual sharpener.

"Well, if you're going anyway, *acquaintance*, you mind meeting Ms. Savoie at the Jiffy Stop and escorting her to the cabin?" Sarcasm cut through Meizel's voice. Guess Gentry's feigned disinterest hadn't been very convincing. "I'm farther south than you and can get to the cabin faster if I don't have to backtrack. You know, since you're already *acquaintances* and all."

"No problem." With or without Meizel's go-ahead, Gentry had every intention of meeting Ceelie. He sped up as the rain eased slightly, now more of a gully-washer than a frog-splasher. He recognized Meizel's attempt to banter with him over the *acquaintance* business, but he wasn't taking that bait. He needed to make sure Ceelie was okay, and damn the reasons he shouldn't get involved. Then he'd ponder the status of their relationship.

You do not have a relationship, jackass. Guilt. Professional concern. A little physical attraction. Nothing more.

He flipped on the blue emergency-light bar that crossed the top of his truck, both to help people spot him in the still-steady rain and to spur them to get out of his way. The drive was still slow, with water ponding on the road in low spots. One of these days, the rain would fall and the swamp would rise and this land would be gone for good. Not in his lifetime if he could help it, but he wasn't optimistic that humankind could hang on to it forever.

Finally, he spotted the old Chevy pickup in the Jiffy Stop lot and let out a breath of relief when he saw Ceelie's silhouette through the rain and the truck window. He'd been afraid she'd called up her stubborn streak and gone back to the cabin alone, or else she'd been followed here by the waste of humanity who'd left a skull on her porch. At least, he thought that's what she'd said in her disjointed description of what happened. And something about red paint.

He whipped his truck into the parking spot next to her, and the fury in her face when she turned to look at him through the window took him aback. She'd been shaky when she called, frightened, and rightly so. Now she looked like a volcano on the verge of covering some poor village in molten lava. She didn't need comforting anymore; she needed calming down.

He motioned her toward his truck. Better to go in his vehicle since they were *acquaintances* anyway. He had plenty of firepower should Meizel need backup; LDWF agents were nothing if not well armed. The state equipped them to handle the wide variety of crap they might encounter. They'd even been armed with high-capacity rifles, since agents had taken gunfire while doing search and rescue in New Orleans after Katrina.

Ceelie jumped out of Eva's beat-up Chevy and climbed in his passenger's seat, throwing a gray plastic Walmart bag ahead of her. He picked it up and peered inside at a tactical knife still in its packaging.

"Planning to cut somebody?" From the look on her face, the answer would be yes.

"You better believe it." Water beaded on Ceelie's black hair, and she swiped an already-wet sleeve across her face and shook her head like his dog Hoss after Gentry had insulted him with a bath. Her wet black top clung to every curve. He jerked his gaze back to the knife. Acquaintances didn't notice things like curves.

The woman had no clue how sexy she was, which made her even sexier. And wet. Gentry reached behind him in the extended cab, grabbed a roll of paper towels, and handed it to her. He tried not to watch as she pulled off a few sheets and scrubbed them over her face and hair.

He failed; that was sexy too. Damn.

She snatched the Walmart bag out of his lap and stuffed the wet paper towels in it, retrieving the knife. She handed the paper-towel roll back to him. "That son of a bitch gets close enough to me, he's going to know how Tante Eva felt. I'm not afraid of blood."

Celestine Savoie might be mighty and fierce, but she was too petite to take on a six-foot-plus killer, especially using a knife straight out of the Walmart display case. That wasn't sexist; it was just fact. He'd explain that to her. Later.

"Tell me what happened before we go to the cabin," he said. "I called the sheriff's office and they have a deputy en route. It's probably better for him to get there first and look around."

She'd been tearing at the knife's packaging and almost had it open. "Thanks for calling them. I realized after I got you on the phone that it was probably something the sheriff's office would handle. I just . . ." She stilled her hands and looked up at him. He'd give half his next paycheck to read her expression, but he couldn't. He could read a criminal's body language like a pro, but women had always been a mystery. Good thing he didn't encounter many female criminals as an LDWF agent or he'd have to find a new line of work.

"I don't know why." She shrugged. "Calling you felt like the right thing to do."

He smiled and cleared his throat when their gazes stayed locked too long. Good thing her skin flushed and she looked away so she wouldn't see him practicing his Creole tomato impression.

Yeah, there was chemistry, all right. He was out of practice but he wasn't blind.

"Tell me what happened." Gentry kept his focus on the bright-green-striped awning of the Jiffy Stop, since he apparently had lost his ability to remain professional while looking at her.

Ceelie described her early-morning activities before driving to Houma to deal with Eva's estate. "Do you think he was watching me, waiting for me to leave?"

Gentry shook his head and finally cautioned a look her way; she stared straight ahead, so he did the same. "No way to know unless we find some kind of evidence on the bank, and the rain's probably ruined that chance. You said you smelled cigarette smoke, though, so he couldn't have been gone long." Or he was sitting out there watching her, more likely, which both pissed Gentry off and scared the hell out of him. The guy was a predator, no matter who he looked like, and Ceelie was in danger.

"What happened when you got back from Houma?"

"I got out of the truck, smelled cigarette smoke, walked around the porch to the front of the house, and ran right into that skull. God, it scared me." She hunched her shoulders. "Then I saw the writing on the door. I thought it was blood, but now I realize it's probably just red paint. When I saw a shadow moving on the bayou, I panicked and ran."

"That was the smartest thing you could've done." Rage settled in the pit of Gentry's stomach. Jena had been right; he needed a conversation with Warren ASAP, to let him know his concerns about Lang. Even if his brother hadn't risen from the dead—and Gentry didn't believe he had—he could give them a more detailed description.

If it *was* his brother, risen from the ashes like some psychopathic phoenix . . . Gentry didn't want to think about that.

He leaned forward and cranked the truck. "The deputy should've had time to get to the cabin by now. It's Adam Meizel. You probably met him when you first got back to the parish." Which would make them acquaintances.

"Name sounds familiar." She opened the passenger's-side door and turned to slide out. "I'll meet you over there."

"No, wait." Without thinking, Gentry reached over and settled a hand on her arm. It felt fragile beneath his fingers. "Ride with me. You can get your truck after you decide where you're going to stay tonight."

The look she gave him was anything but fragile, and she tugged her arm free. "I know exactly where I'm staying tonight: in *my* cabin on *my* land." Her voice rose. "This freak is not going to scare me away."

"*This freak* murdered your aunt and we don't know why. It sure sounds like he wants back in that cabin." Gentry took a deep breath. *Stay professional. Stay detached.* "Look, why don't we see what Deputy Meizel has found and get his input before you decide anything."

Let Meizel be the heavy-handed officer coercing the stubborn victim to act like a sensible human being.

"Fine, but I'm taking my truck."

He couldn't help but smile at her defiance, which only increased the clench in her jaw. He threw up his hands. Call him a chicken and fry him for dinner. "Go for it. I'll follow your lead."

For now, anyway.

While they'd been talking, the rain had slowed to a light sprinkle and the sun had already reappeared. Gentry followed the old Chevy onto the highway and, in a mile or so, turned left into the muddy, puddle-filled drive. A white patrol car with the Sheriff's Department logo on the side sat at the edge of the parking area, empty.

Gentry glanced at the mud between the patrol car and the edge of the porch—the deputy's footprints were almost submerged. Good.

He'd been here long enough to make an assessment without feeling as if Gentry were butting in where he didn't belong.

Because he was just an acquaintance . . . or something.

They met Meizel on the front porch, where he knelt in front of the door, scraping flakes of the writing into an evidence bag. He glanced up as they approached. "It's paint, not blood. I'm taking a sample to the lab in case it has any unusual properties."

"Can I clean it up when you're done?" Ceelie crossed her arms and looked at the door as if she'd like to set it on fire rather than try to remove the paint.

"I've got a paint sample and photos, so it should be okay." He put the evidence bag in a case he'd brought with him. "I need to take the skull with me."

"Want me to pull it down?" Gentry had a few inches on the deputy, so it would be an easy reach.

"Yeah." Meizel looked up at the ceiling of the porch. "Ms. Savoie, was that hook already up there?"

Ceelie nodded. "When I was a kid, my aunt had wind chimes hanging there."

"We don't need the hook, then," Meizel said. "Broussard, see if you can get it down touching only the ropes. That way we don't have to worry about your prints on the skull. And Ms. Savoie, you're going to need to tell me everything. That skull wasn't already here, was it?"

"You mean because my aunt was the great voodoo queen?" Ceelie snapped, then closed her eyes. "I'm sorry, that was uncalled-for. No, I have no idea where the skull came from."

"That's good, actually. It's another clue." Meizel smiled at her. Gentry recognized the smile and the tone of voice—it was standard law-enforcement conciliation. Calm down the victim. Minimize the drama.

Ceelie spoke softly as she repeated her story twice more, thinking about her answers before responding to Meizel's questions and keeping her anger under control.

While they talked, after checking with the deputy to make sure he wasn't interfering, Gentry picked up the groceries that had gotten scattered around the porch, putting them back into the gray plastic bags. He recognized the makings of red beans and rice, although there was an industrial-sized package of ramen as well. Almost everything she'd bought was inexpensive. Her only splurges appeared to be a couple of pounds of good andouille and the biggest container of salt Gentry had ever seen. Maybe she had a sodium deficiency. Or really high blood pressure.

The legal papers had gotten wet, but he wiped them off the best he could and stacked them. They'd be fine once she could spread them out to dry. Ten acres of prime bayou property. Nice.

Ceelie's smartest purchase was the last thing he found—a new deadbolt lock. Gentry pulled the multitool from his duty belt and made quick work of removing the old lock and replacing it with the new one.

He looked up from a crouch to find Ceelie looking down at him. Her lips were curved into a small smile but her eyes were red-rimmed; she'd been crying. Meizel had upset her. The man had the finesse of a rampaging bull gator.

"Broussard." Meizel gestured him over to the far edge of the porch while Ceelie took the new deadbolt keys from Gentry and went inside the cabin. The deputy held up a plastic evidence bag. "Found this on the porch. Don't know if it'll give us anything, but Ms. Savoie's visitor is careless with his smokes."

Inside the bag was a cigarette butt, smoked down to within about a quarter inch of the filter. "Maybe we'll luck out and get fingerprints. Should definitely get DNA."

God, he hoped they weren't a match for his brother's, who'd had a few minor police skirmishes before his death—or undeath. "Might get DNA, although that'll take until Christmas to get processed in Baton Rouge."

"Ain't that right." Meizel folded the bag around the evidence and tucked it in his uniform pocket. "Listen, can you talk some sense into Ms. Savoie? She's insisting on staying here tonight, and we both know that's just plain dangerous. I don't think it's a stretch to say whoever killed her great-aunt did this, and he wants her out of this cabin. We can't force her to be smart."

Gentry nodded. While he'd been installing the new lock, he'd been thinking the same thing. "There's something this guy wants. He either didn't get it before or didn't get all of it." Whatever the hell *it* was. "So he wants another crack at that cabin. If we could get Ceelie to leave, I could stay in the cabin tonight and see if he shows up."

Meizel gave him a long, steady look. "No, you couldn't. This isn't your case, Broussard. If anyone stakes out this cabin, it'll be the parish, not you."

Shit. Gentry held up his hands. "You're right. Since I was the one who found old Eva, it feels personal. But I know it's your case." Last thing he wanted was to piss off Meizel or Sheriff Roscoe Knight. For now, Meizel was sharing information, and Gentry didn't want him clamming up and seeing him as a problem.

Meizel looked past Gentry at the open door of the cabin. Inside, Ceelie hummed that haunting song that had captured Gentry from the beginning. Her voice was remarkable.

"Look, I get it, okay? You want to protect her and get the guy who did this." Meizel dropped his voice and nodded toward Ceelie. "We've just gotta play everything by the book here so once we do catch this guy—and we will—there are no loopholes. Think you can talk her into leaving?"

Gentry doubted it, but he'd already come up with a Plan B. "Let me see what I can do."

"Turn on that coonass charm you Dulac boys have." Meizel grinned.

Gentry seemed to recall the deputy was from the northern part of the state. "Yeah, a redneck cracker like you can only dream of such charm."

Gentry picked up the bags of groceries and took them inside. Ceelie stood in the little kitchenette, looking inside the refrigerator. As near as he could tell, it was almost empty. Time to turn on whatever coonass charm he possessed.

"Here's your food. I set the papers on the rocking chair outside." He piled the bags on the counter. "Want to go to dinner? My treat."

Well, that was smooth as sixty-grit sandpaper.

She looked up at him, and a playful glint shone in those remarkable blue-gray eyes. He'd seen her angry, sad, determined, frightened. He hadn't seen playful, and he liked it.

"You're only asking me to dinner so I'll leave the cabin. Then you think you can flash your dimples at me a few times and I'll let you talk me out of coming back here tonight." She paused. "I have the gift of reading people, just like my Tante Eva. She taught me well. How am I doing?"

Gentry scowled with effort. She'd noticed he had dimples, which shouldn't make him so damned pleased with himself. "Out of curiosity, had you not seen right through me, would that tactic have worked? Is there any way I can talk you out of spending the night here other than physically hauling you out?"

Ceelie picked up the andouille and stuck it in the fridge. "Not a chance, and if you manhandle me, I'm suing Wildlife and Fisheries. I could use the money." She turned to face him and propped her hands on her hips, but her expression wasn't combative. "Look, it really hit me today: I own this place. It's mine, and I've never owned anything more valuable than my guitar. I can't let this jackass scare me off that easily. If I go, then he's won, hasn't he? And I don't want him to win."

She began wrestling the outer wrapping off the megapack of ramen noodles, the favorite fare of broke college students everywhere. Gentry reached out and put a hand over both of hers, stilling them. "This isn't about winning, Ceelie. It's about making sure you're safe."

"I have a new knife," she said. Stubborn had set in and was trotting toward pig-headed. "And an old ax."

Gentry shook his head and pulled his hand away. "Fine. Dig in your heels, then. Get these doors and windows locked as soon as I leave. Don't open the door for anyone."

She cocked her head. "Even you?"

He wasn't joking anymore and gave her a hard look. "Even me, unless I call first. You hear anything, even if you aren't sure what it is, you call me or the sheriff's office. I'll check on you first thing in the morning."

She cocked her head. "Why do you care?"

Damned good question. "Because I obviously have a weakness for women who don't have the good sense to take care of themselves." And he was an idiot in general.

"Don't waste your weakness on me."

After he walked back onto the porch, Ceelie slammed the door behind him and he heard the lock click.

"She's determined to stay." Gentry shook his head at Meizel, who waited by his car. "You guys got anybody patrolling this area tonight?"

Meizel nodded. "I'll make sure we do. I don't like her being out here by herself, though." He raised his eyebrows. "Thought maybe you'd say you were gonna spend the night. You know, as an *acquaintance* and all."

"Acquaintance only gets you so far with a woman that stubborn," Gentry said, walking toward his truck. "I'll check on her tomorrow."

"Call me directly if you hear from her during the night. I go off duty in a couple of hours, but I want to know if there's more trouble."

Gentry agreed, climbed in his truck, and drove back to the Jiffy Stop. He bought a turkey sandwich that looked about three months old, along with two chocolate bars and a couple of bottles of water.

Next, he made a quick run to his friend's place in Chauvin and bought a nice little AC unit that looked like new.

Finally, he called Warren to let him know he was going off duty as planned, drove back down the bayou, and switched his truck into all-wheel drive just past Ceelie's driveway. He pulled to the side of the road until he saw no vehicles in sight, then cut the truck into a muddy stand of trees a dozen yards south of the drive.

Gentry parked where he had a reasonably clear view of her front and side porches but was hidden from the road. He killed the engine and watched the cabin a minute before pulling the cellophane off his dinner. It was going to be a long night.

CHAPTER 10

Ceelie stood on the edge of the porch, squinting through the early-morning sunlight toward the small stand of trees a few dozen yards south of the cabin.

"That man is more stubborn than I am," she muttered. "Not to mention a control freak."

It wasn't a compliment. Whoever sat in the black pickup wasn't visible to her except in silhouette, but she doubted Tante Eva's murderer drove a pickup the size of a tank that happened to be the same color as the ones driven by the state's wildlife agents. The sheriff's vehicles all seemed to be either brown or white.

Dusting flour off the front of her light-blue tank and smoothing her braid, she left the door open and returned to her kitchen. She poured a second cup of coffee and set it next to her own. Unless he'd fallen asleep, which she doubted, Gentry had seen her watching him and knew he'd been busted.

At least she had extra biscuits in the oven. Only because she could save the leftovers for dinner, of course, and not because she'd thought he might drive by this morning, instead of calling, to make sure she hadn't been murdered in her sleep. The man had called her stupid, and the fact he was right made it sting even more. Plus, he'd put in the deadbolt. She figured a biscuit would be apology enough.

Ceelie barely had time to pull out a pan for the eggs before he stomped into sight outside the open door, stopping to knock mud off his boots by banging them on the front side of the porch that overhung the bayou.

"Sleep well?" She propped her hands on her hips and made note of the pickup-truck version of bedhead, dark circles under his eyes, and a healthy case of stubble. The rumpled hair and stubbly jawline looked disturbingly good on him. The dark circles wouldn't rock anybody's world.

"I slept like shit, plus you caught me." He grinned, and she shook her head, turning back to the important work of cracking eggs into a big stoneware bowl.

"That I did." She didn't want to catch him. How many sins had been forgiven by one look at those dimples and those melted-chocolate eyes? Plenty, she bet. Senior Agent Gentry Broussard and his pheromone-emitting weapons belt probably had strung a line of broken hearts all across Terrebonne Parish. She didn't plan to be one of them.

"When did you know I was out there?" He took off the offending belt and laid it on one of the dining chairs—within easy reach should a raving murderer come storming through the door, although Ceelie doubted that would happen.

"I only knew for sure this morning that you were out there." She set a cup of coffee in front of him. "What I knew last night is that I was safe; I just didn't know why."

Gentry sipped the coffee, then got up to add some of the milk and sugar she'd set on the counter. "Explain."

"You like andouille?" When he nodded, Ceelie chopped bits of sausage into fine chunks and set it aside, along with a few cubes of cheese. "Look at the throwing table—the little table in front of the window where Tante Eva had her ritual stuff."

Frowning, Gentry took his coffee cup and walked over to look at the table. Ceelie didn't need to look: she'd unrolled the leather scroll last night and spread it over the cleaned tabletop. The two tallow candles she'd placed at northwest and southeast—rituals required the opposite poles from divination. A white circle had been outlined in salt on the middle of the leather. Inside the circle sat a small basket of yellow, red, cream, and black, a centuries-old piece made from woven river cane and passed down through generations of the Chitimacha branch of her family.

He looked back at her. "I still don't understand. Are you a voo—" He caught himself. "Are you a practitioner?"

Ceelie was tempted to spout a bunch of voodoo-sounding nonsense at him but decided to cut him some slack. After all, the guy had worked all day and then stayed up all night, sitting in a truck in the woods to make sure she was safe. All because she'd trusted her intuition. It had rarely failed her, but that was a hard thing to explain to a nonbeliever.

Plus, he was no tourist. He'd grown up around this stuff, so he'd respect it even if he didn't believe in it.

"A practitioner? Yes and no." She finished the andouille omelet she'd made by adding a light sprinkle of cheese. Then she halved it and slid the halves onto two of Tante Eva's old plates. The dated green-and-yellow floral pattern that danced around the rims was crackled with age and heavy use. "Sit down and eat breakfast, and I'll explain."

He walked back to the table and pulled out one of the chairs. "I'll trade you what's in the back of my truck for breakfast if you'll throw in one of those biscuits." When she turned to look at him, Ceelie was struck by a couple of things—how much room he took up in this tiny cabin and how much she liked seeing him here.

The man was a danger to womankind.

"I bet you have a dog, don't you?" Too bad Sonia wasn't here to make a bet with her. "I bet you have a big dog. Or two of them."

"What?" Gentry looked puzzled. "Just one. His name is Hoss and he's lord of the beastmasters. Why?"

"Hoss." Because he was probably the size of Hoss Cartwright from the old *Bonanza* reruns . . . or he was the size of an actual horse. Probably a stallion.

It confirmed her worst fears. They might have chemistry, but getting mixed up with a born-and-bred Terrebonne Parish man would ruin her life, never mind stall her career plans. Said plans were admittedly vague, but she was pretty certain hooking up with a Louisiana game warden wasn't part of them.

Still, it was just breakfast. He hadn't so much as hinted at anything more.

"What's in your truck that's worth so much?" She dumped the hot biscuits into a napkin-lined plastic basket and held it just out of his reach. "I don't serve my homemade biscuits to just anyone. They come at a high price." And there she went, flirting, and he wasn't even wearing the belt with the dangly bits.

He reached for the basket and wrapped his fingers around her forearm, tugging the biscuits close enough to grab one. "I was over by Chauvin yesterday after I left here and stopped at my friend's place. The one I was telling you about. He had a sweet little AC unit in a corner that needed a home."

He'd bought an air conditioner for her? Wasn't that, like, tantamount to an engagement ring around here? A twitch set up in her right eye.

"Thanks, but I'm kind of on a fixed income. I appreciate the thought, though." Although if she had to keep the doors and windows closed all the time, she might have to become a nudist, at least until it started cooling down a little, which might happen by Thanksgiving. Maybe.

"I didn't say I *bought* it from him." Gentry shoveled a forkful of the omelet into his mouth. "Damn, this is good."

"It's sausage and eggs." No changing the subject. "Why would he give you an AC unit?"

Gentry hooked the breadbasket with one long forefinger and slid it closer to fish out a second biscuit. "Sinclair—Jena Sinclair, my partner—and I caught a guy who'd been stealing from him, and I helped him haul all his stuff back to his shop on my day off. People work by barter around here, you know?" He chewed a few seconds before gesturing over his shoulder toward the throwing table. "So, what's with the candles and stuff?"

They'd be revisiting the free AC.

"You know much about the Chitimacha?" A lot of folks down here had some connection to the Native American tribes indigenous to South Louisiana, but especially those in the lower reaches of Terrebonne Parish. The ancestral grounds of the Chitimacha lay down the bayou in Isle de Jean Charles, along with their chief and what was left of the undispersed tribe members.

"I know some. Thanks for breakfast; that was a lot better than what I get at the Country Cajun most mornings." Gentry pushed his plate back. "One of the agents I work with, Paul Billiot, is part Houma, part Chitimacha. He's really involved in tribal discussions over how and if they're gonna get more folks to move away from Isle de Jean Charles or dig in and try to force the state or feds to include them in the levee system."

Ceelie jerked her head toward the throwing table. "Tante Eva taught me to throw the bones—that's voodoo—but also some rituals she said came from her mentor, who was Chitimacha. One of our ancestors made the basket."

Her dad had caught her using one of the rituals in her bedroom in Houma when she was sixteen and forbade her to visit her great-aunt again. Her regret over obeying him rested like a bitter pill in her gut. He'd been dying by inches from cancer and she'd been desperate not to upset him. But Tante Eva must have felt abandoned by the girl she'd treated like a daughter, and that thought ate at her.

"So this"—he jerked his head toward the table—"is Chitimacha ritual?"

"One of their rituals is for protection. That's what the salt is for, and the candles are probably from some weird mysticism-voodoo mash-up. You know how things are around here. Everything's scrambled."

He nodded. "Got that right."

Catholicism might be the official religion of South Louisiana, an odd pocket in the middle of the protestant Bible Belt, but voodoo and Native American mysticism had infiltrated this area deeply enough it'd give the pope a heart attack if he were aware of it.

"What did the ritual tell you?" Gentry looked curious but not skeptical, and he wasn't laughing at her. Points for him.

"It told me I was in no imminent danger."

He raised an eyebrow at that. "But—"

She held up a hand. "I know you don't believe, but if it had said otherwise, I would have left last night." Although the closest hotels were in Houma and she wasn't sure she'd be safer staying in any roach motel she could afford.

He scooted his chair closer to hers and looked at her hand on the table. For an awkward second, she thought he was going to take her hand in his. But he just fidgeted.

"It isn't that I don't believe, not exactly. It's that I don't want to gamble your life on it. The stakes are way too high if your ritual steers you wrong."

She should stop this conversation now. She should thank him for watching over her last night and get on with the outing she had planned for the day. She should do anything other than sit here and feel this awkward attraction.

She glanced up at him. "Why does it matter? Why do you care?"

He'd been staring at her hands again, but jerked his gaze up to hers as if surprised by the question. He answered quickly, almost automatically. "I'm a law-enforcement officer. I found your aunt and saw what . . . that animal"—he seemed to struggle with the words—"I saw what he did. And we don't know why."

Ceelie nodded. "So this is how you'd treat anyone whose case you got involved with?" And damn her for feeling disappointed.

He reached out and tightened his hand around hers. "No, that's just the answer I needed to give you. That's the answer I'll give my lieutenant if he finds out I sat out here in my truck all night holding a shotgun."

Ceelie's heart sped up. Her voice came out in a whisper. "So what's the real answer?"

He leaned across the space that divided them, cupping his left hand around her jaw and pulling her toward him as if she were fragile, breakable. His kiss was soft, a pressure of lips, a slight parting, a promise of more. His stubble scratched her chin.

"That's the real answer." His voice was so soft the air around him seemed to soak it up. "And don't ask me what it means because I'll be damned if I know."

"I understand," she said, leaning back in her chair and extracting her hand. "It's called a bad idea. A tempting bad idea." A really, really tempting bad idea. "I'm pretty sure your lieutenant wouldn't like the real answer. Better stick with the first one."

"Anyway, you're a short-timer in the parish, right?"

"Definitely." She sighed. Who the hell knew. That was her automatic answer too, but the longer she stayed, the more anywhere else sounded dull and white-bread. Which meant she needed to get the hell out of here as soon as she could sell this land.

They looked at each other another moment before Gentry coughed and pushed his chair back. "I'll get that AC unit set up for you." He practically ran out the door.

Well, that had been beyond uncomfortable. And yet the pressure of his lips on hers remained, like the kiss of a ghost.

As soon as his footsteps no longer sounded from the porch, Ceelie slapped both hands over her eyes. "What the hell you be doin', Celestine?" She spoke softly, in the heavy patois of her Tante Eva. "*Ça, ça va te coûter.*"

Yeah, kissing Gentry Broussard again—that would cost her plenty.

In the meantime, it was almost ten a.m. and she needed to get moving. After she'd done the protection ritual last night, she'd spent some time in quiet thought, trying to recall as many names from Tante Eva's stories as she could. She'd returned to one again and again: Assaud. She was pretty sure it had been the name of Eva's mentor and that he'd lived farther south in the parish, probably down around Isle de Jean Charles, where Eva's grandfather had come from. Ceelie's great-great-grandfather.

Considering Eva's age and figuring this mentor had to be even older, chances were slim she'd find him still alive.

But it was a lead, at least. If anyone knew what secrets Tante Eva or her cabin held that might have led to her death, it could be this mentor. And maybe he had shared the story with someone else who *was* still alive.

Using her phone, she had searched for Assauds who lived south of Montegut and found only two, Joseph and Brandon. Brandon was a young man's name, so she rolled the dice and called Joseph, who lived in Cocodrie—practically at the end of the world. She got voice mail.

Her stumbling message had intrigued him enough to call her back an hour later. His accent had been thick as the Whiskey Bayou mud Gentry had scraped off his boots. "You be talkin' 'bout my grand-père Tomas and great-grand-père, also named Joseph, like me," he said. "Tomas and your Tante Eva learned together from old Joseph. Spent a lotta time down the baya, them, down round Isle de Jean Charles. I was real sorry to hear what happened to Eva."

Her heart had leapt at the names that immediately sounded familiar. She remembered hearing of Tomas. "Are either of them still living? I need to talk to one of them if I can."

"Joseph, he been gone for years with the cancer. Tomas is still sharp enough—lives off Little Caillou Road, north of Cocodrie." He paused. "You want I should meet you over there tomorrow? I ain't checked on the old man in a while."

After some debate, they'd agreed to meet at noon in the parking lot of a church in the area, and then she'd ride with Joe Assaud in a boat to his grandfather's place. She wasn't sure what she'd ask him, but Tomas had known Eva, had apparently learned alongside her. Maybe she had confided in him.

While she was at it, Ceelie also had done a search for LeRoy Breaux on the off chance that the man she'd called Nonc LeRoy was still alive and in the area, although she felt sure if that were the case, the sheriff would've already talked to him. No luck on that one.

A slamming vehicle door at the back of the house was quickly followed by Gentry, stomping off more mud before coming inside with a little window unit that looked brand-new.

Ceelie scanned it for any sign of a price sticker. "You sure you didn't buy that?" Gentry Broussard struck her as having a bit of a savior complex, which was probably pretty common in law enforcement, although she tended to think of game wardens as a different breed from regular cops. It wouldn't surprise her to learn he'd paid for it and was now lying about it so she wouldn't mistake him for a nice guy. "'Cause it looks new."

"Nope, got it from my friend Zack. He does good work." Gentry looked around. "Which window you want it in?"

The window near the throwing table was the most centrally located, but she didn't want cold air messing with her rituals, should she decide to do more. It would be too cold right over the bed. Which left only the other front window. "By the dining table."

The installation took all of ten minutes. "Close the door and windows and let's try it out." Gentry squatted in front of the little unit and pressed a button; it roared to life with a gratifying surge of cold air Ceelie could feel from across the room.

"God, that feels good." She closed her eyes and enjoyed the sensation of sweat cooling on her skin. You couldn't escape the humidity in South Louisiana, but you could at least chill it.

"Now." Gentry came to stand in front of her, and she looked up at him. Had he been this tall before, or was he just standing closer, or was she just too aware of him? "What are your plans for tonight, because I have a night shift starting in about eight hours and I need to catch some sleep."

She swallowed the urge to tell him that her plans for the day—and night—were none of his business. Then she swallowed the urge to tell him he could sleep here at the cabin. Urge-swallowing was liable to give her a bad case of indigestion.

Instead, she'd try the truth. What a novelty. "I found an old guy who lives down near Cocodrie—he knew Tante Eva pretty well when they were young. So I'm going to drive down there and talk to him this afternoon. Then I'll decide whether I'm going to stay here or get a hotel room in Houma. The short answer to where I'm staying tonight? I don't know yet."

He sighed. "That's probably as good as I'm gonna get out of you, right?"

She nodded.

"Will you call and let me know what you decide?"

"Sure." If she was smart she'd never call him again.

CHAPTER 11

Celestine Savoie was the most stubborn, exasperating woman Gentry had ever met. If it were possible, he'd keep her under lock and key until this whole cluster was sorted out—with himself providing personal guard duty, of course. Which spun his mind into a hot fantasy image he didn't need.

Worse, she was endangering the keep-it-simple, keep-it-solitary way of life he'd built over the past three years. When the hell had he decided it was acceptable to kiss the victim of an ongoing investigation?

His inner alter ego piped up: *Not your investigation, though, dude. You've just gotta reel that fish in.*

That might be true if not for the questions about Lang. Until Gentry came clean to Warren, he was right in the middle of this case, intended or not.

He needed sleep but he needed information worse, so he swung over to Dulac for a run past Tommy Mason's trailer on stilts. A late-model white pickup was parked beneath the piers, so Gentry whipped his vehicle into the driveway behind it. He jotted down the pickup's license-plate number in case he needed to run a check on it, then got out.

He strapped on his duty belt, weapons, and radio. This wasn't an official call, but if Tommy Mason assumed it was? That was Tommy's problem.

Gentry made plenty of noise climbing the steep stairs to reach the front door, and knocked hard. Sneaking up on anybody out here in the land of the armed and the free could be deadly. A child wailed inside, followed by a woman's voice: "Hold on a dang minute."

The woman who opened the door looked at Gentry with an expression that told him one wrong step could send her over the edge. She held a fussy toddler on her hip but, despite her less-than-glamorous surroundings, wore a heavy coat of makeup congealing in the humidity.

Ceelie doesn't wear makeup, at least not that you can see, alter ego said.

Not helpful.

"Morning, ma'am. I'm looking for Tommy Mason. Is he around?" Polite and professional, that was Senior Agent Broussard.

"Lord, what's that no-good sonofabitch done now? Wait, you ain't a cop; you're a game warden. What'd he do, run over a fish?"

Gentry gave her a small smile and a few seconds to let her laugh at her own joke. At least it had improved her demeanor. It wasn't the first time he'd heard that one, either. "Is Mr. Mason here, ma'am?"

Her laughter faded, replaced by a sullen pout. Her makeup caked around the laugh lines beside her mouth. Old and tired before her time—she was probably thirty going on sixty.

"He's out back in the garage, working on my car. It's his day off."

Gentry wondered where Tommy worked, but he'd ask the man himself. No point in getting his wife or girlfriend involved. Besides, as far as he knew, Lang was dead and Tommy hadn't been involved in the drug-trafficking case that went down in New Orleans.

Still, if Lang was alive and had come back to Dulac, Gentry's gut told him Tommy would know.

He walked down the stairs and cut under the house to the back. Before he'd crossed half the length of the backyard, a man stepped out of the detached garage and stood waiting with his arms crossed. Either he'd seen the truck or he'd gotten a warning call from his significant other.

Gentry had left Dulac for LSU and life in Baton Rouge shortly after he turned eighteen and hadn't seen Tommy Mason since, so it took a few seconds for him to reconcile early-twenties Tommy with this midthirties incarnation. Same white-blond hair, now receding amid its short cut. Same blue eyes and smart-ass demeanor, though. Probably couldn't beat that out of him with a stick.

"How come I rate a visit from a game warden? Don't hunt. Don't fish. Don't . . ." He trailed off when Gentry took off his sunglasses and hooked them in his pocket. Gentry traced the flit of nerves that crossed Tommy's features before his expression settled back into deadpan arrogance. "Gent Broussard. Heard you'd come back to Terrebonne Parish after murdering Lang. Couldn't stand the heat of the big city anymore?"

"Hey, Tommy." Gentry put on his best blank face. Only Lang had ever called him Gent. Had Tommy remembered that, or had he talked to Lang lately? "What're you up to these days?"

Tommy turned and went back into the garage. "Working over in Chauvin at Landry's Auto Repair. You need a good mechanic, or is this an official visit? Either way, I got no time and nothin' to say."

Gentry followed him into the dark interior of the single-car garage. A portable light hung on the edge of the upraised hood of an older-model silver Honda Accord. As Tommy leaned over the engine with a wrench, Gentry said, "Just wanted to stop by and ask if you'd seen Langston lately."

Tommy dropped the wrench, which bounced off the engine and came to rest on the battery. He wet his lips and fumbled to retrieve it. "That's cold, man. You playin' some kinda sick joke?"

"No joke." Gentry studied the man's body language. He'd retrieved the wrench, but was his hand still shaky? Yep, old Tommy definitely had a tremor. "You seem a little rattled, Tom."

He walked to the opposite side of the car and leaned on it so he'd be on a level with the mechanic. "See, here's the deal. I don't think Lang's dead. I think he's here, back in Terrebonne Parish, and I think he's doing some bad shit. If I was a betting man, I'd bet you know all about that."

Tommy gave him a quick glance before looking back at the engine. "I don't know nothing. You talkin' crazy. Lang's dead. I was at his funeral, sittin' in the back while his mama cried and her fancy new husband and the brother that murdered him sat next to her, all dry-eyed."

Gentry stood up straight. "It's a funny thing about funerals, Tommy. Without a body, they're nothing but ceremonies."

"Lang's dead, man. You need to have your head examined and let that shit go."

Gentry wouldn't learn anything here today, but Tommy was sweating way more than the morning's humidity called for. Gentry pulled out his wallet and laid a business card on the Honda's engine. "You have second thoughts about protecting Lang, give me a call and I'll make sure nothing comes back to you. I strongly advise you to take that offer, Tommy."

He got halfway to the door and turned. "And if you decide to be a stupid fuck and warn Lang I'm on to him, tell him not to worry about his brother the possum cop. Lang's about to hit the Terrebonne sheriff's most-wanted list."

Gentry had no proof, but he had enough gut reaction to Tommy's demeanor that talking to his lieutenant had gone from important to urgent. He tried Warren's cell phone as soon as he got in the truck and backed out of the Mason driveway, but it went to voice mail. Next, he called Stella and learned that Warren would be in meetings all day at LDWF regional headquarters in Thibodaux.

"He should be back by six when you come on duty," Stella said. "Can anybody else help you? Paul's the senior agent on duty right now."

"I've got his number, or I'll wait and catch the lieutenant tonight, Stella. Thanks."

Gentry stuck the phone back in its dashboard holder and considered calling Paul Billiot. He had a lot of respect for the agent, but Paul wasn't up to speed on the Savoie case and chances were good that all he'd do would be advise Gentry to wait for Warren. Or, more likely, Paul would bitch Gentry up one side and down the other, and then advise him to wait for Warren.

He couldn't call Meizel or the sheriff's deputies investigating the case without Warren being blindsided.

Damn it. If he was right about Lang, and Tommy warned him, Lang would be desperate. Desperate men who thought they had nothing to lose might run. Or they'd call the bluff and do stupid things. Things that got innocent people like Ceelie Savoie hurt.

No way he could sleep now, so Gentry called Jena Sinclair. Red was working a day shift.

"I'm about to stop for lunch at the Kountry Kettle and I have a flash drive with the items you asked me to get for you," she said instead of a simple *hello*. "Wanna join me?"

Gentry's breakfast had settled on his stomach like an anchor, but he'd rather talk to Sinclair in person and he wanted the case files from New Orleans. "On my way."

He swung by the cabin and gauged by the empty drive that Ceelie had left for her meeting with the voodoo guy or medicine man or whatever he was, which made Gentry feel better. At least she wouldn't be sitting there if Lang made a quick, careless move. The cabin could be replaced. The thought of anything happening to Ceelie made him jittery. Despite his determination not to get involved with a woman who had no intention of hanging around the parish, he'd gotten way too invested in her welfare.

Ten minutes later, he parked in an empty spot behind Sinclair's truck at the restaurant. It wasn't quite noon, so things were still quiet inside and the ice-cold air hit him with a blast as soon as he entered. In another half hour, the dining room would be deafening and not nearly as cold.

He spotted his partner in a booth at the back and slid across the red vinyl bench opposite her. "Iced tea, extra lemon, no food," he told the waitress.

"On a diet?" Jena took a sip of her soda.

"Late breakfast." He pulled off his LDWF cap and set it on the bench beside him, then slid the salt shaker on the table in front of him so he'd have something to do with his hands. "And a bad case of indigestion."

The waitress, a young woman with a shock of pink hair, brought his tea along with Jena's burger. Gentry thought he might barf.

"What a face. Breakfast was that bad? And stop twirling the salt shaker—you're giving me motion sickness." She snatched it away from him and salted her fries, then set it out of his reach. He snaked out a hand and got the pepper shaker instead.

"I just paid a visit to my brother's best buddy. Or at least his best buddy when we were growing up. I figured if there was any chance that Lang was alive and back in the parish, Tommy Mason would know about it."

Jena froze with a French fry halfway to her mouth. "And?"

He shook his head and focused on the pepper shaker, twisting it round and round with his fingertips. "Man, I have a bad, bad feeling. Tommy was nervous. He should've been pissed off, or sad, or shocked. But his hands shook like he'd been mainlining caffeine the minute I asked if he'd seen Lang."

Jena set the French fry back on her plate. "You've gotta talk to Warren now."

"I tried to call him as soon as I left Mason's house, and he's out of pocket until tonight. Billiot's the senior agent on duty today, but I think he'd tell me to wait and talk to Warren before going to the sheriff."

"You just ruined my appetite." Jena made a face at her burger, wrapped it in three layers of napkins, and stuck it in her bag. "You're probably right about Paul. It's just a few more hours."

A few more hours. That was the problem. A properly motivated criminal could do a lot of damage in a few hours.

"What if I'm right and it is Lang? If Mason calls him, he could get to Ceelie before I even have a chance to talk to Warren." He shoved the pepper shaker toward its resting place near the window. "I screwed up by not talking to him in the beginning."

Make that screwed up *again*.

"You're missing something obvious," Jena said.

"Not possible. Everybody knows I'm perfect." At her frown, he shrugged. "What am I missing?"

"You're worried about him going after Ceelie Savoie. Seems to me the one you should worry about him going after is the brother who's threatening to expose him. You gotta watch your back, Broussard."

Gentry looked out the window. She was right; it hadn't occurred to him that Lang would come looking for him. "I should have tried to shoot him in the shoulder or leg three years ago, so he could've been apprehended. He'd be cooling his heels in a federal prison instead of maybe-not-dead and out committing murders." Never mind the three years Gentry had spent tearing himself apart with guilt.

But Lang had been ready to take a shot at Gentry's partner, betting his little brother wouldn't shoot him, and he'd lost his gamble. Gentry had reacted like a law-enforcement officer, not a brother, and it had cost Lang his life.

Only maybe it hadn't.

Jena pulled a flash drive from her bag and handed it to Gentry. "It's easy to say you should've done things differently in hindsight, but you had no reason to think your brother survived the drug seizure in New Orleans. I read the files this morning. Every reporting agency agreed he couldn't have survived your shots, and that your quick action is the only reason your partner survived.

"It says clearly: Langston Broussard died, and you deserved the commendation you got."

"Unless he didn't die." Gentry sighed and tugged his fingers through his hair. He'd thrown the commendation away. He didn't want to be reminded of that night, much less be rewarded for it, although he'd done what he had to and would do it again.

Gentry didn't know how to feel about the possibility of Lang being alive. For the first time in three years, since Warren had offered him a lifeline in the form of a transfer to Region 6, Gentry wanted to drown himself in a fine bottle of whiskey. He hadn't touched a drop of alcohol since moving back to Terrebonne.

A half hour later, with nothing else to do and his energy level bottoming out, Gentry took one last run past Ceelie's empty driveway before heading to his little house in Montegut. He needed to feed his dog and master, Hoss, and make some attempt at sleeping.

The steps to the raised front door seemed steeper than usual, or maybe he was suffering the aftereffects of his all-night vigil on Whiskey Bayou. Several years of hurricane-driven flooding had forced most folks to raise their homes in an attempt to survive, but climbing those steps also added an extra fatigue factor after a long day and night.

Hoss met him at the door with a round of barking and ankle-biting. "Hey, stop that, boss man. Your needs were met."

When he'd decided to stake out Ceelie's cabin last night, he'd called his neighbor to feed and walk Hoss and refill the dog's water bowl. Mrs. Vallieres's brindle pit bull, Moose, was Hoss's best friend, although Hoss knew he was the biggest badass on the block and bit Moose's ankles, too. With Gentry's unpredictable work hours, it was great having a neighbor he trusted to take care of his dog.

He opened the back door and propped against the doorjamb, watching Hoss fly down the steps and engage in a frantic search for the best place to take a leak. Gentry wished his biggest decision of the day revolved around bladder relief.

Gentry's roommate was moving fast; the day had already passed ninety-five degrees in the shade, and it wasn't long before Hoss was ready to come back inside rather than punishing Gentry for his absence by making him wait.

He checked his messages, stuck a couple of dirty coffee cups in the dishwasher, and shucked off his boots, which set off another round of ankle-biting. "C'mon Hoss, naptime."

His coworkers knew about Hoss—rather, they knew he had a dog named Hoss. Gentry hadn't exactly told them his dog was a pit bull or Rottweiler, but he hadn't denied their assumptions that a badass agent would have a badass dog.

"You are a badass, and don't let anybody say otherwise," he said, flopping on the bed and rubbing behind the dog's giant black bat ears when he hopped up and settled on Gentry's chest. "They're just jealous of your *je ne sais quoi.*"

He'd found the French bulldog puppy abandoned in a drainage ditch in Plaquemines Parish while on patrol one night about five years ago. He'd turned the tiny dog over to the shelter for about twenty minutes, then turned right around and put a claim on him, sucked in by the enormous ears and bulging brown eyes. Now, Hoss was a hefty twenty-pounder and, in New Orleans, had proven quite the chick magnet.

Gentry's coworkers in Terrebonne had big hunting dogs, muscular and masculine. He hadn't shared that his badass pet had legs about four inches long and bore a striking resemblance to Winston Churchill in a black bat costume.

Hoss was snoring within minutes; Gentry didn't last much longer. He'd optimistically set his alarm clock for four thirty p.m., which would give him time to check on Ceelie before driving to Warren's house. He'd wait on his lieutenant, confess everything, and hope to hell he had a job after the conversation ended.

In reality, he expected to lie awake and spend three hours being chased by ghosts.

To his surprise, the high-pitched beep of the alarm woke him from a sound, dreamless sleep. Neither he nor Hoss had moved, and they stared at each other and blinked. Gentry was trying to remember what day and time it was; he wasn't sure what was going through Hoss's mind. Probably kibble or a new spot to take a leak.

"Let's move it, big guy." Hoss jumped down and Gentry shuffled to the shower. By the time he'd washed off as much grime and guilt as he could, his brain had awakened. He pulled out a clean uniform, fed Hoss, and let the dog wander his backyard kingdom for a few minutes while Gentry wolfed down half a leftover shrimp po-boy.

He made sure his spare house key was in place under the loose board on the back deck so Mrs. Vallieres could take Hoss on his evening constitutional. Then he climbed back in his truck.

The sleep had energized his muscles but hadn't done much to stem the dread of talking to Warren.

First things first. He drove south through Montegut and slowed down as he passed the drive to Ceelie's cabin. Her truck was still gone, and nothing looked amiss. No boats in the area.

He turned around at the first opportunity and called her on his way back toward Houma. Then he'd call Warren to see if he was at home or the office.

"Hey, game warden." Ceelie's voice, husky and sultry, caused a shift in his gut that told him he was in so far over his head with this woman he couldn't be saved. He barely knew her; if they ever were able to have a normal conversation, they might not even like each other. Plus, she was already halfway out of the parish on her way toward her real life.

Yeah, he'd keep telling himself that and see when he started believing it.

"Everything good with you? I'm heading to work." Just an agent checking on a casual acquaintance. Right.

"I'm fine. Just about to call you, in fact." She paused, and over the line Gentry could hear the rattle of the old Chevy. "I learned some interesting things about Tante Eva today, and it might give you some clues. I'm on my way home now."

As soon as he talked to Warren and the sheriff, they'd be able to get someone to watch the cabin round the clock, maybe even get the parish to put Ceelie somewhere safe. Hell, she could stay at his house. Hoss liked music.

No, scratch that thought. Talk about inappropriate. If the parish couldn't find a place for her, maybe Ceelie could stay with Sinclair and far, far away from him and his ankle-biter.

"Want to meet for lunch tomorrow? We can compare notes; I learned a few things today too." He winced; his mouth obviously hadn't received the leave-the-woman-alone memo. But he did want to hear about Eva, and he had to tell Ceelie about Lang.

"Or I could cook you breakfast."

She was not making it easy to be detached and professional. "Eight too early?"

Jesus, but he was weak.

They confirmed plans for the morning and hung up after he'd made her promise twice to keep the doors and windows locked. And if Warren fired him, he'd have plenty of time to stake out the swamp by her house.

The phone rang again before he had a chance to hit the speed dial to call Warren. His pulse sped up at Tommy Mason's name on the screen. Was he going to admit Lang was alive? Did Gentry *want* his brother to be alive?

"Broussard."

"Hey there, baby brother. You and me, we got some lousy timing." The familiar voice made his heart stop.

"Lang." His brother sounded the same. Same drawl. Same attitude. Alive and well.

Gentry let the truck drift across the center line and had to jerk the wheel to avoid hitting an oncoming car. He pulled the truck into the gravel drive of an abandoned, hurricane-ravaged shell of a house to avoid killing himself or someone else.

Good God. Despite his gut reaction to Tommy this morning, Gentry had still, deep in his heart, thought Lang was dead, had prayed it was all a mistake. Some people need to be beaten over the head with the truth before they'd believe it; he appeared to be one of them.

"Guess we need to talk, little brother. I'm guessin' since you was the one that stopped by Tommy's house this morning, you ain't told anybody yet. Maybe you didn't believe it was me. Maybe you was feeling guilty for what happened three years ago. Mom ever forgive you for murdering me? Heard you got an award for it."

Shock gave way to anger at the voice of the brother he'd idolized until they'd gone so far on their separate ways that the gulf was too wide to cross. The brother he'd mourned. "We do need to talk. Name the time."

"Tommy's place. Out back in the garage. Don't let his old lady see you." Lang laughed, which sent a flinch of anger across Gentry's shoulders. He was buzzed on something. Last time they'd been together long enough to have a conversation, Lang had shown up at Gentry's place in New Orleans, looking for drug money. His devils of choice at that time were coke to get up and H to come down. Who knew what he was into now.

"When?"

"Hey, I'm here now, just hanging out, bro. You workin', or are you getting ready to bang on that sweet little niece of Eva Savoie's? I might try to get a taste of that myself."

If he touched Ceelie, Gentry would have to kill him. Again. And this time, there'd be no coming back for either one of them.

He swallowed the anger and wrapped his training around him like a cloak. He kept his voice serious, but calm. "I'm just south of Houma. I can be there in thirty minutes. That work?"

"I guess I don't have to tell you to come alone, Gent." Lang's voice, so much like Gentry's had been before four years of college and seven years in New Orleans had smoothed out the accent, grew soft. "Just you and me. A conversation between brothers."

"I'll be alone." Gentry ended the call and sat for a moment, taking deep breaths and thinking. Lying had bought him a little time. He was nowhere near Houma and could be at Tommy's in ten minutes. But he had to handle this right for a change. Start thinking like a law-enforcement officer and stop thinking with his heart and his dick.

He called Jena Sinclair's cell phone, gave her a brief rundown, and asked if she'd go straight to Ceelie's house and stay there until they heard something. She was coming off a long workday, but he trusted her. More important, he thought Ceelie trusted her. "If you need to tell Ceelie there's a credible threat to get her to cooperate, that's okay. I might've had my doubts before, but this is real."

"On my way."

"And Red? I owe you."

Jena chuckled, but it was strained. "Don't worry, Broussard. I'm running a tab."

Next call: Warren, who answered on the first ring with a gruff, "Doucet. Why've you been looking for me?"

God help him. Gentry took a steadying breath and talked fast, sticking to the facts. How he was sure he'd been mistaken about it being Lang, deciding he should approach Tommy, and ending with the phone call from his not-so-dead brother. The "I'm sorry" at the end of his spiel sounded lame even to him.

"Save it," Warren said, and the snap in those two words said worlds. "Where are you?"

"I'm about ten minutes from the rendezvous." Five if he drove fast. He swallowed hard and tried again. "I'm sorry, Warren. I should have told you from the get-go."

"You damn well should have. Give me Mason's address."

Gentry read it off. "You want me to call the sheriff?"

"Hell no." Gentry winced: Warren only cursed when he was really pissed off. "You keep your ass where it is until you see a shitload of deputies coming your way. You take directives from them. You understand me? No more Lone Ranger. I'll be right behind them."

"Yessir." Gentry ended the call and sat in his truck, feeling like the worm he was. No more than two or three minutes passed before an unmarked black sedan pulled up in front of him, followed by a truck with the TPSO shield emblem on the side. He got out, ready to take grief. He didn't know the two guys in the sedan, but Adam Meizel exited the SUV.

"Broussard, what the hell's going on?" Meizel shook his hand, which Gentry appreciated. It might help the detectives see him more as a toad than a worm. A slight improvement.

He gave them as brief a version as possible. "We thought Langston Broussard was dead; I still don't know how he survived, but he did." Gentry's head threatened to explode from the pressure building between his temples. How could his own brother have done the things that had been done in that cabin?

He told his story with his hands holding up the bottom of his shirt, letting one of the deputies strap a wire under his uniform. He tugged the shirt down when it was secure, then took a transmitter disguised as a cell phone so he could communicate if the wire failed.

"We'll stay out of sight until he incriminates himself or it goes south," said the lead detective, who'd introduced himself as John Ramsey. "We haven't gotten prints on anything; he's been careful. So get him to talk."

Finally, they set out. Gentry pulled onto the highway and cut west to Dulac. His training kicked in now that they were moving. A Zen-like calm settled over him and he gave in to it. His eyes were sharp, his nerves steady. Emotion might drag him under later, but he could do this. Again.

All he needed for motivation was to think of a cabin filled with blood and the soft lips of a woman he'd helped to put in danger.

CHAPTER 12

Ceelie glanced at the plastic sandwich bag lying on the seat as she drove the battered pickup up the long, rutted expanse of Little Caillou Road, aka Highway 56. She'd hoped to be heading home with a clue as to why Tante Eva had been killed.

She hadn't expected to come back with family curses, more mysteries, and a bag of blessed chicken bones. Not to mention marching orders to bury Tante Eva's throwing bones and make this new set her own.

Ceelie braked to let an alligator mosey across the highway toward Bayou Petit Caillou, which the road hugged as it meandered northward, along with a steady line of raised houses, boat launches, and private fishing piers.

The number of people living in the bottom portion of Louisiana's second-largest parish, half of which was composed of water or semisubmerged land, had surprised her. She'd steeled herself to spend the day cruising down and back up a long, isolated road surrounded by water, sawgrass, and sugarcane fields, which is what she remembered from her childhood. There was still plenty of tall grass and cane fields, but also a lot of people living their lives, too stubborn to let erosion and increasingly violent storms run them off their own patch of mud.

She understood how they felt, only her storm—Tante Eva's killer—had two legs and doled out a different brand of violence.

Tomas Assaud also had been a surprise. She'd expected a tiny, wrinkled Chitimacha relic when Joseph Assaud, himself in his forties, took her to meet his grandfather. She'd met Joseph at the church parking lot, then he'd taken her in a boat to Tomas's raised cabin at the edge of a marsh, just past the Cocodrie water tower.

Instead of being the shriveled, frail, male equivalent of Tante Eva, Tomas was tall and brown, and looked strong as a Chitimacha warrior should. Only an arthritic hip that slowed his gait and the wide streaks of gray running through his black hair gave away his age.

The meeting had begun on a chill-inducing note when the old man had greeted her not with a handshake or nod, but by pressing his palm against her forehead. He'd bowed his head as if in prayer, speaking softly: *"Vous avez été maudit. Lâche pas, fille de Eva."*

It had freaked the hell out of her. She'd backed away from him until she ran into Joseph, who'd remained in the doorway. She understood his words: *You have been cursed. Do not give up, daughter of Eva.*

"I'm Celestine, Eva's great-niece." To make sure he understood, Ceelie added: *"Petite-nièce de Eva."*

A week ago, she'd have sworn that she'd forgotten every shred of Cajun French she'd learned from Tante Eva as a kid, but necessity was scouring off at least the top layer of rust.

The old man had smiled and approached her again. Trapped by the immovable Joseph, she assumed a rigid stance and waited for another creepy proclamation. This time, however, Tomas hugged her and spoke in his thick, singsong accent. "I know you, child. You don't remember Nonc Tomas but he remembers you. Eva always said you had the gift." He stepped back. "Your Tante Eva, she knew her part in the curse would have to be paid for, but . . ." Tears glistened in his black eyes. "So much pain."

He turned and slowly walked through another door into a small den. "Come, come."

"Go with him; I'm gonna stay here." Joseph sat on a worn sofa covered with a knitted throw in the traditional Chitimacha colors of black, cream, and brick red. "That's his ritual room. Follow him on in there, now. Don't make him wait. He ain't as healthy as he looks." That proclamation made, Joseph picked up a copy of the Houma newspaper lying on the coffee table, flapped it a couple of times, and settled back to read.

Awesome.

Actually, Ceelie would've liked nothing more than to get in Joseph's boat, haul ass to the pickup, and drive back to the cabin. That would accomplish nothing except to prove her cowardice, though—and get her awfully wet and possibly tangled up with a moccasin or gator. She was here. She'd initiated this meeting. She had to see it through.

The room had been small, square, and dark. When her eyes had adjusted, she realized the darkness came from all the textiles hanging from floor to ceiling along the walls. Woven rugs. Strips of leather. Beaded squares. Embroidered rectangles that might have once been bits of tablecloths. It was like a room wrapped in an ornate shroud.

Tomas had settled into a threadbare armchair in one corner. "You look much like her, you know. Like Eva."

Ceelie had pulled a chair away from a small table—his throwing table, she'd bet—and tried to exorcise the thought of shrouds from her mind. "Do I? I don't think I ever saw photos of her when she was my age."

With the ice broken, they had talked for more than two hours. He spoke of his father, Joseph, who'd learned the ways of the Chitimacha from *his* grandfather. About Tante Eva's grandfather Julien, who'd left Isle de Jean Charles and built the cabin on Whiskey Bayou.

He also had said it was with Julien that the curse had begun and had passed to Eva's parents and brother and then to Eva herself.

"What is this curse?" Ceelie didn't know whether to find it comforting or disturbing that it wasn't just she who'd been cursed but multiple generations of her family. "Who created it?"

To those questions, Tomas had no answers. He'd told her Eva never spoke of it in details, only whispered of a secret her grandfather had kept, then her parents, and then her. The secret had brought evil into all their lives, but Eva had claimed that when she died, it would be over.

"I told Eva that the curse might not be hers to end, and only after her death would the fates decide."

Judging by the way her aunt had died, and the things that had happened since, Ceelie suspected the curse hadn't ended at all.

The visit with the old man had gone smoothly until Ceelie asked about Nonc LeRoy. "Did you know him? Do you know why he left?"

Tomas made a slashing sign in the air, and Ceelie recognized the warding off of evil—like a Catholic making the sign of the cross, except creepier.

She waited while the old man recovered, unsure if he'd say more or if their visit was at an end.

"LeRoy Breaux was not a good man." Tomas's voice when he finally did speak was so soft Ceelie had to strain to hear him. "He was *un coquin, un voleur*. He drove Eva to continue the curse of violence."

"I don't understand." Ceelie wracked her brain for a translation. *"Je ne comprends pas."*

"He says the man was a rascal and a thief." Joseph had come to stand in the doorway but wouldn't enter the room, even when Ceelie offered him the chair. Apparently, one entered the room only at Tomas's invitation.

"A thief. What did he steal?" She turned back toward Tomas. "Did he steal from Eva? Did he get in trouble with the law?" Surely the sheriff's investigators would have discovered it if the man had a record.

Ceelie continued to ask questions for a while, but Tomas had fallen silent and stayed that way. She wasn't even sure he heard her anymore. After another fifteen or twenty minutes spent mostly in awkward silence, Joseph announced that it was time to leave.

"He is tired, and has said all he'll say." Joseph headed for the door, but Ceelie paused before leaving the old man with his thoughts and his elaborately shrouded walls.

"Merci, Nonc Tomas." She thought about hugging him, but wasn't sure it would be appropriate. "Thank you for bringing my Tante Eva back to me, at least for a while. I can tell you cared for her. For what it's worth, I loved her too."

She had turned to leave, but before she'd reached the door, Tomas told her to wait. The bones had been in a small drawstring bag in a drawer of his throwing table. He placed them in her palm and wrapped her fingers around them with both of his brown hands. They trembled slightly, the first physical sign that the warrior had grown weary.

"These are blessed, daughter of Eva, but it will take you to make them yours."

She didn't want them. "I have the ones that belonged to Tante Eva, and I don't really know how—"

"You have the sight, and each sight must have its own guide. Bury the bones of *mon amie* Eva Savoie, little one. They are no longer meant for the living."

A dollop of rain on the windshield jerked Ceelie back to the present. The visit with Tomas had been like traveling to a different world—like getting lost in a novel featuring a time-traveling heroine. What must it be like to live almost a century, to see how much the world changed, and how much it stayed the same? To see your people being absorbed into the broader culture but for the few who continued to fight? To see your ancestral lands sinking by fractions into the Gulf of Mexico?

What hadn't changed, and yet was ever changing, was the weather. In her years away, Ceelie had forgotten how much rain this place got.

How quickly the sky would turn pitch-black in the middle of the day, storms exploding into wind and electricity and water. Then, just as quickly, they'd either wear themselves out or move on.

After a tense fifteen or twenty minutes trying to see the road through the downpour and hoping she didn't meet an oncoming truck, Ceelie drove out of the storm. In a matter of seconds, she was scrambling for her sunglasses. The rain reminded her of the call from Gentry and left her with a warmth in her chest—well, okay, maybe lower.

To avoid thinking about things that would leave her more hot and frustrated, she let her mind wander back to what she'd learned today, and what she hadn't.

Nonc LeRoy was a thief. What had Tomas meant by that? What would Tante Eva have that LeRoy would want to steal? Was it the same thing being hunted by Eva's dark-haired murderer, or had LeRoy shared whatever secret Eva kept, maybe told someone else . . .

A memory hit Ceelie with such force that she lost control of the pickup for a moment and left the road.

"Shit!" She steered along the shoulder and slammed on the brakes only a couple of feet before the shoulder disappeared into the concrete side rails of a narrow bridge. Canals crisscrossed the larger bayous throughout the southern part of the state, leading into lakes and smaller bayous and hundreds of winding, isolated waterways. If she drove this stupid truck off the road and into any of these murky bodies of water, she'd never be found.

But she had remembered something, although the memory was as murky as the water around her. Nonc LeRoy had a nephew who came to visit him occasionally, sometimes when Ceelie, as a young girl, would be there. She hadn't much liked him and didn't remember his name.

But one summer when she'd been eight or nine, the nephew had brought a friend with him, a boy whose name Ceelie also couldn't remember. Both boys had stayed for a couple of weeks when Ceelie was visiting Tante Eva. The adults had made pallets for their visitors on opposite sides of the cabin floor, and they'd rolled something—a marble or a ball, Ceelie couldn't remember—back and forth across the cabin in the semi-darkness until LeRoy got up, opened the front door, and threw it into the swamp.

She couldn't remember the friend's name but she remembered what he looked like, because she'd developed a bit of a crush on him, or what a girl that age called a crush. He'd been older, maybe even fifteen. Old enough for her to think of him as dark and dashing.

She'd asked Tante Eva when he'd be coming back, but he never had, or at least not while she was there. It hadn't been too long afterward, maybe that same summer, that Nonc LeRoy had left.

The boy had been tall and thin and lanky, with gangly arms and legs and big hands, like a puppy who'd eventually fill out to become a big dog. She'd loved his hair, dark and glossy and down to his shoulders, falling in curls she'd wanted to touch because her own hair was so straight and heavy. He had dimples and deep-brown eyes.

That boy looked just like she'd imagine Gentry Broussard might have looked when he was fifteen or sixteen. It was why he'd looked familiar.

The boy's name hadn't quite come back to her yet, and he might not even be important. LeRoy, though, was very important. That's who she wanted to talk to Gentry about—and probably the sheriff's investigator, since Gentry kept reminding her it wasn't his agency's case. LeRoy could be the key to this whole mystery.

CHAPTER 13

The white pickup was still parked beneath Tommy Mason's house, so Gentry parked behind it as he'd done yesterday. He scanned the rest of the property for another vehicle but saw nothing. Whatever Lang had been driving could be behind the garage, though, or inside it.

Hell, for that matter, it could've been Lang's silver Honda that Tommy had been working on, rather than the woman's. She could've been lying.

His shoulders itched as if a parade of ants marched across them, and he couldn't shake the feeling that something was wrong. Well, even more wrong than going in alone to meet his strung-out, homicidal brother and his badass buddy Tommy. Bad odds from the start. But if he'd arrived with anyone visibly in tow, no way Lang would talk to him.

Of course, if Lang had any common sense left at all, he'd be smart enough to assume Gentry was coming with backup, which was true. The sheriff had a SWAT team watching his every move and sitting on go.

"No visuals," he said softly. Warren, a couple of parish deputies, and Sheriff Knight himself were ensconced in an unmarked van parked at a boat launch a few hundred yards down the bayou. "Getting out of the truck now."

He exited slowly, knowing SWAT had his back but also knowing things could go wrong fast and they couldn't get too close without blowing cover. The team had debated whether or not he should go in with his rifle or shotgun, but had decided to send him in wearing only his usual duty belt, to appear as normal as possible. He pulled out his SIG Sauer and camouflaged it against his thigh, scanning the area as he neared the stairs leading to the front door of the home.

Through the support piers beneath the house, he caught a flash of movement near the side entrance to the garage and ducked behind the pickup to assess. The front bay of the structure remained closed, but a small side door stood ajar.

A shrill shriek sounded from the garage, was cut short for a split-second of silence, then was followed by a full-out scream. A woman, damn it.

"You hear that? Advise." Gentry pulled out the fake phone and spoke softly. "Woman's inside the garage. No one in view."

The woman's screams turned to loud sobs, and Gentry watched as the garage side door opened wider and the woman he'd encountered at Tommy's house on his previous visit staggered out. She dropped to her hands and knees, and vomited. He relayed this to the others. For the moment, he was their eyes.

"Let her see you, Broussard." Sheriff Knight's deep, authoritative voice came through the phone. "Don't make entry into that garage. See if you can pull her to cover."

"On it." Gentry reholstered his pistol to make himself look as harmless as possible. He didn't snap the strap to hold it in place, though. He might need it. He knew where the woman was, but Tommy and Lang could be inside the garage with guns pointed at his head.

He stepped from behind the truck and walked slowly from the cover of the house's support piers until he was within the woman's line of sight. He didn't think he'd ever felt more vulnerable, despite knowing a shitload of firepower was hidden around him. "Ma'am?"

She stood on her knees and looked around wildly until she spotted him. Dark rivers of mascara ran down cheeks that had turned a mottled shade of grayish-white, the contrast with her sprayed and styled blond hair giving her a macabre, funhouse look. Nothing fun reflected in her wide, frightened brown eyes.

She staggered to her feet and ran toward Gentry. "Help me, please. Tommy . . ." The woman got within a foot of Gentry and crumpled; he reached out and caught her, pulling her behind a support beam to shelter them both from sight of the garage.

"Ma'am, how many people are in that garage?"

"Tommy . . . Tommy." She fell against his chest and, when her legs gave way again, he lowered her to the ground, kneeling beside her.

"Is Tommy in there alone?"

She'd begun to whimper, rocking back and forth, her arms crossed tight over her chest. The question froze her movement long enough for her to look at him. "You were here this morning."

"Yesterday." He noted her clammy skin and rapid breathing. Her confusion. The woman was in danger of going into shock. "You can call me Gentry." If she knew Lang and heard the name Broussard, it might frighten her more. "Is anyone inside the garage with Tommy?" She shook her head and clutched her arms around herself more tightly, as if she could forcibly stop her own trembling. "Tommy's dead."

"You hear that?" Gentry spoke into his phone, and got an immediate response.

"We're going in. Broussard, wait until we clear the building before you break cover."

Gentry closed his eyes for a second. If Tommy Mason was dead, it meant he knew enough for Lang to consider him a threat. Or maybe it was Lang's way of sending a message to Gentry to back off and keep his mouth shut. Too bad. That ship had sailed.

Movement on the left side of his peripheral vision caught his attention, and the woman saw it too. Her whimpers returned, and Gentry feared she'd start screaming again if she saw SWAT on the move. He needed to distract her in case Lang was still in that garage.

"Mrs. Mason—are you Mrs. Mason?"

She turned to look up at him. "Y-yes. Jennifer."

"Okay, Jennifer. When I was here earlier you had a baby. Where is your baby?"

The question brought some awareness back into her eyes. "He's . . . he's in the house, taking a nap. He takes a nap every afternoon at three, but I was late putting him down today."

Gentry had caught more movement as the tactical entry team moved in stages toward the garage. She didn't need to see it. "Is anyone else in the house besides your son? What's your boy's name?"

Under his steady barrage of questions, her trembling calmed to a slight, rhythmic shake. "Cameron. C-Cam."

"Is anyone in the house with Cam?"

"N-no."

"Okay, I'd really like to meet Cam. Will you walk upstairs with me and introduce me to him? Can you do that, Jennifer?"

She sniffled and nodded. "Jenny."

He gave her a smile as absent of impatience and worry as he could make it, although he feared it came out more like a grimace. She didn't seem to notice, but walked under the middle of the house toward the bottom of the front stairway. He placed a hand lightly under her elbow, not only to catch her if she collapsed again but to steer her in areas with as much cover from the garage as possible.

She stumbled once on the climb up the stairs, but seemed more in control. Gentry relaxed a little. Unless Lang was in the house, they were out of sight of that garage and whatever waited in there.

Outside, he heard the SWAT team making dynamic entry into the building. A lot of shouting, but no gunfire. Lots of cursing. Whatever they'd discovered was bad.

He itched to run down the stairs and see what they'd found, but he needed to secure the house and make sure Tommy Mason's family was safe. Not to mention letting the sheriff's officers do their job. *Their* job, not his. He'd be lucky to even have a job by the end of this day. He just hoped he could keep Jena Sinclair out of trouble.

The ice-cold blast from the air conditioning turned the sweat on his body and face to clammy cold as soon as he followed Jennifer Mason into the house. She'd obviously taken over the decorating duties; the small living room was neat and clean, but every surface held some little, breakable doodad. Ceramic animals, ceramic houses, baskets made of glass. Jennifer stood in the middle of the roomful of stuff, lost and broken herself.

"Jenny, where's Cam's room?" So far, the noises outside hadn't registered, nor the barrage of flashing lights Gentry glimpsed out the front window as reinforcements arrived. "Can we check and see if Cam's still asleep?"

The mention of her son got her moving again. "His room is all the way in the back."

Jennifer led the way into a long hall, past enough doors to make this a two- or three-bedroom house. Modest, but neat. Gentry let her move ahead of him as he checked each room, including a quick look in the closets. His gut told him the house was clean. That whatever Tommy had been involved in—or whatever Lang had roped him into—he'd kept it out of his home.

Had Gentry gotten Tommy killed by coming here? He didn't want to think about that. Not yet. It would provide plenty of nightmare fodder later.

He caught up with Jennifer at the last door, leading into a small room that clearly had been decorated for a little boy. Blue walls, bright yellow and red toy trucks scattered across the top of a low table, books with trains on the cover, each engine with its own mocking, laughing face.

The tiny boy lay on his back, a pacifier stuck in his mouth, limbs splayed in the unconscious way of a child who had never experienced fear or need. Whatever else Tommy Mason had or hadn't done, he'd taken care of his wife and this child—or so it seemed.

"He's a fine-looking boy."

Jennifer stood looking down at him, tears forming new rivulets of mascara on her face. "He adored his daddy. What am I going to tell him?"

"Let him finish his nap, and I'll get someone to come and talk to you. Would that be all right? They can tell you how to help Cam." The department had grief counselors on standby and, if Tommy were dead, they'd make sure Jennifer Mason had help, although little Cameron would still grow up without his father. How would Gentry's own life have been different—and Lang's—if Hank Broussard had lived?

She nodded, but Gentry wasn't sure anything was registering. He hated to leave her alone, but he wanted—no, *needed*—to see what was in that garage. Out of fear or self-doubt or whatever, he'd hindered this investigation without intending to. Now, he could help. He didn't know much about Lang's habits or contacts, but he knew the way his brother thought, or he used to.

He assured Jennifer someone would be coming to help her, and on his way outside called Warren and asked for a counselor. "She says Tommy is dead."

"Oh, he's dead all right." Warren's terse voice held more anger than a bayou held water after a hurricane surge. As soon as he saw Gentry, it would probably overflow the banks. "Get out there to that garage and see if you can help for a change. If they tell you to leave, haul your ass over here to the van. I'll have someone stay with Mrs. Mason."

"Got it." Gentry hung up, swallowing yet another apology because Warren wasn't ready to hear it. Before the night was over, he expected there to be not only apologies but lots and lots of groveling.

Walking outside was like entering a refinery. September in South Louisiana was as miserable as August, and prime hurricane season. So far this year, they'd lucked out.

Gentry trotted down the stairs and cut under the house, noting the extra sheriff's-department personnel who'd arrived and now scurried around the garage. The bay door remained down, so he entered through the side entrance, a single wooden door that led into a small workroom filled with a scattered array of hand tools, old paint cans, and a table saw.

A twin-sized blue air mattress covered by a tangle of sheets had been shoved into one corner. Gentry squatted next to it, careful not to touch anything. The one pillow had been punched into a ball. Blue-and-white floral sheets and pillowcase covered the plastic. A window AC unit above it churned out a noisy flow of cold air.

"Think our killer was staying here?" Adam Meizel squatted next to Gentry. "Seen anything to confirm it was your brother?"

He said it without judgment and, for the second time today, Gentry felt grateful. Meizel was a good guy.

Gentry studied the mattress. "No way to tell, but if he's been sleeping here, maybe your guys can find some fingerprints."

"They'll dust it. He got any DNA samples on file from the drug bust in New Orleans?"

"Doubt it, although he'd had a couple of run-ins with the law earlier, so there might be samples. As for the drug bust, we didn't know he was involved until the end." Gentry pressed his lips together. He shouldn't be surprised that Meizel knew his story. First, it had been all over the news—"Wildlife Agent Takes Down Wild Brother" made a good headline. Second, this was a parish of small towns, and gossip traveled. "Obviously, there was no body."

"Hey, from what I've heard, everyone thought he was dead, even the feds. And he's your brother. Don't beat yourself up for getting stuck in a bad situation."

Meizel stood, and Gentry stood with him. "You've been decent about this, more than I deserve. I appreciate it."

"No sweat. You seen the main show yet?"

No, and he might as well see what had befallen Tommy Mason, because he'd always carry part of the responsibility for it. Without intending to, he'd gone cowboy and a man was dead. "Lead the way."

They walked through an open doorway into the main part of the garage, and at first Gentry, trying to look on the floor through a dozen deputies, couldn't see anything.

Meizel jerked his head toward the silver Honda. "Inside the car."

"Aw, shit." Gentry walked to the front of the vehicle and looked over the hood at the figure who'd been Tommy Mason. His face, waxy and white, was frozen with raised eyebrows and mouth hanging open, head tilted back. A heavy wash of blood had spilled out his mouth and down his chin, and blended with the red slit dissecting his throat. The horizontal cut had congealed and turned black in the center, with pinkish-white bits of tissue hanging out at the edges. Here, the blood had run down his neck in streaks, gradually fading into the fabric of his red Terrebonne Tigers T-shirt.

"Is he . . ." Gentry squinted at the face and the blood pattern.

"Missing his tongue?" Meizel nodded. "Yeah. Subtle message, huh?"

Shit. Yeah, it was a message, all right—probably a message to him. Too late.

"Can you give us a positive ID so we don't have to get his wife back down here?" John Ramsey, the lead detective on the Eva Savoie case, walked up and stood alongside Gentry. He was a short, trim, buttoned-and-clipped type of guy with café-au-lait skin and sharp brown eyes. He exuded competence and oozed disapproval.

What was done, however, was done. All Gentry could do now was be cooperative and not react to attitude.

"It's definitely Tommy Mason. Thomas, I guess. Grew up here in Dulac and was running buddies with my brother Langston as long as I can remember. Works up in Chauvin as a mechanic at Landry's." And that's all he knew about this man who, this time yesterday, probably thought his biggest worry was a misbehaving Honda engine and maybe protecting his resurrected childhood friend.

Ramsey shot out question after question, many of them multiple times. Gentry knew the drill, and Ramsey was good. He was trying to get Gentry to trip up on his story.

With a rush of adrenaline that shot through him like bullets from his own duty rifle, Gentry realized for the first time that he might be a suspect—or at least suspected of being an accomplice. He could tell from Ramsey's questions. The detective was trying to decide if Gentry had been covering for Lang, maybe if he'd even been hiding him. Of course they thought that. He sure would, in their place.

Shit. Gentry had just been worried about losing his job. "Do I need a lawyer, Ramsey?"

The detective gave him a smile that dripped with condescension. "I don't know, Broussard. Do you?"

"No." Well, maybe, but not because he was guilty of anything besides being stupid and having a murderous junkie for a brother. Last time he checked, stupid wasn't a prosecutable crime. Otherwise, half the state of Louisiana would be behind bars, led by its politicians. "I'll tell you whatever you want to know."

"Mind telling me about it in Houma later tonight?"

They were going to make him go through an official interrogation, and he had no intention of fighting it. "I don't mind at all. Should I meet you there, or you want me to ride in with a deputy?"

If John Ramsey thought he was going to humiliate Gentry into giving them a reason to lock him up, he had the wrong wildlife agent.

They watched the EMTs pull Tommy Mason's body from the car. "Coroner thinks he was already dead when you got the call from your brother," Ramsey said. "His tongue's been cut out, but I guess you can see that for yourself. We haven't located it."

"Jesus." Gentry rubbed his eyes, wishing for either a drink or a barf bag, or both. "Who does this kind of shit?"

"You tell me." Ramsey looked back at him and Gentry thought maybe, just a little, he saw a shred of sympathy on the man's face. "It's gonna take us a while here, Broussard. Meet me back at the sheriff's office at eight."

"I'll be there."

Before that, he needed to have a come-to-Jesus meeting with Warren Doucet, and he had to warn Ceelie Savoie that the murderer was his brother.

CHAPTER 14

Swamp Goddess. Jena had liked the title when her NOPD friends gave her a camo T-shirt as a going-away gift with the words written across the front in rhinestones. She felt self-conscious wearing it here in the parish, so she slept in it.

Now, as she embarked on her third hour of sitting in her truck in Ceelie Savoie's driveway, she'd been rethinking her love of All Things Dark and Swampy. She was sweating like a boar in heat because she refused to give crazed killers and mosquitoes an easy target by rolling down the windows. Dumb and dumber.

Alligators were amazing animals, little changed from their prehistoric ancestors, and she never tired of watching them. The exploding population of wild boars posed a dangerous nuisance, growing worse by the day—they bred faster than hunters could kill them or gators could eat them. Snakes fascinated her, even the ill-tempered cottonmouths that proliferated in the Terrebonne marshes. The number and type of birds found in this ecosystem filled her with joy. She'd been so excited by her only black-bear sighting that she'd almost peed on herself.

Humans, however, sucked. Well, a lot of them.

Jena had gotten the go-ahead from Warren to stay with Ceelie Savoie until things were resolved at Gentry's rendezvous with his brother; she expected the sheriff's office would be showing up shortly and hoped they'd allow her to stay for moral support. She liked Ceelie and thought she might become a friend when things settled down. Since she'd been in the parish only a few months herself, worked irregular hours, and didn't hunt and fish like most of her colleagues, she hadn't found much common ground for friendship locally.

Only problem with keeping watch on Ceelie Savoie? Ceelie wasn't home from her trip to see her swamp mystic. Jena felt too exposed sitting on the porch, for fear Langston Broussard would show up here instead of meeting Gentry in Dulac.

If he was a smart sociopath who didn't want to be caught, he wouldn't come anywhere near this place again. He'd be on his way to Mexico.

Her time on the NOPD, however, had taught her that sociopaths, while often extremely smart in theory, were impulsive in implementation. Often, they wanted to be caught, at least on some level. They wanted recognition of their brilliance.

She didn't know that Langston Broussard was sociopathic, at least not in a clinical sense. But he'd proven he liked to play games. He'd toyed with Ceelie by leaving the skull and dramatic message at the cabin, where he risked exposure more than anywhere else. He'd toyed with Gentry by setting up this ridiculous meeting, which had little chance of ending well. Gentry had shot him three years ago in the line of duty, so he had to know, on some level, that his brother wouldn't come in without backup.

Jena was no criminal profiler, but she'd pegged Lang Broussard as a classic narcissist. He liked showing off his intelligence, which, of course, was always superior to those around him.

But the big questions hung out there like a Macy's Thanksgiving Day Parade balloon. Why had he killed Eva Savoie in the first place? And what did he want now?

Jena poured some of her bottled water onto a paper towel and scrubbed it over her baking face. Gentry would be making ruthless fun of her for being what he called cheap and she called fiscally responsible. She'd been turning on the AC every half hour or so to cool down the truck cab, but she'd be damned if she'd waste the gas to sit here and run it continuously in this fuel-guzzling truck, even if it wasn't her dime.

Finally, Ceelie's old pickup came into view in Jena's rearview mirror, then pulled alongside her. Did she imagine a flash of disappointment crossing Ceelie's face when she saw Jena instead of Gentry? Call her a matchmaker, but Jena thought they made a good pair—even if they hadn't realized it yet, given the circumstances. Celestine Savoie just might be the one woman stubborn and spirited enough to keep a handle on Gentry Broussard and his unique mix of ego and overactive sense of responsibility.

Plus, he probably didn't realize it, but he was smitten.

Of course he might not have any ego left after the lieutenant finished chewing him up and spitting him out, which would probably happen as soon as the rendezvous went down. She didn't want to be there, but had a feeling she'd get dragged in for a conversation about why she hadn't gone around her partner and reported what he suspected about his brother.

Her only answer? He *was* her partner, and he'd trusted her with his doubts and worries about what he had and hadn't seen. She didn't take that trust lightly. Plus, she'd read the reports from NOPD. There had been no reason to think Lang Broussard was alive. She still couldn't figure out how he'd survived, except that, in her experience, meanness was awfully hard to kill.

Jena climbed out of the truck's cab, stretching like her cat, Boudreaux, after a long nap in the sun. Except Boudreaux didn't sweat.

"How long you been here?" Ceelie got out of her truck and locked it using a key—the old rattletrap predated remote door locks. She carried a wallet and a plastic sandwich bag full of what Jena would swear were bones. "Your face is the same color as your hair."

"Well, *that's* a look I try to achieve—never. Mind if I come in and keep you company?" Jena followed Ceelie onto the porch and ran into her as soon as she rounded the corner. Ceelie had frozen in place four feet from the front door.

Jena's training kicked in. She gently reached out with her left hand and shuffled Ceelie behind her while unholstering her pistol with her right. She scanned the porch, the swamp, the shoreline down the bayou, then shifted her gaze along the same route a second time.

"Did you see anyone or just—" Wait. What the hell was that lying in front of the door?

"Just that." Ceelie stepped around and stood next to her, looking down. "Looks like a skinned animal of some kind. Maybe a rat or frog? Another animal could've dragged it up here."

Jena took a deep breath. "Stay here." She was the big bad wildlife agent, right? She knew about dead things.

She approached the door, which, despite a lot of scrubbing, still bore the faint outlines of GO HOME, BITCH, and knelt in front of the bloody lump. She closed her eyes. Jena wished she was wrong, but she was fairly certain the lump was a human tongue, and a fresh one. Judging by the amount of blood, the tongue's owner had not been dead when it was removed, or at least he or she hadn't been dead long.

Ceelie walked up beside her. "What is that thing? It looks like . . . Oh my God."

They stared at it for a few horrified seconds before Jena finally shook off the shock. "Don't touch it. I need to call the sheriff's office."

"Shouldn't you call Gentry?"

Jena's nerves skittered, but she kept her voice slow and calm. "I'll call my lieutenant as soon as I talk to the sheriff. This is their case, not ours. And Gentry's on a special assignment right now. He's fine." God, she hoped so.

"But . . ." Ceelie took a deep breath and nodded. "Okay. I'm going inside. There are a couple of things I need to do. You want to come in or do you have to . . ." She looked down at the tongue.

Unfortunately. "Yeah, I need to stay out here and make sure a gator doesn't decide it smells like dinner. Go on inside and lock the door behind you. Don't open it for anybody but me, and make sure I'm alone.

Ceelie smiled, but it looked forced. "How will I know if you're alone?"

Jena looked at the solid door and a pair of front windows that wouldn't give a full view of the porch. "My secret code phrase is *swamp goddess*." At Ceelie's raised eyebrows, she added, "It's a long story."

Ceelie unlocked the deadbolt and took an exaggerated step over the tongue to get into the house, taking her bag of bones with her. Jena wasn't sure she wanted to hear that story. It, too, was probably a long one.

First, she called the sheriff's office, identified herself, and reported finding a human tongue on Celestine Savoie's porch on Whiskey Bayou.

"I'm sorry, did you say a tongue?" The dispatcher would have her own tales to share tonight.

"Yes, ma'am, and a fresh one. It might be related to the operation half your department is working in Dulac right now."

That statement was enough to get her transferred straight through to the sheriff, who—after her stumbling introduction—handed her off to Warren. Sheriff Knight, a tad impatient on the best of days, probably thought she was verbally challenged and cursed that he had to coordinate his own operation with LDWF.

"Talk, Sinclair."

She relaxed at hearing the dulcet bark of her own lieutenant. Warren sounded about as cheerful as a mama gator whose nest had been raided, so she kept it brief, ending with, "The tongue looks kind of . . . fresh."

"The tongue probably belongs to the late Tommy Mason, who seems to be missing his," Warren said, to which Jena closed her eyes. Whatever Gentry had walked into, it had been bad. "Stay with the evidence until it's collected by the TPSO. Anything to make you think Langston Broussard is in the area?"

So they hadn't caught him, damn it. Jena turned around on the porch, looking in all directions. It was almost dark. Down the bayou, the gator hunter licensed here for the season had arrived and was wrestling a big reptile into his boat, already so loaded the vessel was sitting low in the water from hundreds of pounds of extra weight. Louisiana didn't allow gator hunting after nightfall, so he probably was bringing in his last line of the day.

"There's no sign of him, but there's a gator guy nearby. I'll flag him down before he leaves. Maybe he saw something." She paused. "Sir, is Agent Broussard okay?"

"Other than the new asshole he's going to get ripped by myself and the sheriff, he's fine. You might get a new one yourself, Sinclair."

Great. Just what she wanted to hear.

"As soon as—" The lieutenant paused at the low, rhythmic hum sounding from inside the cabin, obviously loud enough for him to hear. Jena moved farther from the door. "What the hell is that?" he asked.

Jena lowered her voice. "It's Ceelie Savoie, chanting or singing or something." She paused, but couldn't resist adding, "She has some new chicken bones."

There was a long pause.

"Chicken bones. Godalmighty." Warren sighed. "Well, as soon as the TPSO picks up the tongue, get Ms. Savoie and her chicken bones away from that cabin. The sheriff wants to stake it out since our suspect keeps returning to it. She needs to be gone."

Jena looked at the closed door. Behind it, Ceelie continued to sing in what Jena suspected was Cajun French, but she wasn't sure. "That could be a problem, sir. She's pretty stubborn."

"Then knock her over the head and drag her out." The lieutenant didn't sound as if he were joking. "You're supposed to a smart woman, Sinclair, not that you could prove it by your recent actions. Figure it out."

"Yes, sir." It was going to be a long, long night. "Where should I take her?"

"Wherever she'll go, as long as it isn't anywhere near Whiskey Bayou."

Jena ended the call, unsnapped the holster strap above her SIG Sauer to make sure it was at the ready, and dragged the rocking chair to a spot where she could see all of the bayou. Her only blind spots were the sides and back of the house. The state needed to equip its officers with camera-carrying drones.

She waved the hunter over when he finished tagging his gator and had turned his boat back toward Bayou Terrebonne. It was a long shot, and Jena didn't expect to learn anything, but any tidbit she could uncover might put the lieutenant in a better mood.

"Don't know if it means nothin', but there was a boat pulling back into Bayou Terrebonne when I was cutting back here to check my last lines," he said. The man, from a family whose name Jena recognized as longtime parish residents, said he'd been surprised to see anybody else. "Don't usually find nobody else back here. Didn't get a look at his face, really. It was a skinny guy with dark hair. Mostly, I was lookin' at the boat."

Jena pulled out the small notebook and pen she kept in her pocket. "What can you tell me about it?"

"He wasn't no hunter, is all. Old beat-up boat, no gear. I'm always on the lookout for another poacher." He jerked his head toward the cabin. "I been keepin' an eye on this place too, since Miss Eva's girl come back out here to live. Don't want nothin' happening to her."

And that's why Jena loved it here. People watched out for each other, even for people they'd never met. "You see that boat again, call the sheriff's office or call me and I'll contact them." Jena handed him a business card. "Don't engage with the guy, though. Steer clear of him."

"Don't you worry 'bout that. I can take care of myself. Can take care of him too." The hunter left, saying he needed to get his gator haul to the buyers in Houma before they shut down for the night.

And that's why Jena hated it here. People watched out for each other, and felt perfectly qualified to mete out justice in their own way.

She tensed at the sound of a vehicle door slamming behind the cabin, then chastised herself for getting jumpy. If Lang Broussard showed up here, he wasn't likely to slam a car door to announce his arrival.

She turned as two SO deputies rounded the corner of the porch. She'd seen them both before but didn't know their names.

"Hey, I hear you got an extra tongue," said the shorter of the two. Jena had at least six inches of height on him. In her olive uniform, she felt like the Jolly Green Giant.

She stepped aside and pointed at the darkening lump, which had two big horseflies crawling on it, just in case it hadn't grossed her out enough already. "Get that thing out of here. Please."

Then she had to figure out how to get Ceelie Savoie out of here as well.

CHAPTER 15

The deputies' boots clattered around on the porch, but Ceelie did her best to block out the thumping, along with the low murmur of voices as they examined and discussed their evidence.

She'd also been trying, without much success, to block out the feeling that Jena Sinclair knew a lot more about Tante Eva's murder and the investigation than she'd let on. Otherwise, why sit out here and wait without having any idea when Ceelie might get back? The woman had been on the verge of heatstroke, which meant she'd been here a while. Ceelie's best guess? To play bodyguard until someone from the sheriff's office could get here and talk her into leaving the cabin.

Of course, maybe Jena would've told her more if they hadn't been distracted by the tongue. What kind of sick freak cut out somebody's tongue and left it as a calling card? And did Gentry's "special assignment" have anything to do with this case?

Ceelie didn't like games. She didn't like being lied to or talked around. She didn't like being "handled." She didn't like being kept in the dark "for her own good."

All those things seemed to be happening.

Until she could pin Jena to the wall and make her talk, however, all Ceelie could accomplish while the officers did their job was to do her own: take the new set of throwing bones from Tomas Assaud and make them hers. *The bones never lie,* Tante Eva had told her. *They always fall true.*

One big problem with that: she had no idea how to claim these bones as her own. She spread out the worn square of leather on the throwing table and poured the delicate bones out of their plastic bag onto the mat, hoping for inspiration. She set the candles at northwest and southeast.

Taking the carved wooden box out of the drawer, she pondered how literally she should take Tomas's instructions. Had he meant she needed to actually bury Tante Eva's throwing bones, and, if so, did the box needed to be buried as well? Or was a figurative burial sufficient?

You have the sight, and each sight must have its own guide, Tomas had said. To Ceelie, that translated as *Follow your gut,* and her gut told her to get rid of Eva's throwing bones—they needed to be out of this cabin, and that would be enough.

Since the cabin's only door led straight to the awful gift that had most likely been left by the same psycho who'd killed her aunt and tried to scare her away with the skull and painted door, Ceelie tugged open the back window. She leaned out as far as she dared without losing her balance and threw the latched box as hard to the right as she could. It cleared the corner of the cabin and landed in Whiskey Bayou with a satisfying splash about two feet off the bank. The box floated for a few seconds along the murky top of its watery tomb, then sank out of sight.

Rest easy, Tante Eva.

She sang an old French song she remembered from her childhood as she wandered around the cabin, scanning the shelves and counters for something in which her own throwing bones could live. She stopped at the sight of a worn, leather-covered cufflink case sitting atop the tiny bedside table. She'd seen the flat, rectangular case in a store window in Houma when she was a teenager, after her dad had gotten sick but before he'd been forced to quit his job at the gas plant.

She hadn't known what the box was for, really. She'd never seen her dad wear cufflinks, or any other jewelry except a wristwatch and the gold wedding band he'd never taken off. She'd thought the box was beautiful and might make her dad feel better. The soft leather was the color of dark chocolate, and a shiny gold crest, now flaked and faded, had been stamped on top. The inside was lined in cream-colored satin.

She'd bought it for his birthday, spending money from the "Get Out of Terrebonne Parish" fund both she and Dad had been contributing to since her mom left. He'd chastised her for the purchase at first. Then he'd made too big a fuss over it, realizing how desperate she'd been to make him feel better and how helpless she felt to do so. It was the only thing of his she'd kept, using it for her own few pieces of jewelry.

He'd probably chastise her again, but she knew the box was where her own throwing bones should live. She took out a couple of bracelets, a silver ring, and a few guitar picks—the box's only contents—and stuck them in the zippered outer pouch of her suitcase.

She kept the candles at northwest and southeast for protection, lit them, and sat before the throwing table, humming her in-progress Whiskey Bayou song while placing each of the bones into the case. With each one, she paid homage to the role it had played in the animal's life. Once the bones were inside the box, she prayed to the God of her church, asked the Virgin Mary for intervention, then added a few words of respect for the mystic leader of her Chitimacha ancestors, the guidance of her Tante Eva, and the universe in general. Finally, she made the sign of the cross, to confuse things even more. Somehow, it felt right when she ended with *Amen.*

Gotta love the contradictory nature of South Louisiana.

With a start, Ceelie realized she *did* love it. Maybe Dad had wanted more for her than he'd been able to find here, but it had been wrong of him to make her promise to leave. Maybe not being here was what had kept her from being whole, what had made her music begin to fall silent. Maybe that one song that had come to her before she left Nashville was telling her it was time to go home.

She shook her head to erase those thoughts. The meaning of home was something to ponder later. She blew out the candles, moved them back to northeast and southwest for divination, and lit them again. She held the box of bones over which she had prayed, and, closing her eyes, upended them onto the leather mat.

The bones will fall true, child. You just have to know how to understand what they're tryin' to say. The bones never lie.

They tumbled out like macabre pickup sticks. Ceelie studied the pattern into which they'd fallen, tiny pricks of memory returning to her. The wing bone meant travel; the foot, evil. She sought out the single foot, and a shiver ran across her shoulders when she saw it lying over the neck bone, which represented life. Danger awaited someone, maybe death. But whose death? Not hers, or the foot would have lain across the skull. This pattern foretold danger or death for someone close to her.

Which was ridiculous, because she wasn't close to anyone. Not here, anyway, and she doubted the bones meant Sonia was going to be run down by a Nashville bus.

They mean Gentry. He's in danger.

What a ridiculous thought. She barely knew the man and was letting this weird, long day get to her. Ceelie leaned over and blew out the candles, then jumped like she'd been shot when someone knocked on the door.

She was so rattled that she opened it without asking who was there.

"You're not too good at this staying-safe thing." Jena took a wide step over the threshold even though the tongue was no longer there. In its place was a smear of blood, however, that Ceelie would have to douse in pine cleaner. Otherwise, she'd have gators at her door following the scent.

"Are the deputies through out there?" She went into the kitchen and pulled out an industrial-sized bottle of cleaner, which she'd bought on her first trip to the store and had already used down to the halfway point.

"Yeah—you're going to cover the bloodstain? Good idea. I've already shooed a vulture away from the area."

Damn it. "Big turkey vulture? Red head, mean eyes?"

"Yep, that's the one. Funny, that's what people say about me."

Ceelie smiled. "I doubt that." Jena Sinclair was nice and, under other circumstances, good friend material. Maybe good friend material anyway. "I wish you'd shot the damned thing."

Jena laughed. "Not the thing to say to a wildlife agent."

"Right. No telling agents to shoot animals: duly noted. There's no shortage of those nasty things, though." Ceelie took the cleaner to the door and poured at least a cup on top of the bloodstain. That would do for now. No self-respecting gator—or vulture, for that matter—would come anywhere near it while it reeked of pine.

She closed and locked the door and turned to look at Jena. The agent had taken off her cap and finger-combed her tousle of dark-red hair. With her sharp green eyes, fair complexion, and height, she was downright striking. "You ever do any modeling?"

Jena laughed. "God, no. I have two left feet. I'm pretty sure models need to be graceful. And I have the fashion sense of a forensic biologist—which was my background before I got into law enforcement. Besides, don't change the subject."

Ceelie feigned innocence. "Did we have a subject? You mean vultures?"

Jena walked to the corner of the room where Ceelie had stuck her suitcase. She picked it up and laid it on the bed. "Start packing. You can't stay here, not until this case is wrapped up."

Damn it. Jena was right. The tongue had convinced her of that, coming so soon after the skull. But it galled her to have some nutjob dictate where she could and couldn't go, where she could and couldn't live.

"How do you know when you've crossed the line between being strong and independent and being stupid?"

Jena smiled, but it didn't reach her eyes. "When there a sociopath targeting you, or at least your house, and you refuse to accept help, that's stupid." She pointed at the suitcase. "Not putting some clothes in there and leaving with me right now? That crosses the line into stupid too."

A flush of guilt spread its heat across Ceelie's face at Jena's tense expression. She'd probably been ordered to make sure her charge left for her own good, and wasn't sure Ceelie would do it. Jena wouldn't leave without her, and the idea she might be putting the agent in danger brought clarity. She had to go. For all she knew, Jena could be the one in danger.

The bones never lie.

"I guess you're right." Ceelie opened the suitcase and went into the postage-stamp-sized bathroom to grab a few things she'd hung up to dry this morning. The rest of her clothes, what few she had, were already in the suitcase. The cabin had no closet, and she had yet to figure out what to do with them. Plus, unpacking felt permanent. It felt like more of a commitment to Terrebonne Parish than she had been willing to make.

Now that she'd finally realized how much she loved this place, even this tiny little shack, she was being forced to leave. Ironic.

Ceelie sat on the bed, flummoxed. "I don't know where to go." She'd been feeling intelligent and empowered; suddenly, she nosedived into epic failure. "Maybe one of the fishing camps down in Cocodrie I saw yesterday would be pretty cheap this time of year." She'd feel safer there than in a fleabag hotel.

"You can stay at my place in Houma," Jena said. "It's not much, but I have a sofa that pulls out into a bed. Besides, we're gonna get this guy soon and then you can get on with your life."

"Yeah, my big, fat, successful life." Ceelie laughed, then mentally slapped herself upside the head. Self-pity was an ugly state to live in, and she didn't plan to set up residence there.

"Your voice is amazing." Jena picked up the Gibson, which Ceelie had propped against the wall near the bathroom door. "If you haven't made it yet, all it means is that the time hasn't been right. Or maybe the place."

Ceelie shrugged. "Probably. I used to think I could make it, but Nashville beat me down." Now that she'd been away, even for just a week, she could see how defeated she had become. "Who knows. Maybe I'll try Austin."

"Nope." Jena handed her the guitar. "Lafayette's the place to start, and it's close enough for you to live here if you decide you want to stay. I'll ask Mac about the best music spots—one of the agents in our unit. He's up there every weekend for the music." She shook her head. "Well, he's also up there to pick up women, but that's another story."

"Sounds like one best enjoyed over pizza and beer."

"Definitely. Let's get out of here and find some before it gets any later."

And darker. And scarier. Ceelie agreed. Now that she'd finally admitted she shouldn't stay out here alone, she couldn't leave fast enough.

Jena pulled her pistol from its holster before unlocking the deadbolt. "Let me take a look around first. The sheriff's office was supposed to leave someone on guard, but we're taking no chances."

Ceelie waited inside, straining to hear voices. Part of her—a big part—hated the idea of fleeing from her home like she'd done something wrong. And yes, it had become home.

After a soft knock on the front door, Jena stuck her head inside. "You ready?"

Ceelie took a last look around, her gaze coming to rest on the throwing table. "I need to get one more thing. Can you take this?" She shifted the handle of her rolling suitcase to Jena, then opened the top drawer of the table. Moving quickly, she put the throwing bones into the cufflink case and snapped it shut, then rolled the candles up in the leather mat. Tucking it all under one arm, she grabbed the Gibson with her other hand and walked onto the porch.

This was her life in a nutshell, wasn't it? An old guitar, a box of bones, and the blood that ran through the veins of her people. *Her people*. She could honor her promise to her dad and leave this parish, but she could never leave behind who she was and the people who'd come before her. She'd left for the wrong reasons.

She hadn't understood that until now.

"I'll be back," she whispered, and closed the door behind her. She didn't bother locking it. The cabin on Whiskey Bayou would not be hers again until all this was over.

Jena looked curiously at the box and rolled-up leather bundle under her arm, but didn't say anything. "You want to ride with me or follow me?"

"Follow." She'd be damned if she left the truck here. It represented her last shred of independence. "Are you sure it's okay to stay with you?"

"Absolutely." At the corner of the porch, they ran into the deputy who'd answered Gentry's call about the skull-and-bloody-door episode. The name embroidered on his uniform shirt read "A. Meizel."

"Glad you're leaving, Ms. Savoie." He held a rifle in the crook of his left arm and a long flashlight in his right hand. Another fifteen minutes or so and full dark would fall. "Hopefully, we'll catch this man soon. We're close."

"Okay, enough." Ceelie stopped, giving them no choice but to stop with her. "I can tell something's happened. I want to know what it is."

"As soon as we get to my place, I'll fill you in," Jena said, her voice low. "I promise. We need to go so Deputy Meizel and his colleagues can do their job."

"I'm holding you to that." Ceelie clenched her jaw and gave a tight nod. She followed Jena off the porch and set her throwing materials and guitar in the passenger's seat of the truck.

"Okay if I put your suitcase in the back of my truck?" Jena already had it wedged halfway behind the driver's seat.

"Sure." Between the Gibson, the bones, and the suitcase, the luggage was the least important. She wouldn't take off without the former, but the latter didn't mean much. Clothes could be replaced.

The sound of a generic ringtone could barely be heard above the swamp noises beginning to rise around them as night fell. Jena cursed. "Hang on." She finished shoving Ceelie's suitcase in the pickup and unclipped a phone from her belt. "Hey, Broussard."

Tension drained from Ceelie's muscles; she hadn't realized it was there. Even before she'd thrown the bones, she'd had a feeling Gentry was in trouble. The bones had given birth to a fear that he was injured. Maybe worse.

Sometime when she'd begun to realize Whiskey Bayou was home, she'd also begun to think of Gentry Broussard as more than a pheromone-emitting uniformed guy with bedroom eyes and dimples. Though he surely to God was all that.

She wrenched her thoughts from bedroom eyes to listen to Jena's end of the conversation, which so far had contained a lot of mild expletives and a few groans. "Okay, okay. Give me the address," she said, pulling the little notebook and pen from her pocket. "Where's the key? What about the dog?" Jena's voice rose. "Broussard, we are not going to stand outside your house until you get home. If the dog doesn't like us, he'll have to get over it. I have a stun gun."

Ceelie slapped a hand over her mouth when Jena held her phone a foot away from her ear while Gentry had a fit over what sounded like her threat to stun his dog. Did that mean a change of plans?

"See you when we see you." Jena stuck her phone back in its belt clip. "I have to meet Gentry and our lieutenant at his place when he finishes up—he's on his way to the sheriff's office right now and doesn't know what time. Want me to drop you at my apartment first?"

And miss a chance to check out Chez Broussard? "No way. I want to meet Hoss, and I want to know what's going on. You promised."

Jena smiled, and Ceelie thought she looked even more worn-out than Deputy Meizel. "So I did."

CHAPTER 16

Gentry was ready for somebody to stick a fork in him. He'd been grilled and fried and was past well-done by ten p.m., and that had been an hour ago.

The halos from the scant streetlights scattered around the unincorporated community of Montegut bled together into a haze. He turned down Pelican Street toward his house, which backed up to an earthen levee and, beyond that, Bayou Terrebonne.

As if the night hadn't already been bad enough, he had no doubt that two women had been rifling through his stuff and terrorizing his dog for hours; they'd probably sent out a memo to everyone in the department that his Big Bad Beast was a wriggling twenty-pound pudgeball with bat ears. Warren still wanted his own pound of flesh. To top it off, he had to call his mother and break the news that her dead eldest son the junkie was now alive and committing gruesome murders around his old hometown, including extracting the tongue of his former best friend.

Gentry swore he'd shoot himself with his own SIG Sauer if he didn't fear that he'd fail and end up filling out reams of paperwork while detective John Ramsey hammered him with questions.

Maybe he could take care of Warren by reciting the same answers he'd been giving Ramsey for hours.

No, he'd had no idea his brother Langston had survived the shooting in New Orleans, nor how he'd done so.

No, he hadn't heard from Lang prior to the phone call this afternoon.

No, he hadn't been protecting Lang by not telling anyone the killer looked like his brother; he'd believed the resemblance was a product of his own guilty imagination.

No, he hadn't been letting Lang hide out at his house.

Yes, they could search it all they wanted, if they felt the need to waste their time instead of being out searching places where Lang might actually be.

No, he had no idea what Lang wanted from Eva Savoie. He knew of no connection between them.

No, he hadn't known that Lang was staying with Tommy Mason nor for how long; he'd visited Tommy on a simple fishing expedition.

No, he wasn't screwing Celestine Savoie in order to help his brother get information or access to her cabin.

That one really pissed him off.

Warren had finally shown up with the sheriff, publicly chewed his ass up one side and down the other to make sure Knight and Ramsey heard his humiliation, then told him to get his worthless carcass home and wait so Warren could come by later and chew him up again.

The worst part? He had to own it. Well, maybe not that part about Ceelie—she deserved better than for them to think she'd fall prey to such a ruse even if he had been some heartless, manipulative son of a bitch. She was smarter than that.

Plus, he wasn't a user. He wasn't a game-player. He was just an idiot.

Gentry's heart sped up and pumped adrenaline through his system at the sight of a dark figure moving between the support beams beneath his raised house. Jamming his foot on the brake, he stopped the truck with a lurch behind Jena's and Ceelie's vehicles. He killed the engine and had boots on the ground in a split second, gun drawn.

"Stop!" he shouted. "On the ground! Now!"

The figure froze, and two muumuu-clad arms flew into the air. "Don't you be shootin' at me, Gentry Broussard. It's Maxine!"

Awesome. Now he'd almost killed his elderly neighbor, Maxine Vallieres. That would've made his night complete.

"Maxine, what are you doing under my house?" Gentry holstered his gun and pulled his rifle and a bag of burgers from the truck. A dark blur sped across the yard at him before he could react, followed by a sharp pain that shot through his ankle like a knife blade.

An outburst of angry growls and tugs on his pants leg followed. "Hoss? Why are you outside? Stop biting me."

The whole world had gone nuts.

"I've lost Moose." Maxine wandered over, wringing hands covered in a half dozen sparkling rings. His neighbor was a self-admitted home-shopping-channel addict. Her pink-sequined housedress glinted in the lights from her front porch. "Can you help me find him? He's afraid of the dark."

Moose was part pit bull, part chicken. "Sure. When was the last time you saw him? Why is Hoss outside?"

"I don't know." Maxine burst into tears, which made Gentry feel even worse about ordering her to hit the ground. "And you have a houseful of women, Gentry. Are they supposed to be there? I told them you never had women at your house."

"Yeah, I knew about the women." Awesome. Now they'd know he'd not only exaggerated his dog's fierce-factor, but that he had no social life.

He had a sudden thought. "Maxine, have you seen Moose since the women arrived? Was he outside with Hoss when they got here?"

She stopped crying and settled her hands on her hips, lips narrowing. "Now that you mention it, yes. You think those women stole Moose?"

No, he thought they'd seen two dogs and made a false assumption. "I'll get to the bottom of it; I bet Moose is in my house. You want to come in?" Might as well make it a midnight slumber party. Warren was divorced; maybe he could fix his lieutenant up with Maxine and divert his attention from Gentry.

"No, just send him out if he's in there with those women."

"Gotcha; get Moose away from the women. C'mon, Hoss, we need to stage a rescue." Now that he had bitten and chastised his human minion, the French bulldog had wandered off in search of the ideal pissing spot du jour. Gentry caught him at the foot of the stairs and climbed up, trying to keep the canine and the burgers as far apart as possible.

He rattled his keys outside the door so the women wouldn't be startled, and paused at the realization that no one else had ever been inside his house besides Maxine and the cleaning service that came every other week. There was loner and there was pathetic; he thought he'd settled into Pathetic Town.

Hoss went racing in ahead of him, followed by a flurry of screams from the living room as the Frenchie reclaimed his territory. Gentry stood in the doorway and watched the two dogs reunite on top of Ceelie, who'd collapsed into a ball of laughter on the sofa while Jena, all arms and legs, tried to untangle them.

He grinned, which felt really good after the day he'd had and the night and day ahead of him. Not to mention, Ceelie's husky laugh tightened something low in his gut that had no business tightening.

"Moose! Come!" He had to call twice before the pit bull raised his brindle head, then took a leap off Jena's back to bound across the room. Hoss was busy asserting his dominance over the women, so Gentry hooked a finger in Moose's collar and tugged him toward the door.

"Here you go, Maxine!" He waved and released Moose, who flew down the stairs toward the woman who called herself his "mom."

As soon as he'd made sure Maxine and Moose were safely inside their house, Gentry closed the door and walked back through the foyer. In the living room, things had settled down, or at least Ceelie had been able to sit upright and Jena had collapsed onto the floor. Hoss jumped down and ran to Gentry for an ankle bite. He scooped the dog up before he could draw blood. He'd never been able to break him of that bad habit.

"Where did Hoss go?" Jena asked. "Although I've gotta admit, Gentry, that dog is the biggest, laziest couch potato I've ever seen. Plus, he ate most of the pepperoni-and-sausage pizza we ordered for you."

Gentry grinned, glad Maxine would have to deal with the noxious fallout from that feast. "It's because that couch potato wasn't Hoss. His name is Moose and he lives next door. This"—he hefted the squirming Frenchie—"is Hoss."

Ceelie burst into laughter. "I told you, Jena. That little dog's been sitting outside the door and howling at the top of his lungs since we got here." She walked over to Gentry and ruffled Hoss's big ears. "You sure are cute."

"Thanks." Gentry cleared his throat when Ceelie looked up at him with a playful sparkle in her eyes. A flush of heat spread over him that had nothing to do with the steamy night. "On behalf of Hoss, of course."

"Of course. Jena's filled me in on everything that's been happening." Her expression grew solemn. "You look exhausted. Are you okay?"

So much for pretending everything was normal. He set Hoss down and picked up the bag of food. "I've had better days, but . . . God, I'm sorry, Ceelie. My brother—"

"Your brother is a murderer who likes to torture old women and play games with his victims," she said, steel in her voice. "But he's not you, and I get why you wanted to be sure before saying anything."

He closed his eyes, feeling ten pounds lighter. He hadn't realized how much he wanted Ceelie's forgiveness. How much he hoped she wouldn't blame him or think he'd been helping Lang.

He greeted Jena, sat on the opposite end of the black leather sofa from Ceelie, and wolfed down burgers while they filled him in on the unexpected appearance of Tommy Mason's tongue. He brought them up to speed on how Tommy lost it in the first place, sparing them the worst of the details. The sight of that blood-drenched chin would haunt his dreams for a while.

"His poor wife," Ceelie said. "To have been the one to find him first."

Gentry had been halfway through his second burger; at the memory of Jennifer Mason's desperate face, his appetite took a hike. "It's my fault." He pulled the meat off the burger and gave it to Hoss, who'd been sitting at attention next to his elbow, patient except for the slight butt trembling. "I accelerated things by visiting Tommy. I might as well have—"

"Shut it." Jena speared him with a pointed look. "Did you really think your brother was alive when you went to the Mason house? No, you didn't. And as soon as you realized Lang could be alive, you tried to call Warren."

"You should've tried harder." Warren Doucet's voice preceded him into the living room. "And you should start locking your door. If I were Langston Broussard and I thought the brother who tried to cap me three years ago was trying to get me caught, you'd be the next person I'd visit. It wouldn't be for a friendly family reunion."

Gentry halfway hoped Lang would show up—not while the others were around or could be put in danger, of course. He desperately wanted to talk to his brother, however. He wanted to find out why Lang had made one bad choice after another. He wanted to know how things had gone so wrong. Drug addiction explained a lot, but not everything.

He wanted to talk to his brother, and never mind that at the end of the conversation, one of them would likely end up dead.

First, he'd get his continued groveling out of the way and save Warren the awkwardness of firing his former partner's son. "I'm sorry, Warren. Lieutenant Doucet. If you want me to resign, I under—"

"Shut the hell up, Broussard." Warren Doucet might be in his forties, with short-trimmed hair that had a good bit of salt joining the pepper, but he was tough as they came. The lieutenant could hold his own with his younger agents physically and outthink all of them put together. "Any more pizza?"

"Gentry's neighbor Moose ate most of it, but there are a few slices left," Jena said, ignoring Gentry's *eat-shit* look. "Have you met the infamous Hoss, Gentry's guard dog?"

"That's Hoss?" Warren looked down at the dog, and Gentry could tell he was trying not to smile. The light in his eyes gave him away. He shook his head and grabbed the pizza box. "Is it a dog or a bat?"

Jena returned to her seat on the floor with her back against the hearth. "Take the recliner, Lieutenant. Have you met Ceelie Savoie?"

"Not until now." Warren introduced himself and took Jena up on the recliner offer. Gentry figured he should have offered his own seat, but he was almost too tired to move. Besides, he liked sitting on the sofa with Ceelie, even if Hoss was stretched out between them. At least so far, the dog hadn't started snoring or farting. There was plenty of time for that to start, though.

"I need to be brought up to speed, Broussard, but first let me say this," Warren said. "You've apologized, and as far as I'm concerned that's all I need to hear. But you're gonna have to apologize to Sheriff Knight, to our regional captain, and to Detective Ramsey—formally. That means a personal visit and a letter."

Gentry nodded. He'd expected that, and he knew it could be a lot worse. "I know Ramsey thinks I'm working with my brother, but I swear to God I'm not."

Warren chewed a bite of pizza and gave him a long, steady look before speaking. "I knew both of you boys when you were little kids. You're probably too young to remember much, but I can tell you this. Your dad worried about your brother until the day he died. Hank never worried about you, not for a single day. You were just like him as a kid, and you still are. That's a compliment. You're welcome."

He dug in the pizza box for another slice. "So save your breath about being an accomplice. Let it go. I never thought for a second that you were working with your brother. The sheriff's just pissed off that we're in the middle of his case. Not just you. Us. We're all a team. Don't forget that."

Damn, he must be even more tired than he thought, because Gentry felt the burn of tears behind his eyes. So he kept his gaze trained on the floor. "Thank you, sir. For everything."

Warren cleared his throat as if he, too, might be having a Moment. "Now, start at the beginning, from the minute you saw the killer who looked like Langston leaving the cabin. Don't leave out anything."

So once again, this time with help from Jena, who contributed the conversations they'd had about it, Gentry went through the story. It was a lot easier this time, without John Ramsey's insinuating questions.

"I still don't know why, though." Gentry looked apologetically at Ceelie. "I don't know why he would go after your great-aunt. There's just no connection there."

Ceelie scratched behind Hoss's ears. The dog had moved to curl up in her lap, ignoring Gentry. Smart dog. "Do you and your brother look alike at all?" Ceelie asked, frowning and staring down at the dog. "I remembered something on the way back from Cocodrie today, although admittedly it's a stretch."

"Gentry and his brother could've been twins except for the height and age difference, at least when they were kids," Warren said. "Why were you in Cocodrie?"

Oh boy, Gentry thought, *this should be interesting.* Warren was a Baptist, a religious minority in South Louisiana. Baptists weren't known for their tolerance of voodoo and Native American mysticism.

"I wanted to visit with a mystic who learned the practice alongside my Tante Eva." Ceelie had set up a rhythmic stroke along Hoss's silky ears, and the dog sighed with contentment. How sad was it that Gentry envied his dog?

Warren stared at her. "Practice of what?" Then it registered. "Oh." He blinked a couple of times but recovered quickly. "What did you remember?"

Ceelie turned to look at Gentry. "You remember the first day I met you, I thought you looked familiar?"

"Yeah." He smiled. "But I would've remembered you."

She returned his smile, and damn if that now-familiar heat didn't settle somewhere in his nether regions again. "Well, I remembered who it was that you reminded me of. It was a boy who came to the cabin one summer for a couple of weeks with Nonc LeRoy's nephew—or the man I called Nonc LeRoy. It would've been about 1996."

Gentry and Warren exchanged looks. "That was the year my dad died." Still, he saw no connection. "What does it have to do with me or my brother?"

Ceelie shrugged. "Probably doesn't have any connection at all. It's just that he looked a lot like you, or like you might've looked back then. He was a friend of LeRoy's nephew and was fifteen or sixteen. I kind of had a crush on him."

"Do you remember this boy's name?" Warren lowered the footrest of the recliner and leaned forward.

"I think the nephew's name was Tommy. But the other boy . . . I can't remember for sure, but it was a funny name you didn't hear very often. I think it was Lane or something like that. What's your brother's name?"

Chill bumps had set up along Gentry's arms and shoulders and he looked at Warren again.

"His name is Lang."

CHAPTER 17

Ceelie closed her eyes and coaxed her muscles to relax under the hot water from the shower in Gentry's guest bathroom. It was the first real hot shower she'd had since her return to Terrebonne Parish. The cabin's jerry-rigged shower spit water in uneven spurts and was more tepid than warm.

Gentry's house wasn't large, but it felt palatial after the confines of the cabin on Whiskey Bayou.

From its dark-blue siding and white trim to its interior that looked like it had been put together by a furniture-store decorator told to create a "bachelor-pad ambience," the house had been exactly what Ceelie would've expected from a single man who worked long hours and hadn't given two thoughts to home decor. The only things that told her anything about the owner were a flat-screen TV the size of a spaceship, an unmade king-sized bed, a spare room full of workout equipment, a desk, a docking station, and speakers for a digital music player. Plus, of course, the spoiled-rotten French bulldog.

Hoss was Gentry Broussard's biggest tell. He was all macho talk covering a soft-hearted, good man who wanted to save the world and all the puppies in it. She wouldn't be voicing that opinion, however. She wasn't sure he was even aware of it, and might find it insulting.

The more Ceelie learned of Gentry Broussard, the more she liked him. A few days ago, she'd sworn a man didn't figure into her future plans. She'd also sworn Terrebonne Parish didn't fit into those plans. Now? She wouldn't swear to anything.

As exhausted as she was from spending the entire night listening to the three agents spinning theories about the possible link between Lang Broussard and LeRoy Breaux, Ceelie couldn't stop her brain from continuing to hash and rehash it.

Tante Eva hadn't liked LeRoy's nephew much, or at least she hadn't wanted Ceelie spending time alone with him. She'd thought it was because he was an older boy and her aunt thought it wasn't proper. Now, however, she wondered if it wasn't their age and gender Tante Eva didn't trust, but something about Tommy himself.

Gentry had finally told her that Lang Broussard's best friend was Tommy Mason, and it was Tommy's tongue that had ended up on her porch.

Gentry had been twelve when his dad died, and although he didn't say so, Ceelie could tell he'd idolized his father. Lang, at sixteen, was already rebellious, and while Gentry remembered his brother going away for two weeks that summer, he'd thought Lang was at Tommy's house. There had been no reason to tie his visit with Tommy to LeRoy Breaux.

It all kept coming back to LeRoy.

Ceelie finished her shower, pulled on a clean pair of jeans and a red tank top she'd brought in from Jena's truck, and wandered into the kitchen. Gentry was pouring a scoop of coffee into a fresh filter for a new pot. They'd started one just before her shower, so he must have been mainlining caffeine.

She watched him for a moment; he was rubbing his temples as he watched the water drip through the filter with a gurgle. He looked sexy, in an exhausted kind of way.

"How're you doing?" She poured herself a fresh cup of coffee as soon as the drip slowed and took a sip. Strong, with chicory. Not her favorite, but probably a taste he'd picked up in New Orleans.

"I can't stop thinking about Lang. It had to be him that visited LeRoy Breaux at Whiskey Bayou. But how does that relate to what he's doing now?"

She leaned against the counter. "If anybody can fill in that blank, it'll be your mom. When are you going to call her?" Ceelie and Gentry himself had both wanted him to make the call early this morning, about three a.m., as soon as they'd connected the dots between LeRoy Breaux and Lang Broussard. This was a murder investigation, after all, and if Gentry's mom had to be awakened from a sound sleep, too bad. Langston Broussard needed to pay for what he'd done to Tante Eva. What he'd done to the guy who was supposed to be his best friend. And yeah, for forcing Ceelie out of her own home.

But Lieutenant Doucet had ordered him to wait until morning. "There's no reason to upset her in the middle of the night," he'd told Gentry. "Wherever Lang is hiding out, he's probably going to lay low until the Tommy Mason murder dies down. And I need to bring the sheriff up to date. The man's getting a little prickly that we're all up in his business."

Gentry added enough cream and sugar to his coffee to turn it the color of a lightly toasted marshmallow. "Warren said he'd be back here by seven, and Jena too. I'll call as soon as they get here. I want my mom to hear about this from me, not the morning news show, but I want Warren here as well."

Ceelie didn't blame him. The media had quickly picked up the story of the newest murder in the rural parish. Every headline they'd seen or heard this morning was worse than the one before: "Murder in Bayou Country." "Serial Killer Stalks Swamps." "Tongue-Tied in Terrebonne."

At least Lang's name hadn't been released in connection with the murder—not yet—nor had Tommy Mason's murder been formally connected with that of Eva Savoie. The sheriff's department was in charge, however, and the sheriff would decide what did and didn't go to the media. Warren had expected that a combined task force with the sheriff's office, the Louisiana State Police, and Wildlife and Fisheries would be formed in short order. A photo of Langston Broussard would be on every TV station in Louisiana by midday and an all-out manhunt would be officially under way.

Ceelie looked out the window as the sun rose over the stretch of Bayou Terrebonne that ran behind Gentry's house. When Jena and Warren had gone home to shower and change, Ceelie had asked to stay. She didn't think Gentry needed to be alone.

She looked at his profile, strong and serious, beautiful in the soft light creating reddish-gold glints on his dark hair. He'd showered and changed into a simple white polo and jeans, not an ounce of vanity or guile about him this morning, the uniform swagger absent. When he finished his coffee and turned toward her to set it in the sink, his expression was that of a man with a heavy heart.

"It's going to be okay." Before she could talk herself out of it, Ceelie wrapped her arms around him. Gentry froze at first, and she could practically hear the thoughts racing through his head—not wanting pity, not wanting to step over the line with someone whose family member his brother had murdered, not wanting to cross any lines, period.

Ceelie didn't give a crap about lines. She'd come to care about this man, even if her feelings had been born out of fear and loneliness, and at the worst time in the world. She wanted to give him comfort if he needed it. She'd learned many things from Tante Eva, and one of them was to own her feelings.

Ceelie pulled back, but kept her hands resting on his waist. "I know you're torn in a million different directions right now, but can you do one thing for me?" He wouldn't do anything to help himself, but he'd help her. She knew him that well already.

He blinked. "Okay."

"Hold me." She wrapped her arms around him again. "Just hold me."

Some dam inside him seemed to give way, and he pulled her close, resting his cheek against her hair. He smelled of soap and something citrusy.

Ceelie raised on tiptoe and it seemed to be all the direction Gentry needed. He leaned into her, seeking out her mouth, kissing her like she hadn't been kissed in . . . maybe ever. It wasn't like their first kiss back at the cabin, tentative and sweet. It was hot, hungry, and when Ceelie molded her body against his, she felt the hard press of his arousal.

Which was fine, because she wanted him. Now. Here. If the last couple of weeks had taught her anything, it was that life was short and you never knew when it would be taken away.

He lifted her onto the counter, but then wrenched his lips from hers. "Are you sure about this? I mean, we—"

Good grief. This man, with his overinflated sense of responsibility, was going to force her to be the aggressor. Well, so be it. She hooked her legs around his hips and hauled him toward her, creating heat and friction that made her breath catch. She grinned at his wide eyes and northward-hiking eyebrows.

Ceelie leaned in and tugged his earlobe between her teeth, just hard enough that it should sting. Her breath puffed against his ear. "Do I seem like I'm not sure? I think you're scared of me."

He wrapped his hands around the curve of her hips and jerked her tightly against him so she could feel exactly how scared he wasn't.

CHAPTER 18

Moving against her, Gentry let himself get lost in her heat and the salty-sweet taste of her skin. The world shrank to the two of them, the doubts and worries that had been plaguing him pushed away by the soft moan of this amazing woman. The doubts would come back soon enough, but for now, she took away his ability to think of anything but having her.

She reached down to untuck his shirt.

"Too slow." He took the fabric from her and ripped the shirt over his head, tossing it on the floor. He wanted to feel her against his bare skin.

There was still a tank top between them, and that damn thing needed to go. He slipped his hands underneath the red fabric and pushed it up, revealing a glimpse of full breasts in a simple white bra. That needed to go too, because his mouth wanted to be there. Now.

He was halfway there when a blaring horn sounded outside the window, freezing him in place.

That would be the window they were well on the way to having sex in front of.

That would be the window through which he could see his partner getting out of her truck and pointing at them, at her eyes, and back at them again. Shit. "It's Sinclair."

"Think she saw us?" Ceelie was breathing as hard as he was, and he wanted to cry when she tugged the tank top back in place. Damn it.

"Oh yeah, she saw us." He helped Ceelie down from the kitchen counter—now his favorite spot in the house—and snatched his shirt off the floor. "I'm putting her on desk duty."

Ceelie laughed. "Five minutes later, and she would've had blackmail material. Make that more blackmail material; she already has Hoss."

"I'm completely confident in my masculinity. I own a pink shirt and a French bulldog." Gentry kissed the tip of her nose before pulling his shirt back on.

He made Sinclair wait a few seconds before he answered the door. At least he'd locked it this time so she hadn't let herself in, which had spared her from getting the shirtless, breathless partner-with-a-hard-on view.

Just to be safe, since that last problem hadn't quite gone away, he left the shirt untucked and thanked God for tight jeans.

Jena wore jeans and a green button-front shirt and had her hair tucked into her LDWF baseball cap. Today was supposed to be their first of three days off.

"Can't leave you kids alone for a minute." Her voice was lively, but she had dark circles under her eyes that Gentry suspected matched his own and Ceelie's. Warren had looked ready for the glue factory when he left.

"You better hope that bag you're holding helps make up for your bad timing." He would never, ever hear the end of this. He snagged the white paper bag from her hand and looked inside at an assortment of doughnuts. "You could've given us a few more minutes, though."

"Only takes you a few minutes, huh? Bet that's great for her. Not." She grabbed the pastry bag back. "Don't finger the doughnuts. I don't know where those hands have been."

"Nowhere, unfortunately." Ceelie stuck her head out the kitchen door, and she didn't look nearly as embarrassed as he felt. Women had no shame these days. "You want coffee?"

While the shameless women puttered in the kitchen, Gentry went back to the combination living room–dining room, stacked up the pizza boxes to take to the trash later, and moved the landline phone to the dining-room table, where it sat like a ticking bomb. He didn't like calling his mom on normal days because he never quite knew what to say to her. Things had been awkward after she'd remarried and downright strained after Lang's death, when she'd kept asking him why he hadn't aimed for an arm or leg.

Gentry had asked himself the same question, but the truth was, in the heat of the moment, he'd fallen back on his training. People saw LDWF agents as "possum cops," but they had paramilitary-style training on top of regular law-enforcement training. That stormy night on the boat, he hadn't seen Lang as his brother, but as an armed drug dealer about to shoot Gentry's partner. He hadn't been trained to take out an active shooter with a hit to the leg.

Today's call about Lang's sudden return to the living and his resurrection as a murderer was not going to be a good conversation.

Ceelie set a fresh cup of coffee on the table beside the phone, cream and sugar already added. He took a sip and smiled. "Perfect. You're a quick study."

"Yeah, well, don't get used to being waited on. That's pity coffee over having to call your mom. Nobody can do guilt like single parents."

"My mom remarried." She'd only made it two years as a single parent.

"Yeah, but you're playing semantics," Ceelie said. "Did you ever think of your stepfather as a father? If not, she might as well have been a single parent."

It hadn't been fair to his mom or to Louis, her husband, but Gentry hadn't wanted another father. He'd been a typically self-absorbed fifteen-year-old when they married, and he saw his mom's new husband as an insult to his dad's memory. By the time he realized what a tool he'd been, there had been too much to overcome.

He sighed and stared into the pale-brown liquid swirling around in his coffee cup. "I never gave the poor guy a chance. We haven't ever been unfriendly, exactly, but we have nothing in common."

He sat at the table nearest the phone; Ceelie and Jena took the chairs on either side of him and set the plate of doughnuts in the middle. They ate in near-silence, waiting for Warren.

Gentry wanted his lieutenant to hear every bit of his conversation with Marie Broussard Jackson. Even the painful parts, and there would be many. As he'd told Warren last night—or in the wee hours of this morning—he needed to be transparent as cellophane from here on out. Warren hadn't disagreed.

At the sound of a truck door slamming outside, Jena went to the foyer and, a few seconds later, returned with a freshly pressed and laundered—if not exactly rested—Warren Doucet. His dark hair might have been turning silver at the temples, but he still wore it in the buzz cut Gentry had always known.

Warren had been wrong about Gentry being too young to remember him from when he and Hank Broussard used to patrol the parish. They'd become almost like a single person to him in his memories, not sure where Hank ended and Warren began.

"You ready to do this?" Warren clapped him on the shoulder after retrieving a cup of coffee for himself. "It's not going to be an easy call."

"No, it isn't." He hadn't dreaded anything more since Lang's funeral.

"I'm gonna take Hoss for a walk," Ceelie said. "I think it'll be easier if I'm not here."

Gentry gave her a sharp look, then exchanged glances with his partner.

Jena nodded. "I think I'll go with you. Gentry, is it okay for us to take Hoss up on the levee to walk?"

"Yeah, I take him up there a lot when I go running." At Jena's snort, he clarified. Hoss wasn't the speediest dog on the block. "I take him up there a lot when I go walking."

"Do we have to worry about him getting off-leash and going in the water?" Ceelie asked, taking the leash from the hook beside the door and clipping it onto the dancing Frenchie's collar.

"Hoss wouldn't go near the water if you threw him in there—he'd find a way to levitate over it. He doesn't like to get his feet wet."

The women were laughing when they left with his happy dog, and once again, Gentry was thankful for one smart partner. Ceelie wanted to give him privacy for the phone call, which he appreciated. Jena was going to make sure Ceelie was safe, which he appreciated even more.

Jena had picked up a backpack and taken it with her, and he'd bet next month's salary that her service pistol was inside.

The clock on the phone handset read seven a.m. His mom would be up, and Louis would still be home. He wanted her to have some support there, and both of his stepsisters were grown and living their own lives. So the time was now.

He took a deep breath, punched in her number, and put the phone on speaker.

Louis answered and had the good grace to sound pleased when he heard Gentry's voice. More guilt. He really needed to do a better job of staying in touch with his mom and trying to be a part of her family. Maybe even find a way to think of it as *his* family, if it wasn't too late.

"I need to talk to Mom, and I think you need to stay with her if you can," he told Louis. "It's going to be a tough conversation. It's about Langston."

"Ah . . . right. I'll get her."

Marie Broussard had been a real steel magnolia, a force to be reckoned with, when Gentry and Lang were little. Gentry remembered his parents arguing more than once—way more than once—about Hank Broussard's job and the hours he kept. Of course, Gentry was "Hank made over," according to just about everyone who'd met the family, so he'd never taken the time to see his mom's side of things.

Now he got it. He worked long hours. He worked holidays and weekends and in the middle of the night, because that's when most criminals were out being criminals, whether they were drug dealers or poachers or hunters trying to bring in an illegal deer. The job was more dangerous than anyone outside the agency imagined. Most of his fellow agents, especially in enforcement, were single or divorced, or were married to other law-enforcement officers. It wasn't an easy life, especially for a spouse who hadn't bought into the culture.

"Gentry?" Mom's voice sounded . . . like Mom. God, he hated to do this to her. They might not be close, but he didn't want to hurt her.

Warren pointed to himself, brows raised. Offering to break the news.

Gentry shook his head. "Hi, Mom, sorry to call so early, but I needed to talk to you as soon as I could."

"Louis said it was something about your brother?" Her voice sounded older.

Gentry look a deep breath. He'd thought and thought about how to do this gently but hadn't come up with a better way than just telling her. "Mom, first of all, I don't know how he survived, but Lang's alive."

Gentry and Warren exchanged grim looks as the silence on the phone told them the depth of Marie's shock.

"Where has he been?" Louis spoke this time, maybe giving his wife a moment to absorb the bombshell. "Have you seen him?"

"I don't know where he's been the past three years, but at least for the last couple of weeks, he's been here in Terrebonne Parish, probably in Dulac."

That shocked his mother out of silence. "Did he call you? Have you seen him? Why hasn't he called me? I know he . . ."

She stopped without finishing that sentence. As far as Gentry knew, Lang hadn't given her the time of day since she'd married Louis.

"Mom, Warren Doucet—Dad's former partner and my lieutenant here—is with me. I haven't seen Lang yet, but I did talk to him on the phone. The reason I know he's here in the parish is that he's, well, he's in legal trouble. A lot of trouble."

Which was sort of like referring to a T. rex as an oversized gecko.

"Oh my God." Louis again. "What has he done now?"

"Louis, don't." Marie's voice was muffled, but her sharp tone came through loud and clear. Then she put on her Southern matron persona. "Warren, it has been a long time. I hope you're doing well."

"It has been a long time, Marie. I'm sorry we're calling you with this kind of news."

"The fact that my son is alive is good news, I'd think."

Only because they hadn't told her anything else. Gentry waited for her to ask about Lang's legal troubles. It took less than a minute, so he had to give her credit for a quick recovery.

"Gentry, what has he done?"

Here came the fun part. "Mom, we have every reason to believe he killed a woman, an elderly woman who lived just south of Montegut. And then he killed Tommy Mason in Dulac—don't know if you remember him. We think Lang might have been hiding out with him."

"Tommy Mason was his best friend. He wouldn't kill him."

"I'm sorry, Mom." Gentry considered admitting his role in what happened to Tommy and couldn't handle it. Not yet.

Another long pause and Gentry thought he heard his mother crying. He looked at Warren and gave him a *what-now* look.

"Marie, I need to ask you a couple of questions. I know it's all a shock," Warren said. "But you're going to be hearing from the Terrebonne Parish Sheriff's Office soon with the same questions, and you're going to be seeing Langston's photo on the news. I want you to be prepared for that." He paused. "Can I ask you some questions?"

"Does it have to be now?" Louis's voice was shaky too. "Can we process this and let Marie call you back?"

"I'm sorry, Louis." Gentry picked up the baton in the interrogate-Mom relay. "It really has to be now. There are people still in danger, including me." Not that he was his own main concern, but he figured it would snap his mother to attention.

He was right. "You think Lang's going to try to get back at you?" Her voice had risen an octave, and he closed his eyes as if the surge of guilt washing over him were physical.

He decided to evade that question and get to the real things they needed to know. "Mom, do you know a man named LeRoy Breaux?"

Dead silence. Then, "Why in the world would you ask about LeRoy Breaux? I haven't heard that name in years."

Gentry and Warren exchanged glances. "So you know who he is?"

She let out a short laugh. "Or who he was. Far as I know, that man left Terrebonne Parish twenty years ago and never looked back. He's probably dead by now. He'd have to be going on close to eighty-five or ninety."

"Who is he to you, Marie?" Warren asked. "Is he related to you in some way?"

"Oh my goodness, no." She made a few more noises to let them know this was not a subject she considered worthy of her time. "He was related to Tommy Mason, actually. His uncle by marriage or something like that. You know, half the parish is related if you go back far enough."

Damn. "Mom, did Lang ever go to visit LeRoy Breaux? Specifically, did he spend a couple of weeks with him the summer Dad died?"

"Yes, although I didn't know about it until after the fact. And it was a mistake, let me tell you."

Holy mother of God. There was the connection, confirmed. "Why was it a mistake? We need to know everything you remember about that visit and about LeRoy."

Marie's annoyance and impatience sounded through the phone's little speaker. "Why does this matter, Gentry? That was an awful time. Lang had started running with a bad crowd and acting out, and Tommy Mason's mother offered to let him stay with them a couple of weeks. I thought it would be good for him. I didn't know until later that both boys went out to stay at that cabin on the bayou with LeRoy. Why dredge up all of this old history?"

"Marie, we believe that Langston killed Eva Savoie, and that visit is the only thing we've come up with that would link the two of them." Warren tapped a pencil on a notebook he'd opened and on which, so far, he had written nothing.

"Eva Savoie? That voodoo woman who lived out in the bayou with LeRoy back then?" Marie's voice quivered. "Why would Langston kill that old crazy woman?"

"That's what we're trying to figure out, Mom. Do you remember anything Lang might've said when he came home, or if he ever went back to visit LeRoy?"

"He certainly *did not* go back." Marie said something to Louis in the background. "He came home talking about all that voodoo nonsense. He said LeRoy was about to come into a fortune and he wanted Lang and Tommy to help him get it. I told him loud and clear, no son of mine was going back to visit any voodoo practitioner."

"Bet Lang took that well." Gentry couldn't help himself.

"Sarcasm is not called for, Gentry Broussard."

Gentry slumped down in his seat. He was a thirty-two-year-old man with a college diploma and a commendation for champion marksmanship, and he had just been dressed down from three hundred miles away by his mama. Some things one just didn't outgrow.

"Marie." Warren came to the rescue. "Did Langston tell you any details about this fortune LeRoy Breaux was supposed to be on the verge of getting?"

"No. I refused to listen to such nonsense." Her firm tone underscored her words, and Gentry had no doubt they were true. What Marie didn't like or believe in, Marie didn't want to hear. Never had. "And, as I recall, it was only a month or two later that I heard down at the church that LeRoy Breaux had left that voodoo woman and gone God only knows where. Maybe he got his fortune and took off. At least, that's what everyone figured."

Gentry couldn't resist poking the bear. Something about talking to his mom brought out his inner tween. "You were gossiping about the voodoo queen at church?"

"I'll have you know that woman was on our prayer list every single week. It wasn't gossip." Marie paused, then seemed to remember what had started this conversation. "Why would Langston kill her? Did he . . . did he shoot her? Was she robbed?"

Gentry had debated how much to tell his mother and had decided to tell her the truth, although not every gory detail. If he sugarcoated it too much, though, she'd hear worse on the news. So he told her that Eva had been stabbed, that he'd found the body, that he'd seen who he thought was Lang leaving the cabin.

He left Ceelie out of the equation. He doubted the sheriff would release information that the murderer was trying to scare off his first victim's heir.

Warren asked her a few more questions, but Marie had told all she could. She promised to think some more about it and be cooperative with anyone who called her from the sheriff's office.

Before he ended the call, Gentry had to add a warning in case the unthinkable happened. "Mom, if Lang calls you, you need to let me or Warren or the sheriff know, okay?"

"He's not going to call me, Gentry." Suddenly, Marie sounded tired and much older than her sixty-two years. "Your brother hasn't called me since I left the parish. He stopped by the morning the moving van was pulling out. June 30, 2002. The day I moved to Shreveport."

This was news to Gentry. "He wanted to talk you out of moving?"

Marie laughed. "We're talking about Lang," she said, bitterness creeping into her tone. "He wanted money."

CHAPTER 19

Ceelie and Jena walked down the steep, grass-covered bank of the earthen levee toward Gentry's house.

"Warren's gone, so I guess the phone call is over." Jena stopped to scrape some mud off her shoe by dragging it along the edge of a rock. "Bet that wasn't an easy one."

Ceelie couldn't imagine the pain on all sides of the conversation. "I'm sure it was awful, but I hope they found out something. Nothing personal—I like you guys—but I want my life back."

Jena glanced up from retying her shoelace, a slight smile on her face. "You like some of us more than others, though, right?"

Ceelie closed her eyes. "I plead the Fifth."

They resumed their walk toward the house. "You think you'll stay in Terrebonne Parish once this is done, or are you still determined to leave?"

Ceelie wasn't sure how to respond, because she no longer knew the answer. "It's starting to feel like home here, but I'm not sure if it's where I'm meant to be or if it's just familiar. Does that make any sense?"

"I don't think familiarity makes a place feel like home. We just resonate with some places," Jena said, stopping to look around at the scattering of small houses on stilts. "I grew up in the city, in New Orleans. Lived there my whole life. But I swear, the minute I set foot in Houma and started working in the parish, this felt like where I belonged."

"Home. I'm not sure I even know what that means anymore," Ceelie said. After finally admitting she'd left the parish to please her dad and not because it was what she wanted, Ceelie also had to admit the guilt over having pulled away from Tante Eva for the same reason. To follow her dad's dream more than hers, to stay away from the woman who'd been more of a mother to her than Ceelie's own mom had been, just to please him. "But I'm beginning to think I belong here too."

Jena gave her a sidelong glance. "My partner got anything to do with that?"

"No." Ceelie thought about it, reconsidered, but her initial reaction felt true. "Gentry's not the reason. We don't really know each other that well yet." Yet. "Would it bother you if we got . . . I don't know, involved?"

"Are you kidding?" Jena laughed. "No, once this mess gets resolved—and it will—maybe you'll mellow him out a little. He can be a pain in the ass."

"Somehow I don't find that hard to believe." They walked the rest of the way in silence. Hoss already sat in front of the door, waiting for them, his round eyes bugged out in what Ceelie interpreted as impatience. Long walks were not his cup of kibble.

"I'm gonna head back to the apartment and see if I can make up for some of the sleep I didn't get last night. You want to come with me, or just get directions?"

"I'll follow you." Ceelie figured Gentry would want some alone time after talking to his mom.

They walked in the front door without knocking, but Ceelie saw no sign of Gentry. Jena stuck her head in the kitchen, but shrugged. "Not in there. I'll check in back and tell him we're leaving."

Ceelie was having second thoughts about going. The expression on Gentry's face as he got ready to call his mom had been one of absolute misery. It sounded like there had been so much damage to that relationship already, and now this. He needed support, whether he knew it or not.

Jena was gone less than a minute. She grabbed her keys and backpack. "Let's go. He's more ill-tempered than a gator with a treble hook in its gullet."

Ceelie hesitated. She already had her suitcase here. Why not stay? "If he's that upset, shouldn't we hang around?"

"No way I'm subjecting myself to that." Jena raised an eyebrow. "I told him we were leaving and his exact words were, and I quote, 'Good. Get the hell out of here.' He needs to stew in his own juices for a while."

That did it. Ceelie threw her bag on the dining table and dug out her cell phone. "Give me your address. I think I'm going to stay here, at least until he throws me out."

"Yeah, well, good luck with that." Jena gave her a street address and apartment number in Houma. "Gentry goes in dark places sometimes, and in my admittedly brief experience, it's best to let him work through it."

"I'll give him space if he needs it." The sight of the bones she'd thrown yesterday at the cabin weighed on her. Ceelie wasn't sure she could keep Gentry away from danger, but she could at least try to distract him.

That kiss weighed on her too. For a few minutes, they'd gotten lost in each other. Both of them. He might throw her out the front door and sic Hoss on her, but she was determined to either talk to him or distract him. Whatever he seemed to need.

First, she had to face down the gator, as Tante Eva used to say. She locked the door behind Jena, squared her shoulders, and walked into the center hallway that stretched the length of the house. From her earlier snooping, she knew her way around. A quick glance in Gentry's empty bedroom told her he was in the spare room that held his workout equipment and his computer.

She stopped in the doorway, watching him. He'd changed into a pair of navy drawstring workout pants and was pounding the treadmill with his cell phone strapped to his right bicep and earbuds jammed in his ears.

She could wait. Besides, the view was good. The man had a fine body. It was a pity he ever had to wear a shirt.

After a few minutes, he cycled the treadmill down gradually and finally stepped off.

"Nice technique."

He twisted to look at her briefly, then grabbed a towel off the side rail of the treadmill and scrubbed it over his face. "You need to leave."

Fine, he would be abrupt and she'd be direct. "Jena's gone, but I'm not leaving you like this, not after what you went through this morning."

"You can't help and it's dangerous for you to be here. Go to Sinclair's and I'll talk to you later."

The subject obviously over, he tossed the towel back on the treadmill and lay on his back on the weight bench. He lifted one heavy-looking stacked set of weights in his left hand, then a second set in his right, doing chest-presses with enough aggression that he had to be in serious danger of popping a hernia.

But damn. If she could video those abs and biceps during his workout, she could sell copies to every woman in Terrebonne Parish and make a fortune.

This was getting ridiculous. She either had to get his attention or get the hell out, not stand here like a voyeur. What was it Tante Eva used to say? *You see what you want, girl, you gotta take it. Ain't nobody givin' you nothin'.*

She walked up to the weight bench, straddled his waist, and sat. He dropped one set of weights on the floor and had to catch the other to keep it from landing on his head. His expression teetered between outrage and shock. "What the hell are you doing?"

Ceelie grinned. "Getting your attention."

"Well, stop it."

"No, I don't think I will." She wriggled a little farther down his body until both his sharp intake of breath and the pressure on her core told her she'd hit the sweet spot.

The fierceness in his dark-brown eyes softened, and he closed them when she gently rocked against him. "You can't . . . We can't . . . Warren said . . ."

"I don't care what Warren said." Well, she cared, but not right now. "Later, I'll care. Right now, I don't want to care about anything. I don't want to think. I just want to feel."

She moved in exaggerated slowness, taking hold of the bottom of her tank top and pulling it over her head. Gentry was getting harder; that, she could feel. And he was distracted, judging by the glazed look in his eyes and the rise and fall of his chest, as if he were still working out.

"God, you're amazing." His voice was hoarse, breathy. "Take your hair down. I've never seen you with your hair down."

With languid movements, she removed the bands at the bottom and top of her braid, then reached up and ran her fingers through her hair to work out the thick strands that wound around each other.

He sat up so abruptly she had to grab his shoulders to avoid falling off his lap. "Let me do that."

Ceelie smiled and dropped her hands, closing her eyes as he wove his fingers through her hair. "That feels good."

"Feel this." He grasped her hips and pulled her more tightly against the hard length his workout pants did a poor job of disguising.

Then, just as suddenly, he turned it off. "We can't do this, Ceelie. Not while he's still out there and you're a target."

"I'm not a target; my cabin is a target." She shifted slowly in his lap, earning a soft groan. "So you're telling me that I'll have to go in your bedroom alone and relieve my own needs, all by myself? Don't think I won't do it either, and if you aren't going to participate, then you can't watch either."

His eyes narrowed a fraction of a second before the dimples appeared and held. "You wouldn't."

She shrugged, removed his hands from her hips, and eased herself off his lap. She looked pointedly at his misshapen pants as she slipped down the straps of her bra and pulled it off slowly.

"God." His eyes lost focus. She hung her bra around his neck, unzipped her jeans, and eased her hips out of them with a slow shimmy to exaggerate her curves. He cursed under his breath in unintelligible syllables.

Finally, she stepped out of the jeans and kicked them aside. "See you later."

She turned and headed down the hallway, clapping her fingers over her eyes as soon as she was out of his sight. What the hell had she just done? Obviously channeling her inner stripper, for God's sake. Knowing he wanted her had turned her into an insta-trollop.

She walked into his bedroom, at a loss. Okay, *Fifi La Celestine, what's next, eh, chère?* If she had—

She gave a startled gasp as strong hands gripped her waist and turned her. Gentry was on her before she could react. His hands slid through her hair, tilting her head to move in for a kiss. Not just demanding, but devouring. Forceful.

His hands slipped down her body, moving, restless, stroking until she couldn't breathe, using fingers that dealt authority and violence to pluck her like the strings of her old Gibson.

"Make me forget," she said. "Make me forget everything."

They made quick work of the few clothes remaining, and he was as beautiful as she suspected, heavy and hard, every cut of muscle defined.

"We've gotta slow down or I'm not going to touch you the way I want to, slow and sweet, until you're begging me to be inside you." His voice was low and hot against her throat.

"We can do slow and sweet later. I want you fast and rough, and I've been begging for a while now." She hooked a leg around his, bringing their bodies together as close as possible. "If you missed the memo, buddy, I've been trying to get you inside me half the day."

With a low groan, he picked her up and lowered her to the bed, his mouth and tongue setting up a rhythm to match the fingers he slid inside her. "Not that," she said. "You. Now."

"Bossy Cajun woman." He gave her a tousle-haired, lopsided grin as he rolled into the cradle of her thighs, positioning himself at her entrance.

"Is this what you want, Ceelie?"

He slammed into her with one long stroke, then set up a hard, frantic rhythm that erased all thoughts from her mind. She could only feel. This was not a sweet lovemaking but a claiming, a marking, as he filled her and brought her to the edge, and then took her over the cliff with him.

Then they lay together, still connected, foreheads touching. "Hold me," she whispered. Neither of them had slept, and her muscles felt so warm and loose that she didn't think she could stand up if she tried. She just needed to touch him.

"Bossy Cajun woman," he whispered, kissing her, sweet and deep. Then he shifted to lie beside her and pulled her to him.

She tucked her head between his shoulder and neck and, for the first time in longer than she could remember, slid into sleep feeling both satisfied and safe.

CHAPTER 20

Gentry sat in his truck, making sure all his gear was in place for his shift. He couldn't remember a more miserable or more satisfying trio of days off.

He'd had to grovel before Sheriff Knight and Detective Ramsey, who had insisted he extend his groveling to the whole TPSO detective team and all the personnel who'd worked the Savoie and Mason murders.

He'd dodged reporters after the manhunt for Lang hit the media and someone had quickly made the connection to the New Orleans case three years earlier.

He'd spent most of one day writing reports on what he'd done related to the investigation, and when, and why, and how.

He'd made lists of everyone he could remember who'd known Lang, talked to Lang, looked sideways at Lang, or thought about looking sideways at Lang, using a set of high-school yearbooks to refresh his memory with names and faces and stories.

He'd provided every photo of Lang he could get his hands on, which were sadly few and none more recent than from seven or eight years ago, when they'd run into each other in New Orleans. Lang had hit him up for drug money.

Three miserable days. Three glorious days. Whatever time he wasn't playing witness or informant, he'd spent with Ceelie. Talking about everything except the case. Finding common ground in music and a love of this land and culture. He had thought she'd rejected it, but she hadn't. She was part of it. She sang to him, worked on new songs, cooked a mean red beans and rice with andouille and an even meaner seafood gumbo.

And yeah, they'd spent a lot of time gathering firsthand knowledge of each other's bodies. She was experimental and adventurous with sex, and he loved her openness and lack of self-consciousness. She said he had a lot of work to do in that department but he was damn good once she got him where she wanted him. Like on the weight bench or the dining-room table. He'd never look at the laundry room the same way again.

She knew he got weak-kneed when she sucked on his earlobes, and he knew the sensitive spots on her breasts and a certain way to move his fingers that would make her moan and writhe and beg him to take her.

The memories forced him to shift to a more comfortable position in his truck as he backed out of his drive, waving to Ceelie. She sat on the landing at the top of the stairs to the house, sharing a slice of toast with Hoss. He'd rather go back and make good on what the memories had started, but he was technically on the clock.

They'd both be working on the case today, but from different directions. Jena Sinclair would be taking Ceelie back to visit Tomas Assaud, to see if she could get more information on LeRoy Breaux. He'd called the man a thief, which meant there was something worth stealing. Maybe with Jena and her badge there, he'd be more willing to elaborate.

Whatever there was to steal, had LeRoy told the teenage Lang Broussard and Tommy Mason about it? And if so, why would Lang be going after it now, after all these years? Maybe Tomas could fill in some blanks.

Ceelie had feared the old man wouldn't meet with her again, but when she'd sent a message through his grandson, Tomas had agreed.

As for Gentry, he'd gotten the go-ahead from both the sheriff and Warren to embark on a little fishing trip today in the name of inter-agency cooperation. It had occurred to him that, while everyone was looking for Lang Broussard and digging into the background of LeRoy Breaux, no one had been looking at Eva Savoie.

He figured the sheriff had agreed to let him get involved because this mission was virtually guaranteed to keep him out of the deputies' way, but Gentry would take whatever they gave him. He needed to stay involved. Plus, he was a believer in the old adage that so often proved wise: follow the money.

Eva Savoie operated on a system out of step with the rest of the world except those living off the grid: cash and barter. She didn't have a bank account, and she'd inherited the land and the cabin with no debt attached to the estate, so there was no conventional trail of finances to follow. Still, she had property taxes to pay and gasoline and food to buy. She had electric and water bills. She had expenses, in other words, so she needed income.

Last night, Gentry had contacted the hunter who leased alligator-hunting rights on Eva's property each year, and got confirmation: the man always paid her in cash and sealed the deal with a handshake. A couple of times, when the cabin or the truck had needed repairs, she had bartered part of his fee for that.

He paid her a nice sum, but not enough for her to live on.

Next, he tracked down her utility accounts and, in both cases, she'd paid her bills in person, in cash, and always on time.

Gentry had stewed about it all night before bringing the subject up with Ceelie. "In cleaning up the cabin, did you find any kind of ledger where Eva kept up with money? Any receipts?" Often, people who lived on the cash system—especially older people—were obsessive receipt keepers.

"A lot," she'd said. There had been papers and receipts scattered all over the room. The ones covered in blood she had glanced through and thrown away. As for the others, she'd found an empty shoebox she figured they had been in when Lang ransacked the cabin, so she put them in there and stuck the box under the bed.

This morning, he'd gotten permission from the TPSO to visit the cabin. The driveway was empty, but he figured there were deputies or state police either in the adjacent wooded areas or nearby in a boat. He made plenty of noise, slamming his truck door, jingling his keys, and taking his time on his way to the cabin so anyone watching would see his uniform.

Being mistaken for Lang could get dangerous. The more he thought about it, the more he wondered if Jennifer Mason had made that mistake when he found her outside the garage. No way Lang could have been hiding out there for three years, but he could've been there overnight, which meant she might know more than they'd thought.

Gentry let himself inside the unlocked door. It was hot as hell from being closed up for several days, but nothing looked out of place. He figured Lang would be laying low for a while, but if he were still in Terrebonne Parish, his brother would take another run at searching this cabin eventually. He'd bide his time, wait until he felt safe, and try again.

A squawk from his radio almost sent Gentry through the ceiling. If he got any jumpier, he'd be screaming like a girl—a comparison about which Ceelie and Jena would have plenty of commentary.

It was Stella, verifying that he was in the cabin after she'd been called by a member of the TPSO surveillance team. "Yeah, I'm here." He was glad they were on their toes. "I should be here an hour or less."

"You get out of there as soon as you can, Gentry Broussard. The whole idea of that place gives me the creeps." Stella managed to put a shudder in her words.

Yeah, apparently it was working on his last nerve too.

He turned on the AC and took a seat at the dining table with the shoebox in front of him. A pair of sad-eyed basset hounds stared at him from the scuffed brown-and-white box. Eva had bought herself some Hush Puppies shoes once upon a time—a long time ago, judging by the state of the box.

He spent the next half hour going through receipts for electric bills, water bills, property taxes, automobile taxes. All paid in cash. Receipts for groceries bought at the Piggly Wiggly.

Finally, he found one that sent his heart rate into a gallop: a pawn-shop receipt from a place in Houma. Eva Savoie had received five thousand dollars in cash for what was described only as "two coins." The receipt was dated six months ago.

The money scattered around the cabin must be all she had left, or maybe Lang had taken some cash after all.

What kind of coins would a pawnshop pay five grand for? One way to find out.

Gentry sped through the rest of the receipts, but his gut told him he'd found what he needed. Once he finished, he took a cell-phone photo of the receipt from Houma Quik Kash as he'd found it in the stack. One never knew when a time-stamped photo would be helpful in a court case.

He stuck the receipt in his pocket, stacked the rest of the papers back in the box, and returned the basset hounds to their spot under the bed.

He sat on the bed for a few minutes. Ceelie's bed. The house still smelled of pine, but also of her shower gel. His focus flitted from a place in the corner that looked as if the foundation pier was sinking, to a water stain on the ceiling over the throwing table, as Ceelie called it. Considering its age and the storms that had blown through here in the last century, the cabin was in pretty good shape. Eva had kept it up. With a little work, he could turn it into a nice place for Ceelie to live. Or a weekend spot for the both of them.

Gentry shook his head, hoping to rattle some sense into it. He was getting way ahead of himself. He felt as if he'd known Celestine Savoie all his life, but they were still virtual strangers. Hell, maybe he was just lonely.

He'd keep telling himself that.

Using the radio clipped to the collar of his shirt, he roused Stella and asked if she'd find someone from the sheriff's office who could drop by the cabin. He wasn't going to sneeze without the TPSO being involved. Lesson learned. He didn't like groveling so much that he wanted to give a repeat performance.

Less than ten minutes later, he opened the door to welcome Adam Meizel.

"We gotta stop meeting like this, Broussard." Meizel stepped past Gentry into the cabin and leaned over in front of the window unit, letting the cold air hit him on the face. "Nice humble pie you served up yesterday for the department."

"Yeah, well, amazing what the desire to keep a paycheck coming will make you do." Gentry pulled the receipt from his pocket. "What d'you make of this?"

Meizel pursed his lips and studied the receipt, dark brows lowered. Deeply tanned, with dark-brown hair cut short, he wore the top button open on his light-blue short-sleeved uniform shirt. "Looks like Miss Eva had some money. Any idea what kind of coins these were and where she got them?"

Gentry filled him in on Tomas Assaud's comment about LeRoy Breaux being a thief, and his mom's contention that LeRoy had had some kind of get-rich-quick prospects back in 1996 that had enticed his teenage brother. "Thought someone from the sheriff's office might want to run up to this pawnshop and ask some questions. Might be that Eva Savoie has some assets hidden around here that we didn't know about. Maybe that's what Lang was looking for."

Meizel tucked the receipt into the shirt pocket beneath his shiny TPSO badge. "And let me guess; you'd be happy to ride shotgun."

Gentry nodded. "In the spirit of interagency cooperation, of course."

"Of course. C'mon. It's almost time for me to go off duty anyway. You'll have to drive, though. My partner needs to stay with the boat."

Like most towns that had seen more prosperous days, Houma was a mixture of historic buildings with small-town charm, modern parish-government structures, and urban sprawl, with the Gulf Intracoastal Waterway meandering through the middle of it all.

Houma Quik Kash was housed in a concrete rectangle tucked amid an industrial corridor. It was a big rectangle, though, and judging by the number of cars filling the lot and the size of the place, it did plenty of business. Gentry figured it had to be prosperous if they could afford to pay $5K for a couple of coins. If it was like most pawnshops, those coins were worth a hell of a lot more than Eva got.

They parked Gentry's truck in the lot and studied the storefront a moment before getting out. "This is my show," Meizel said. "Just in case you were wondering."

Gentry held up his hands. "I'm just observing."

He followed the deputy inside, aware of the stares they got from the customers. They probably didn't often see a sheriff's deputy and a wildlife enforcement agent together, both armed and in uniform, and Gentry doubted their presence would help business.

"Can I do something for you, Officers?" The manager, a short, round, balding man in a rumpled pink shirt, came bustling from the back of the store, introducing himself as Jerry Dorchand.

Meizel showed him the receipt. "We need to talk to whoever con-ducted this transaction. Looks like your name signed at the bottom."

He looked at it briefly. "Right. That would be me. Come on, let's go in the back. Nothin' personal, but you guys are bad for business." Which made Gentry want to stand around the front of the store on principle, but he followed Meizel's lead. They trailed Jerry through the junk heap of a store and into a back-corner office, a dark-paneled 1970s special complete with cheap green indoor-outdoor carpet. The pawn-shop manager motioned them to a couple of metal folding chairs and took his seat behind the desk.

"First, I want you to know this was a straight transaction—nothing funny about it." Jerry compulsively straightened the papers on the edge of his desk, which struck Gentry as an awfully nervous tell for a guy who only conducted straight transactions. "Sellers sign a form sayin' they got the right to sell what they're sellin'."

"Don't worry, sir." Meizel's voice was patient but firm. "We aren't here to accuse you of anything. We're trying to learn exactly what these coins were, and anything you can remember about the person who sold them to you."

"That old lady complain about somethin'? 'Cause she agreed to the price without no fuss, and she seemed to understand English well enough. Can't always tell with them country folks. But she can't come back after six months and send the sheriff to do her complainin'."

"Ms. Savoie is not complaining. Ms. Savoie is dead," Meizel said, and the way Jerry absorbed that news, with relief, made Gentry want to blacken one of his beady, greedy little eyes.

"That's too bad, too bad. So what do you think I can tell you?" He remained on the edge of his chair as if he might bolt at any minute, but he had stopped reorganizing his paperwork. "Can I see the receipt again?"

Meizel handed it over.

"You get that many valuable coins in here that you need to look it up?" Gentry asked as Jerry flipped through a ledger and held the receipt alongside an entry.

"You'd be surprised at some of the stuff people bring in here, Officer. Half the time, they don't have a clue as to what they got. They usually think it's worth three times what it really is." Jerry returned the receipt to Meizel but squinted at Gentry. "How come a game warden's involved?"

"Never mind that." Meizel folded the receipt and put it back in his pocket. "You remember enough about this transaction to talk here, or would you remember better over at the Justice Complex?"

"No, no, no. I remember it." Jerry leaned back. "It was for two 1861 gold dollars. 1861-Ds, as they're called. Don't see 'em very often. In fact, the only other ones I've seen were from this same lady—she brought three of 'em in a few years back."

Gentry racked his brain for anything intelligent to ask about coins, but his knowledge was limited to how many it took to get a soda out of a machine. "What's special about these coins?"

"Well, 1861 was during the Civil War, you know?" Jerry turned to the bookshelf behind his desk, pulled out a book of coin values, and began flipping through it. "There were only a couple of places in the Confederacy that minted coins, and 1861 was the last year there was any gold in the South to mint. Don't see many of 'em around."

Gentry looked at Meizel as Jerry slid the catalog across the desk and thumped on the left-hand page with his index finger. "There's the 1861-D."

Meizel looked at the catalog a moment before handing it to Gentry. "Did Ms. Savoie say where she got the coins, or how many she had?"

Gentry scanned the page and almost choked to see the prices those coins sold for at auction. Jerry should be arrested for only paying Eva Savoie five grand for coins that were worth more like fifty grand apiece.

"No idea, and believe you me, I asked her, 'cause those are quite a find," Jerry said. "She said her granddaddy left 'em to her. You know there's old wives' tales about Confederate gold and pirate gold being buried all over South Louisiana. Gotta figure at least some of them stories is true."

Gentry frowned. The curse. Ceelie had told him the Savoie curse that the old man Tomas talked about began with Eva's grandfather. Had he found a cache of these coins?

If so, LeRoy Breaux might, indeed, have found himself a fortune. Or maybe Lang thought Eva still had the money.

"Has anyone else come in and asked about these coins or about Ms. Savoie?" Gentry asked.

Jerry leaned back in his chair and waited. He was doing them favors now and wanted to make sure they knew it.

"We'd appreciate anything you can remember," Meizel added.

"Yeah, now that you mention it. There was a guy who came in a few minutes after her that day, wanting to see the coins and asking a lot of questions."

Gentry didn't look at Meizel but he heard the tension in his voice. "This guy have a name?"

Jerry shrugged. "No, and I hustled him outta here when it was clear he was fishing for information on the old lady." He paused. "I didn't tell him nothing about her. Nothing at all."

Jerry was able to give them enough description to determine that the man fit Lang's profile.

"Looks like we hit pay dirt," Gentry told Meizel on the way back to the truck.

"Yeah, let's take a detour to the department while we're in the vicinity," he said, climbing back into the passenger's seat. "I think we found your brother's motive."

CHAPTER 21

As soon as Gentry's truck had turned off Pelican Street and driven out of sight, Ceelie threw the bones. She didn't know how he'd feel about her doing rituals at his dining-room table, but he'd seemed pretty accepting of her mixture of mysticism and faith. Then again, he'd grown up in the parish, so he'd seen it all his life.

Jena wasn't due for another half hour, so Ceelie locked the front door as she'd promised to do, then turned off the lights, closed the blinds, spread out the leather mat, and lit the candles. She gathered the bones from her dad's old cufflink case and prayed over them before raising them in both hands over the mat and letting them fall as Tante Eva had taught her so many years ago.

"The bones never lie," she whispered. "They always fall true."

Would the chicken foot still lie across the neck bone? Or had the sign of danger disappeared since she'd last thrown them three days ago?

She opened her eyes and stared at the pile of bones on the mat. A chill stole across her scalp at their new configuration. The foot had landed across the neck bone again, but this time instead of being apart, the tiny skull had gotten tangled with them. One claw of the foot, crooked and awkwardly jointed, stuck through the eye socket.

Not only was someone close to her in grave danger. So was she.

The bones never lie.

Maybe not, but they could be misinterpreted. Ceelie wasn't sure what old Tomas would think of it, but she took a photo of the bones with her cell phone so she could show him. She'd been thinking about asking the old man if he would teach her the rituals. At least maybe he'd help her with this reading, because Ceelie knew there was meaning in every nuance of the bones with relation to each other. She'd forgotten most of what Tante Eva had taught her, and what she did remember was rusty and unreliable.

At least she hoped so, in this instance.

Her hands shook as she blew out the candles and placed the bones back into the case. At a soft knock on the front door, she almost bolted to the back of the house.

She needed to get a grip and remember that she might not even be reading the bones right. She took a deep breath and looked through the peephole in the front door to see a funhouse view of Jena Sinclair.

"You're early," she said, stepping aside to let Jena in. "Give me about ten minutes to finish getting ready."

"I'm not early. Gentry must have preoccupied you." Jena stopped as soon as she saw the mat and candles on the table. "Or maybe something else did."

"Uh, yeah, sorry. Back in a few minutes." Ceelie had no idea where Jena stood on the whole topic of faith and mysticism. As a New Orleanian she would've been exposed to the touristy version of voodoo but probably not to real practitioners. She probably hadn't been in the parish long enough to have run across the mishmash of local beliefs. Even a decade ago, when Ceelie had left the parish, the blend of faiths had been dying out here among the younger residents.

She changed into her most conservative clothes, a pair of dark jeans and a button-front white blouse she'd picked up a couple of days ago at a thrift store while Gentry was trying to make nice with the sheriff's office.

It wasn't that Tomas Assaud would think more or less of her because of what she wore, but she wanted to show her respect. She stared in the mirror at her features that had always been part blessing, part curse. The tan skin and black hair, with the blue eyes, marked her as a half-breed. More like a Heinz 57 breed. She could've downplayed it by cutting her long hair or changing the color, but she wouldn't feel true to herself.

And Gentry loved her hair, which shouldn't matter as much to her as it did. She unraveled the braid and pulled it back in a loose ponytail for a change. And realized she was stalling. Something felt wrong today. It had prompted her to throw the bones, and that certainly hadn't made her feel better. She felt as if whatever was destined to happen today wouldn't roll into motion until she walked out that front door. And then she wouldn't be able to stop it, whatever *it* was.

Maybe whatever Tomas could tell her would help. Officially, she was looking for information on Tante Eva's curse and on what LeRoy Breaux had or hadn't done. Unofficially, she wanted nothing less than spiritual enlightenment.

Which, if Jena knew, would probably make her cancel the trip.

Okay, time to do it.

Ceelie went back to the living room, where Jena was playing with a beyond-happy Hoss. The little black Frenchie had adapted well to having women in his life, even though Ceelie had caught Gentry baby-talking him more than once in the past few days. The dog didn't lack for attention, unless it was because of his roommate's long, erratic work schedule.

"You mind riding with me?" Jena waited on the landing while Ceelie locked the door behind them. It had felt weird exchanging keys with Gentry this morning. "Since I'm officially on duty, I need my gear in case there's an emergency call."

"Sure, that's fine." Ceelie followed her down the steps. She'd grabbed her Gibson on the way out the door, thinking maybe she could play for Tomas. She'd also seen some of Gentry's business cards on the coffee table and stuck a few of those in her back jeans pocket. She'd leave them with Tomas and Joseph in case they remembered anything or, God forbid, saw Lang Broussard. "We're better off in your truck anyway. Your AC probably works better than the one in the beast."

She opened the passenger's door of Jena's department-issued black pickup and stared at the amount of gear. She'd thought Gentry was just a techno-freak with his tricked-out dashboard, but Jena's was just as bad.

A laptop computer had been mounted below the center console, and the whole front dash was a mass of cords and equipment. A GPS unit. Two radios, one with "LDWF" written on masking tape across the top, the other reading "TPSO." Binoculars, tools, clipboard, bottles of water.

"Everything okay?" Jena sat behind the wheel, waiting for Ceelie to climb in.

"Yeah, I just hadn't realized how much *stuff* you guys carry with you." She climbed in, twisted to put the Gibson behind the seat, and blinked at the sight of a pile of life jackets, a shotgun, and . . . "Is that a freaking *assault* rifle?"

"We don't actually call them that since we don't assault people— that's a media thing, but yeah." Jena wove her way out of the neighborhood and headed south after cutting over to Highway 56, a long, winding road that went all the way to Cocodrie. When the road ran out, the land ran out, too.

"We're the lead agency for water search-and-rescue operations in the state," Jena explained. "After Hurricane Katrina, some of our agents were shot at while trying to rescue people from flooded homes. You probably remember how crazy it got." She shrugged. "Anyway, after that, the department furnished all agents with the rifles."

"That happened the year before I left Houma." Ceelie's dad had been buried about six months after the hurricane hit. "We didn't get that much from Katrina here in Terrebonne, except farther south, but Rita socked us a month later. And a bunch have hit the area since then."

Jena nodded. "Yeah, it's one thing that makes it so hard to find somebody like Langston Broussard if he doesn't want to be found. Every time a hurricane or tropical storm floods this place, a few more people decide they've had enough. They don't think they have it in them to rebuild again, so they walk away and leave their flooded-out houses behind. There are hundreds of abandoned buildings. Hundreds of places for a criminal to take cover and hide out."

That crawling sensation crept across Ceelie's head again, and as they sped southward, she shivered at the sight of some of those abandoned buildings. She hadn't noticed them on her first trip down; they were so common that they had become a seamless part of the landscape.

About ten miles south of Chauvin, Jena stopped for gas and Ceelie went inside the station for sodas. For the next few miles, Ceelie pulled out the guitar and played some of the songs she hadn't trotted out since Nashville. Somehow the old standards weren't as onerous now that she wasn't singing to a bar full of drunk tourists.

"You're really good," Jena said, glancing in the rearview mirror. "I talked to Mac Griffin yesterday—the agent I was telling you about who likes music?"

"You mean the agent who listens to music while he picks up chicks," Ceelie corrected.

"Well, yeah. But he's going to talk to some . . . damn, that's weird." Jena flicked her gaze to the rearview mirror again.

Ceelie looked out her side mirror at a silver sedan driving a few car lengths behind them. "What's weird about it?"

"That car was behind us before we stopped for gas, so it should've passed us instead of still being behind us."

Ceelie looked at it again. "Maybe they stopped too."

"Maybe." Jena shrugged and sped up. "We'll outrun them. We're on official state business, right?"

Ceelie laughed. "Right."

She started strumming the chords to her still-unfinished song about Whiskey Bayou, but lost her rhythm when the SUV lurched.

"Son of a bitch." Jena reached up and flipped a switch, and in the reflection on the truck hood, Ceelie saw the blue bar of lights atop the vehicle begin flashing. "He butted me from behind." Ceelie twisted to look back and gasped. "He's coming at you again." The sedan bumped the truck with a jolt, and Jena jerked the truck into a quick left, blocking the roadway so the car was coming at the driver's-side door of the truck at a ninety-degree angle. It slowed to a stop.

Everything slowed to a stop.

"Shouldn't we try to outrun him?" Ceelie hated the quiver in her voice, but every nerve in her body screamed *Run*.

"Hell, no. I'm going to arrest the son of a bitch." Jena unholstered her pistol and waited. The driver's-side door of the sedan opened. Looking across Jena, Ceelie couldn't see the driver's face, but she recognized the silhouette of a weapon before he got out. "Jena, he's got a gun!"

"Shit. Get in the back, behind the seat. Now. And stay down."

Jena called out the window as she drew her pistol. "State agent! Stop where you are and put down the gun."

A blast shattered the driver's-side mirror and left it hanging off the truck.

"Damn it. Ceelie, get down and stay down, no matter what. Pull the life vests on top of you." Jena grabbed her radio as she propelled herself across the seat with her pistol in one hand, and grabbed the rifle with the other. She slid out the passenger's door, putting the truck between her and the shooter.

Ceelie thought Jena's voice sounded way too calm; only a slight tremor gave away her nerves. "L-843. Officer needs help. Shots fired. Shots fired! Highway 56 near Bush Canal. Officer—"

Another blast glanced off the windshield, leaving a spiderweb of cracks. A volley of shots followed as Jena returned fire.

Ceelie looked around the storage area behind the passenger's seat. The shotgun was a 12 gauge and looked pretty straightforward. And it was loaded. She stuck her head above the life jackets long enough to see the driver looking over the truck bed, trying to locate Jena. Ceelie got a good look at him, and it was a distorted version of a face she'd know anywhere.

"Jena, he's slipping around the back of the truck," she hissed through the open door. "It's Lang Broussard."

Jena shot again, followed by a shot from Lang. They were circling the truck.

Ceelie pulled out her cell phone, keeping her right hand on the shotgun's trigger, glad she had put Gentry on speed dial. He answered almost immediately. "Ceelie—what's going on? I heard—"

"It's Lang!" she whispered. "Little Caillou Road near—"

A deafening crash knocked both the phone and shotgun out of her hands and she instinctively screamed and covered her face. What felt like a solid wall of glass pellets flew at her from the truck's passenger's-side window.

"Jena?" The world turned gray at the edges, and somewhere in the distance, Ceelie heard Gentry calling her name. Blackness fell.

CHAPTER 22

"Ceelie! Damn it, I lost the connection." Gentry's heart beat erratically. He tried to find his professional calm, but it was gone. He'd jerked the truck into a parking lot, done a gravel-spewing U-turn, and headed south as soon as Jena's call for help came over the radio. His grip on the phone tightened as he punched in Ceelie's number. Meizel was already on his own radio, sharing what little he knew.

Ceelie's phone went straight to voice mail.

If he hadn't been stopped at a red light, he'd have crashed the truck. As it was, Meizel still put his hand on the steering wheel. "Pull over, Broussard."

Gentry ignored him, flipping on his lights and running through the intersection as soon as he was sure cars had stopped to clear the way.

He speed-dialed Sinclair. Straight to voice mail.

"Pull over now, Broussard!" Meizel yelled, and finally broke through the fog taking over Gentry's brain.

He shook his head. "I'm OK. Let your guys know that Ceelie iden-tified Langston Broussard just before the shots."

"Damn." Meizel got on his radio again, and Gentry calmed now that the cavalry had been called. He still didn't plan on wasting time. He was going with lights and sirens on.

He punched speed-dial one on his phone.

Warren didn't bother with a greeting. "All we know is Sinclair called in an 'officer needs help' approximately two minutes ago." Tires squealed in the background; the lieutenant was already on the road. "I don't know the situation and we haven't been able to get her on the radio."

"It was Lang." A welcome numbness settled over Gentry. "Ceelie Savoie called me and got that much out before I lost her. Sounded like a gun blast through the windshield or window. TPSO's en route."

"Everybody in the parish is en route," Warren said, and Gentry struggled to hear between his own sirens and Warren's. "Billiot and Griffin were patrolling near Chauvin, so they'll probably be first on scene. EMS is on the way as well."

Gentry ended the call and almost lost the truck on a tight curve.

"Slow down." Meizel's voice was quiet. "Slow down or pull over. If you kill us both on the way we aren't going to help anybody."

Pride fought with common sense, and he slowed down to a reasonable sixty-five.

"Look, I get it," Meizel said. "Sinclair is your partner and I don't think I'm wrong in saying you and Ceelie Savoie are way more than just acquaintances. Am I right or am I right?"

Gentry let out a long, ragged breath. "Yeah."

"Plus that's your brother out there doing this shit, so cut yourself some slack and just drive. For now, tell yourself it's just another case."

Gentry nodded. If he'd learned anything in the long months after he'd *killed* Lang—what a joke that all seemed now—it was to let himself feel what he felt. Right now he was so angry he'd eviscerate Lang if given half a chance. For three years, he'd wallowed in guilt over his brother's death. Now, he wished like hell he'd killed him for real. And if Jena or Ceelie were hurt . . .

Gentry obsessively called Ceelie's and Jena's phones every few minutes for a while, praying someone would pick up. Every time, voice mail. Finally, he stopped trying.

An ambulance sped up behind them, and Gentry slowed down and waved them around.

They saw the crime scene long before they reached it. A chaotic swarm of blue and red flashing lights could be seen far ahead, and a dozen or so cars were backed up in the southbound lane in front of them at a dead stop.

"Screw this." Gentry swerved into the northbound lane, driving south past the stopped cars. When he came upon a state police car blocking the right lane and a trooper managing traffic, the trooper waved him through.

"Jesus." Ahead, Gentry saw Jena's truck turned almost at a full ninety degrees, blocking the road. A mile farther south and she would have gone in the water making that turn. Sunlight glinted off broken glass, but not as much as Gentry would've hoped—it probably meant either the windshield or one or more windows had been shot *into* and not out of. He could only hope Jena had gotten a better shot at Lang than he got at the truck.

He pulled in behind a TPSO van and lurched to a stop. Gentry didn't wait for Meizel; he jumped out and raced toward the pickup, slowing at the sight of a familiar shock of dark-red hair on the ground a few feet from the front wheel on the passenger's side. Jena.

He scanned the people standing around—a growing crowd of sheriff's deputies and state police and LDWF agents. Sirens everywhere. A chopper swooped past overhead, adding to the deafening sound of a fast-forming manhunt. They were a brotherhood and sisterhood that came together when the place and people they loved were threatened. The color of the badge didn't matter.

Paul Billiot stood near where the EMTs were working on Jena, talking on his phone. Gentry skirted around him, edging as close to his partner as he could without getting in the way.

There was no sign of Ceelie. Where the hell was she?

Jena's face had bleached to the color of parchment, at least what he could see of it. Blood coated her from hairline to waist, and Gentry did a quick assessment: facial lacerations—a lot of them, some deeper than others. The EMTs had already covered chest wounds to keep the lungs from collapsing, so the damage must be significant. She'd lost a lot of blood, but the EMTs seemed to have it under control. No sign of consciousness.

"There were at least a dozen rounds fired," Paul said to Gentry, shouting to be heard over sirens and officers barking orders. "Sinclair took two rounds to the chest; the facial wounds are all from glass pellets. A lot of cuts on her hands where she shielded her eyes; otherwise, she'd have lost one or both. She got off a lot of shots, but no sign of Lang."

"Where's Ceelie—did they already take her in?"

Paul nudged him away from Jena and toward the truck. Gentry recognized a stall.

His voice came out in a hoarse shout. "Damn it, where's Ceelie?"

How could an ambulance already have taken her in without passing him? The nearest hospital was back in Houma. Fear slithered up his backbone like a snake.

"Sinclair's alive, but barely," Paul said. "EMTs are trying to get her stable enough to transport; chopper's on the way from the hospital in Houma. There's no sign of Ms. Savoie. We found her cell phone, broken, on the back floorboard. Her purse was in the front passenger's seat." He paused. "No easy way to say this, Broussard, but we think your brother took her."

Gentry stared at him, not seeing anything for the first shocked seconds except the vision his mind conjured of the bloody, butchered body of Eva Savoie.

Lang had Ceelie, and there were a million places in this wild bottomland for him to hide. And so much worse he could do to her.

He closed his eyes and tried to draw on his training. This was an abduction case now and a state agent had been shot. They'd have all the people and resources they needed. Everyone had mobilized fast, so Lang didn't have much of a head start.

He would make sure they survived, both of them. Jena was stubborn. She would fight to live. Ceelie was tough, and she was smart. She'd find a way to hang on until they found her. He had to help, not fall apart. Losing either one of them was not an option. Especially not like this.

"What else do we know?" The calm in his voice masked the despair in his heart. And the fear; he ached from it.

"With Tommy Mason out of the picture, Lang's gotta need money," Paul said. "Both women's wallets were cleaned out, so if he's stupid enough to use a credit card we'll know it. An APB has already been issued, and the troopers are setting up roadblocks at every access point off the highway—it's not like there are many side roads for him to take. If he tries to get anywhere by car, we'll get him. Troop C's already got a chopper in the air."

"Are Jena's weapons accounted for?" Gentry hated to think of all that firepower in Lang's hands.

"We're still digging through glass—or the TPSO team is. Looks like he took all the weapons except the knife. She still had it on her belt. When she made the distress call, she identified a silver sedan but not the driver."

Gentry nodded. "Ceelie called me as soon as she realized it was Lang." He waited until another cluster of sirens edged around Jena's truck and sped south, and he still had to shout. "So he has a car and plenty of weapons but probably not a lot of ammunition. Is Tommy Mason's silver Honda still impounded?"

"Don't know." Paul pulled out his cell phone and made a note. Then he turned and surveyed the broad, flat landscape. "Where would he take her?" He turned back to Gentry. "You know the two of them better than anybody here. Where would he take her, and why?"

"The where could be anywhere, but I don't think he'll get too far from the Savoie cabin if that's where he thinks he's going to find his payday. I think I know the why." Gentry waited for Warren and the sheriff to join them, pulling them as far from the noise as he could.

He filled them in on his and Meizel's trip to the pawnshop in Houma. "If we assume Lang was trying to torture Eva Savoie into telling him where, or if, she had more of those gold coins, he might also assume Ceelie knows something about them."

She didn't, though. He hadn't even had a chance to tell her the coins existed. All this for money. He'd give his brother every goddamned penny he had just to get Ceelie back safe.

"We're gonna tear through that cabin again, looking for coins," Sheriff Knight said. "And we have to figure Broussard has access to a boat since that's how he reached the Savoie cabin the first time. We can't assume he's gonna travel by car."

"What can I do?" Gentry asked. He needed to contribute. If he went home and saw reminders of Ceelie all over the place he'd go crazy.

"We want people working in teams," Warren said. "You and Billiot take a patrol boat and see what you can find between here and Chauvin, east side to Montegut. I'll send Griffin with the TPSO water patrol for the west side and over to Dulac. Go in every branch and bayou. Check any abandoned buildings. There are a lot of houses along the highway. See if anybody saw anything. Look for the vehicle but also the boat you saw earlier—silver aluminum and shallow, right?"

Gentry nodded, relieved that he'd get to stay busy. And Billiot was a silent, serious SOB but he was a good agent and he wouldn't make Gentry talk. Warren probably knew that. If he'd put Gentry in a boat with the gregarious Mac Griffin, Mac might not live to enjoy his twenty-fifth birthday.

"If you see anything, you know the protocol," the sheriff said. Roscoe Knight was a tall, gruff man in his fifties who oozed power, probably because he had a lot of it in a huge parish with only one metro police department. He was a straight arrow, and from what Gentry had heard, his officers respected him. "Enter the scene only if it's life and death. Otherwise, radio it in and let my team do its job."

While Paul went to move the patrol boat to the designated launch, Gentry walked around the truck. None of the windows remained; the windshield was still in place but a gust of wind would finish shattering it. He looked in the backseat, careful not to touch anything . . . until he saw Ceelie's guitar. The instrument was covered in glass and blood—Jena's blood, or Ceelie's? Part of the body had been crushed.

He stopped one of the sheriff's crime-scene people who was taking photos nearby. "Any way I could take the guitar that's in the backseat? It's my friend's and I'd like to be able to fix it and give it back to her when we find her."

"Sorry, but we need to keep the evidence togeth—"

"Take it, Broussard." Sheriff Knight clapped a hand on his shoulder. "And we *are* going to find her."

Gentry thanked the sheriff, reached inside the SUV, and gently brought out the Gibson. It was Ceelie's most valued possession, and he hoped the fact that it had survived with what looked like repairable damage was a good sign for its owner.

For the next six hours, Gentry and Paul went door to door along Highway 56, the stretch known as Little Caillou Road. They searched abandoned buildings, talked to residents, left business cards until they ran out, and then started writing their phone numbers on scraps of paper.

They made it back to Montegut and went by Ceelie's cabin, where Gentry could find no sign anyone had been there since his visit that morning.

"You ready for a night on the water?" Paul asked when they got back in the truck.

"You're off duty." Gentry didn't plan to go home tonight, but he didn't expect Paul to stay on the water indefinitely. Night marine duty was the worst, and the last few nights had been foggy.

"I'm on duty until we find this homicidal nutcase." Paul glanced at him. "Sorry."

"That's a lot better than anything I've been calling him." Gentry turned his truck back to the south, toward the boat launch Warren had set up for them, and said what had been running like a tape loop through his head all day. "If I'd just fingered him that first morning . . ."

"Chances are nothing would be different." Paul looked out the window. "And I should've offered Celestine Savoie a place to stay besides that cabin."

Gentry glanced at him in surprise. "Why would you do that? Not that she'd have taken you up on it—I tried. You don't even know her."

"She's part Chitimacha and we should take care of our own. We don't always do it."

Gentry pondered that. "Look, we can blame ourselves or say we should've done this or that all day, but the fact is, the person responsible is my brother and no one else."

"Can't argue."

They fell silent for a while, then Paul used his phone to rouse Stella, and he put it on speaker. "Got a status on Agent Sinclair?"

Gentry noticed Stella was a lot more businesslike with Paul than with him or Jena. Or maybe she was as shocked as the rest of them. "They got her to Terrebonne General, and they're trying to get her stable enough for surgery. They almost lost her in the chopper." Stella sounded as if she'd been crying. "She hasn't regained consciousness."

Gentry focused on the road, but if he clenched his jaw any harder, he'd crack a molar.

They bought sandwiches and drinks at a spot near the launch, and transferred their gear from the truck to the nimble marine boat, small enough to get in some tight waterways but big enough to support two engines, searchlights, and blue bar lights.

They set out, moving north and then south at gradually widening waterways, navigating partly from memory and partly by GPS when the light gave way to full dark. Although they had the twin outboards, they were propelling the boat with a quiet trolling motor: the better to slip up on someone.

"Kill your light and kill the motor." Paul raised a pair of night-vision binoculars to his eyes and scanned the south bank of an overgrown outlet of the inexplicably named Billy Goat Bay. He handed them to Gentry. "See what you think."

Gentry took the binoculars and studied the area where Paul had been focusing, passing by and then returning to a faint light coming from . . . something. He dropped his voice to a whisper. "Is that a fish camp?" He patrolled this area fairly often and didn't remember any inhabited camps out here.

"One way to find out."

"I better call it in." They'd muted the radio to minimize their noise, so Gentry used his cell phone to call Warren. When he described their situation and location, Warren didn't mince words.

"Go in slow and keep me informed. Unless you see something to make you think the victim's life is in immediate danger, call it in and wait for backup. You hear me, Broussard? Lang's desperate."

Gentry and Paul exchanged glances in the glow of the cell phone. "I understand. I'll check in." He ended the call.

"You ready?" Paul asked.

"Let's go."

Trouble was, the only way to exit the boat and make their way through the dense growth of sawgrass without breaking their necks was to use a light. Paul, shorter and not as heavy, carried the flashlight pointed downward to illuminate as small an area as possible, and Gentry followed close behind. They both carried their rifles in addition to having their holstered sidearms.

They moved silently through the grass until they were close enough that the faint moonlight lit the outline of a small wooden structure about the size of Ceelie's cabin. And like her cabin, the back end of the structure sat on land and the front was on piers over water, only this place had a fishing dock that stretched from the front porch. And unlike her cabin, this one had a back door.

A light definitely shone from inside, although it was a dim one. They slipped up to the front door and took their positions on either side. Paul still held the light facing down so they could see each other, and Gentry pointed to himself, then to Paul. He held up three fingers. Two fingers. One.

He grasped the door handle and turned gently, not expecting it to give. It was unlocked, however, and swung open with a squeak that sounded loud enough to be heard in Baton Rouge.

So much for the element of surprise. Gentry and Paul conducted a textbook search of the house, finally coming back to the front room, where a candle burned on a round wooden table; it had almost burned down to the end of the wick. An overturned chair lay next to the table.

"I'll check out front." Paul exited the front door and disappeared from view while Gentry continued to look around the cabin. A white card lay near the door and he picked it up and turned it over. His mouth went dry at the sight of his own business card. Whether it had been left by Ceelie as a clue or by Lang as a taunt—or dropped by accident—they had been here.

"Broussard, come out here."

Gentry laid the card on the table so it could be dusted for finger-prints and stuck his head out the door. "Find something?"

"Oh yeah."

Gentry couldn't see Paul but could tell he was off to the right side of the building. He pulled out his own flashlight and as soon as he rounded the corner, he spotted what his fellow agent had found so interesting: an older-model blue Ford sedan.

"I also found one of my business cards on the floor of the cabin," Gentry said. "They were definitely here."

"Maybe not so long ago." Paul didn't touch the vehicle but skirted around it, shining his flashlight into the windows.

Warren told them to hang tight while he and the sheriff sent more personnel to the area. "Any sign they're nearby?"

"No, although it's dense back here with very little light, so it's pos-sible. I'm thinking they might have left in the boat Lang had earlier—there's a dock in front of this camp. It's just too dark out here to see anything, but we'll keep looking."

"Don't go too far; the sheriff will want to coordinate efforts from that fish camp."

Before leaving the cabin, Paul pointed out a smudge of blood on the driver's-side window of the car. "Think Sinclair hit him?"

"Don't know." Gentry shone the flashlight across the window, then on more blood on the back of the driver's seat. "But I don't like the look of the backseat."

Gentry's heart dropped as he took a closer look. Blood, mostly dried, covered the seat bottom and the lower half of the seatback, like someone had been lying on it—someone injured. How badly had Ceelie been hurt? Had Lang left the candle burning intentionally or had he left in a hurry, maybe spotting Paul and Gentry as they crossed the sawgrass?

He turned slowly, scanning the dark marsh. Ceelie was somewhere nearby, and she was hurt. He could feel it.

CHAPTER 23

Burning. Something was in her eyes, burning. They were crusted closed but the sunlight was bright behind her eyelids. Where was she? Sensation of movement.

****

A voice kept talking although no one answered. It was too cheerful. Her limbs moved but not by themselves. Someone was carrying her; the shoulder against which her head rested smelled of blood. In her head, she heard a blast. Saw a flying wall of glass. Jena was dead.

****

Coughing. She lay on a hard, dusty floor but the movement had stopped. The voice again, but not one she recognized. Where was Gentry? She remembered a phone call. Glass flying. Lang in front of the SUV with a gun. He'd smiled when he aimed at Jena. The world exploded.

****

Cool water on a rough cloth scrubbed across her face. The voice said, "Wakey wakey" in its cheerful tone. She asked where Gentry was, but maybe that was just in her head.

****

Ceelie woke up—not for the first time, she didn't think, but for the first time with any true awareness. She lay on a hard wooden floor that hadn't been cleaned in eons, judging by the wafts of mold and dust that tickled her nose and throat. Even though she sensed that it would be wise to feign unconsciousness, the sneeze came without asking.

"About time you woke up. This ain't no holiday resort."

She lay on her right side and her arms had been tied behind her. Not tied, she decided after jiggling them. Maybe taped. With effort, she slit open her eyes just as a pair of blue-jean-clad knees dropped to the floor in front of her face, then a pair of shoulders, then a man's face as he stretched out on the floor in front of her, almost in kissing range, a parody of lovers.

Not a man. Langston Broussard.

Not a man, but a monster with a face so much like the one she thought she might be coming to love.

Gentry. She peeled apart dry, stuck-together lips to form the name, but nothing came out. She was immobile, and she was mute.

"Pretty blue-eyed, dark-skinned Celestine. You remember me?"

She tried to answer but only managed to croak, "Water."

"Water, water everywhere and it's all salty. Don't that figure?" The man disappeared for a few moments, then returned. "Let's see if you can sit up."

He slid a hand behind her neck and pulled her to a seated position, propped against a wall. The room swayed like the deck of a ship for a few seconds before finally righting itself. Lang held a bottle of water to her lips and tilted it. Half dribbled down her chin, but the rest she drank greedily.

"Enough. Too much and you'll get sick, and I don't have time for that. We have business to conduct, you and me."

Ceelie swallowed. "I remember you. You visited Tante Eva and Nonc LeRoy back when we were kids." In a cabin a lot like this one. Traditional South Louisiana fishing camp made of wood. But where? Were they still in the parish?

"When *you* were a kid, you mean. I was sixteen. You were kind of sweet on me. You probably thought I didn't know about that little-girl crush, didn't you? Thought about banging you then, but I was afraid that batshit old aunt of yours would put the voodoo hex on me."

Ceelie's awareness of her situation finally kicked in. The outside of her thoughts remained fuzzy, but a core of comprehension and memory was growing. "What do you want from me?"

"What do you think I want? Same thing I wanted from your crazy old Tante Eva, but she was too damned stubborn to give 'em to me. I want the coins."

Ceelie frowned at him. "What coins?"

Langston Broussard was a thinner, unhealthy version of his younger brother, but now Ceelie saw another couple of clear differences: a hardness in his dark-brown eyes she'd never seen in Gentry's. Meanness. And jittery nerves, which could mean drugs or desperation, or both. "If you're gonna start with that I-don't-know-nothin'-bout-no-coins shit, you and me are gonna have a long day, Celestine."

Ceelie had never heard mention of coins, but Tante Eva talked of a curse and LeRoy Breaux was supposed to be a thief. "You mean the coins Nonc LeRoy stole?"

His hand shot out so quickly she didn't see it coming, not until his fist made contact with her jaw and her head cracked against the wall behind her. Everything faded slowly to gray, then black.

****

A throbbing jaw brought Ceelie back to consciousness. She'd fallen over, her back against the wall that had been serving as her prop. This time she didn't give herself away, but studied her surroundings.

They were still in the fish camp, but she could see Lang's profile standing in the doorway on the left side of the cabin. A small candle flickered in the center of a round table. Lang held something long and narrow in his right hand—maybe Jena's shotgun—and he was smoking a cigarette. A pistol, the rifle, and a roll of duct tape lay on the table.

Darkness had fallen, so she'd been out at least ten hours since he'd taken her. Between her call to Gentry and Jena's radio distress call, there should be a lot of people out looking for her.

God, Jena. Had Lang killed her? There had been so many shots. Ceelie had been covered in broken glass and hadn't managed to get off a single shot before something had slammed into her head and she'd lost consciousness.

She did a mental inventory of the pain signals her body was sending to her brain in a steady march. The throbbing jaw came from Lang's fist. Her face hurt all over, but it was probably due to minor cuts from the glass. She vaguely remembered shielding her eyes at the last second. Her head was sore where it touched the wooden floor, and Ceelie imagined she felt a lump there. Lang had hit her with something. Not a concussion, she didn't think.

Other than a need to relieve her bladder, she didn't think she'd suffered any other injuries.

At least not yet. Fact was, she didn't have the information Lang wanted unless she made something up. Would he kill her as soon as he thought he had the location of these coins? Or would he kill her—only more slowly, playing with that knife as he'd done with Tante Eva, or raping her—if she didn't tell him what he wanted?

Either way, she'd be dead, so it might as well be faster rather than slower.

Lang turned to look at her, and Ceelie was pleased to see the upper part of his T-shirt sleeve was covered in dried blood. Maybe Jena had at least grazed him with her shot, and he hadn't changed clothes, so they were hiding out. He hadn't brought her to anyplace he'd been living for long.

He walked closer and nudged her knee with the toe of his worn leather boot. "Wake up. We gotta move."

When she didn't respond, he kicked her, more to startle her than to hurt. She opened her eyes and tried to sit up, but he had to help her first to a sitting position and then to her feet. She reeled and the room reeled with her. Finally, her equilibrium settled.

Lang's hand on her upper arm slid to her breast; she stiffened when he squeezed, hard. "We'll find a new spot to hide out and then I might have a few ways to convince you to talk."

He turned away to the round table in the center of the room, and Ceelie made a shuffling run toward the cabin door.

He caught her by the tail of her shirt and slung her to the ground, knocking over one of the chairs. "Nice try, bitch." Leaning over her, he slapped a length of duct tape over her mouth.

"Just for that, I'm gonna take a little taste of what my brother's been enjoying as soon as we get to our next stop. First, though, we have a couple of nosy cops out in the marsh who'll eventually work up the balls to come in here. So we're gonna take a boat ride."

Cops! Ceelie's frantic gaze skittered around the cabin, looking for something that would draw their attention without making Lang angry enough to knock her out again. Or at least she had to let the cops know they'd been here.

As Lang pulled her across the cabin toward the door, she remembered the business cards in her back pocket and managed to twist her arms enough to pull one out between her fingers and let it drop to the floor.

Then she had no choice but to be dragged out the door and down a wooden dock, where Lang shoved her into a small aluminum boat. She thought about jumping in the water, or upending the boat, but with her hands tied behind her she'd drown. She hadn't given up on living enough to commit suicide. She just had to wait for an opening, hope Lang made a mistake, and pray that the authorities would find her before it was too late—and Gentry, because she knew he'd be looking for her.

Lang propelled the boat away from the dock with a long pole to avoid making noise, and continued to use it in the shallow cove to make slow but silent progress. Did he know where he was going or was he looking for a hideout of opportunity?

Over the shoulder of his moonlit silhouette, Jena spotted the bobbing light of a flashlight crossing the shoreline toward the cabin. Maybe two figures, but it was hard to tell. It took a few moments for her to realize tears were blurring her vision, adding to those already coursing down her cheeks.

She swallowed down the fear and rage; there was no time for it. Since he didn't want to draw attention, Lang had shut up for a change, so it gave Ceelie a chance to think of a strategy.

Coins. Tante Eva sure hadn't lived as if she'd been wealthy, so either LeRoy Breaux had stolen some coins or the coins were themselves the curse that Tomas had talked about. If the curse had started with Julien Savoie, maybe he had found a cache of coins when he built the cabin on Whiskey Bayou, so their age would make them valuable. Cajuns, Creoles, and Chitimacha alike were proud peoples, but often downtrodden and suspicious. The Savoies were some of all three, so they might well be more likely to hide the treasure than use it, especially if they thought the money might be claimed by somebody else.

If she were a suspicious swamp-dwelling half-breed, which she was, and she came across a cache of treasure she didn't want publicized, where would she put it? Ceelie had looked under the mattress in the cabin, but not inside the mattress. She'd looked under the bed and moved every stick of furniture. She'd gone through everything in the cabin's kitchen. There were open rafters, so there was no attic in which to hide something.

Tante Eva didn't have a bank account; Ceelie couldn't imagine she had a safety-deposit box.

The most likely story was that Tante Eva had told LeRoy about the coins—they'd lived together for years, although Ceelie didn't know how many—and that LeRoy had stolen them and skipped town.

That story, however, wasn't going to satisfy Lang Broussard. He wanted the money. She was going to have to get him talking, at least enough to learn what he thought happened to the coins, and then wing it.

If he thought Tante Eva still had these mysterious coins, she had to have them hidden somewhere on the property, assuming LeRoy hadn't stolen them without Lang knowing about it. They weren't in the cabin, so they were either buried in the swamp or they were underneath the cabin. She decided on the web of lies she would spin. Now she just had to stay alive and keep Lang Broussard in a good mood long enough to trap him in it.

CHAPTER 24

Sometime between one and two a.m., Gentry and Paul finally gave up and made their way back to the fish camp that had become the new central command.

Gentry collapsed on the floor against a back wall of the main front room. He'd found a shred of duct tape and some drops of blood near the wall, and he knew Ceelie had been here, maybe even leaning in this same spot. The duct tape was another sign of her; it would make an easy, cheap, and effective restraint for Lang to use on her.

No doubt they'd been here. Lang hadn't been careful about fingerprints—why bother, at this point? Plus, he'd been in a hurry. Gentry thought they'd surprised him, but not quickly enough to prevent him from slipping out of here with Ceelie. Then, of course, there was the business card, which Warren seemed to think Ceelie had found a way to drop, to let the authorities know they were getting close.

He shut his eyes, sending a prayer heavenward for the first time in three years. When he'd killed Lang—make that when he'd *thought* he'd killed Lang—he'd abandoned the faith instilled in him by his parents. He didn't understand a God who made a man choose between killing his brother or letting his partner die, who let innocent people like Ceelie get caught up in something so evil because a junkie wanted drug money, who let screwed-up people like Lang prosper and survive while someone good and honest like Jena Sinclair fought for her life.

But he prayed his way through that baggage. He prayed for Ceelie to survive both physically and emotionally, for Jena to survive the surgery she was undergoing as of about a half hour ago. He prayed that he would be strong for them and help them move on with their lives no matter what wreckage Lang left behind.

Surely, every once in a while, the good guys had to win. Surely it was time to end the Savoie curse. To end the Broussard curse. Maybe it wasn't just the love of the parish he and Ceelie had in common; it was the ghosts of the past.

He did not pray for Lang. If there was a God, and if he were listening, he'd know a hypocritical prayer when he heard it.

Gentry opened his eyes halfway and watched Warren, Sheriff Knight, and a captain from the Louisiana State Police huddle over a parish map. The cabin, which had no electricity, had been illuminated like a stadium with portable lights running off noisy generators. If the freaking International Space Station flew over, the cabin would probably show up as a bright dot in the middle of a dark, dark swamp.

The map, which covered the entire round table, showed every bayou and bay and bog and gator slide in the parish—thousands of places to tuck oneself away and hide. To commit torture.

Don't go there. If he went there, he'd lose it.

A virtual armada of state and parish marine units had been gathering for the past two hours, ready to launch a massive manhunt from what had become Fishing Camp Central as soon as the first gray predawn light gave them visibility. LDWF agents from the adjacent parishes in Region 6 had arrived during the night.

Sheriff Knight was in charge, but Warren had a major role since his teams knew the waterways better than anyone. Knight thought the most likely area for Lang to hide out would be within the confines of the Pointe-aux-Chenes Wildlife Management Area, more than 35,000 acres of protected wildlife area just east and southeast of Montegut and stretching into neighboring Lafourche Parish. Left to his own devices and absent any emergency calls, the Pointe-aux-Chenes WMA was one of Gentry's favorite places to patrol and one of the state's last stands to protect the rich ecosystem from erosion and storms that pushed in saltwater. It was secluded but for the hunters who were already into duck season, but it had no cabins. Roughing it had never been Lang's cup of tea.

"What do you think, Broussard?" The sheriff speared Gentry with a glare. Apparently the groveling hadn't been sufficient, so he'd further the ill will by disagreeing.

"I don't think he'll go into Pointe-aux-Chenes." Gentry climbed to his feet with difficulty. He was emotionally and physically spent. "I doubt Lang has a tent or anything to protect him from the elements and, believe me, my brother doesn't do physical discomfort. There are only two boat launches if he needs to get back on land, and there are lots of hunters and fishermen this time of year. He'd see it as too risky. Plus, there's a possibility that he was injured."

It was too early to know if any of the blood from the truck was Lang's. Maybe it was all Jena's or some of it was Ceelie's, but as many shots as Jena had gotten off, chances were good Lang had been hit too. Maybe the bastard would bleed to death, doing them all a favor.

Knight crossed his arms, wearing the demeanor of a man who'd just taken a bite out of a lemon. "You think he could find a way to depart the parish?"

Gentry rubbed his eyes. "My gut says no. If Lang took Celestine Savoie because he thinks she can lead him to this alleged cache of treasure, it's easier for him to hide out nearby. I think he'll find another place like this one: an isolated fishing camp where he can get out of the elements, reachable only by boat. I think he'll stay relatively close to

Whiskey Bayou and the Savoie cabin. He has to go back there eventually if he thinks that's where the coins are."

"Except he has to know that cabin is under surveillance night and day," Warren said. "How does he think he can get in there to search right under our noses?"

Gentry had no answers as to his brother's state of mind now, but he knew the way Lang used to think. "He thinks he's smarter than the average bear, and bears definitely include law enforcement." Gentry walked over to look at the map. "He's been playing a game of chicken with us all along, trying to scare Ceelie Savoie away from the cabin, leaving Tommy Mason for us to find the way he did, then setting the tongue outside Ceelie's door."

Gentry had been thinking about something else. "What do we know about that car?"

"It was registered to Tommy Mason over two years ago," Knight said. In honor of the heat, the sheriff had removed his suit coat and rolled up his sleeves. The end of his tie flapped from his right pants pocket. "His wife claims to have no knowledge of it, or of your brother. What about it?" His expression told what he thought of Jennifer Mason's lack of knowledge.

"Since he had wheels, I'm guessing Lang was probably watching my house and followed Jena Sinclair and Ceelie Savoie from there."

As soon as the words were out of his mouth, he wanted them back. The sheriff's eyebrows shot skyward, and Warren shook his head with a *what-an-idiot* expression.

"Let me get this straight, Broussard. The victim of this abduction, taken by *your* brother, was staying at *your* house. I'd been led to believe she was staying with Agent Sinclair." Knight crossed his arms and, yeah, the man was intimidating. Gentry wanted to grovel again. "Son, you're up to your neck in this shitstorm."

"Yes, sir, it would appear so." Gentry shrugged. You couldn't argue with the truth.

Knight shook his head and resumed his study of the map.

Warren walked over to Gentry, put a hand on his shoulder, and nudged him into the back room, which contained a bathroom and a couple of sets of bunk beds. "See that bed over there?" He pointed to a lower bunk. "We can't do anything for the next three hours, when day breaks. Close your eyes for a while if you can. You're our best insight into both Lang and Ceelie. I need you to be sharp, and the sheriff has you on his radar again as a potential problem. Just sleep a while."

Seriously? The man thought he could sleep? Gentry opened his mouth to protest but then closed it. Warren was right. He'd be no good to them if he turned sloppy out of fatigue; nothing he could do about the stress. He couldn't sleep but he could try to relax and slow the thoughts racing through his brain. "Okay, but let me know if anything comes up or you hear about Sinclair's surgery."

Gentry stretched out on one of the bottom bunks and a sweet scent hit him like a blow to the gut. Ceelie had been here; her head had been on this pillow. He could smell her shampoo. He rolled to his side and pulled the hard rectangle of foam to his nose, inhaling her. Twenty-four hours ago, they'd been in his bed, together.

"You all right, Broussard?" Paul Billiot came in and flopped on the bottom bunk on the other side of the room. "Warren's put me in time-out for a few hours too."

Gentry cleared his throat, unwilling to let Paul see how choked up he'd gotten over a faint scent on a pillow. "Yeah, I'm not feeling the whole going-to-sleep shit, though."

"I hear ya," Paul said, then promptly fell asleep. Gentry could tell by his steady breathing.

Just as well. He wanted to think about coins, and about his brother. Lang had been laying low for three years. If their hypothesis was true that he was after a pot of gold at the end of the bayou and that he'd learned about that gold more than fifteen years earlier, what had happened to prompt his sudden interest?

"Broussard! Billiot!"

At the sound of Warren's voice, Gentry sat up and cracked his head on the bunk above him, and saw Paul do the same thing across the room. He'd fallen asleep despite himself.

Gentry was on his feet before he fully awoke. "What happened? Did somebody find her—find them?"

"No, but come out here. We just got an interesting call from the state. Sheriff Knight wants to tell all of us at once and get some feedback."

Gentry followed Warren into the "war room" and noticed the eastern sky through the open front door. It had turned from jet-black to charcoal. Another half hour and they could see well enough to mobilize and discover what was around them.

Sheriff Knight leaned against the room's north wall, looking like he needed a nap himself. Warren's fatigue showed in the dark circles under his eyes. After two hours of sleep, Billiot looked fresh as a water lily. Must be clean living.

The sheriff ended his call. "Okay, we got a report back on the skull that Ms. Savoie found hanging on her porch." He looked at his watch. "Lab's been working overtime to get it to us as soon as possible."

A forensics report in under two weeks and in the wee hours of dawn. That had to be some kind of miracle, but Gentry didn't see the big deal. They knew Lang was the culprit, and compared to his other crimes, stealing a skull and hanging it from a porch roof would probably rank low on the prosecutor's list. Murder trumped grave robbery; that skull had been too bashed and battered to have been purchased.

"The medical examiner had told us the skull belonged to a male, approximate age sixty-five at the time his skull was presumably separated from the rest of his body."

Knight paused for effect. "The DNA, though, matched up with some old information in CODIS; the skull belonged to LeRoy Breaux."

What the hell? Gentry and Warren exchanged shocked looks. How in God's name had Lang Broussard gotten his hands on LeRoy Breaux's skull?

CHAPTER 25

"Time to play, little Celestine."

Ceelie kept her face blank even though the feel of Lang's thumb circling her breast through her torn blouse made her want to do a number out of *The Exorcist* and projectile spew right in the face that was such a twisted parody of Gentry's.

But she'd decided, when they sailed away last night in that boat, twisting and turning through the bayous until she wasn't even sure they were still in Terrebonne Parish, that no matter what he did to her physically, he would not touch her heart, her soul, or her mind.

She was scared, no hiding that, but the anger had begun to take the edge off the fear. He might kill her. He might do horrible things to her before he killed her. But he would not break her. She made that vow to the memory of Tante Eva. To her father. To her people. To Gentry. To Jena.

They lay on the moldy mattress of a rusted iron bed in the remains of a house that had seen serious flooding. The walls had gone way past mold, and the toxic air carried the chalky smell of baked-on mold spores. The doors and windows had been blown out or washed out.

Lang had pushed the bed up against the wall and then hemmed her in with his body. First, he had stripped off his bloody shirt. His upper arm had taken one of Jena's shots, and his anger over that was what had earned Ceelie the first punch to the gut as soon as she'd regained consciousness the first time.

Her captor was thin, pale, and lanky, with lines on his face that told her his years had not been easy, and track marks across both arms that told her how he'd spent many of those years. She hadn't seen him shoot up so far, but he'd popped pills. A lot of pills and no food, which made him unpredictable and volatile.

She was going to have to channel her inner Gentry and Jena in order to protect herself. She'd been with both of them when they were outside the home environment, and both of them constantly scanned their surroundings, pausing long enough to assess a movement or situation, then resuming their scans. Ceelie needed to read Lang's body language, to see what his triggers were and avoid them. If she were unconscious, she'd lose any control over her fate.

Not that she had much control, but earlier, she had convinced Lang to cut the tape off her wrists long enough for her to pee in the deep sawgrass and relieve the pressure on her shoulders from having her arms restrained behind her for so many hours. He also had offered her a packet of peanut butter crackers, the little cellophane-wrapped packs sold at every convenience store and vending machine on the planet. He'd let her have a little more water, although his supplies were running low.

Advance planning didn't seem to be Langston Broussard's strong suit. Otherwise, he'd have realized that if he shot—maybe killed—an LDWF agent, it would bring out every law-enforcement agency in the region. He would've had backup plans. He'd have had supplies. Instead, he had a couple of candles, a roll of duct tape, a knife, a six-pack of water bottles, and a few packs of crackers. And pills and cigarettes. Of those, he seemed to have plenty.

After a half hour, he'd taped her wrists together again, in front this time, and stretched out beside her on the bed, touching her a little—mostly her breasts—before going to sleep. His touch held no heat and she wondered if the drug use had taken its toll in the sex department. She'd come across enough junkies in the Nashville club scene to have heard several bemoan the trade-off of highs for hard-ons. Too many of the former eradicated the latter.

Good news for her, unless he used his fists to take out his frustration over an inability to rape her. Those worked just fine. Twice while he slept, she'd tried to slowly maneuver herself toward the foot of the bed, hoping to escape into the swamp. Both times, he'd moved quickly and without warning, hitting her hard enough to bring tears.

Now he was awake again, and Ceelie thought showtime had arrived. Until finding this abandoned house, he'd been too concerned with survival and avoiding capture to question her about these mystery coins, but she had her story ready. First, she had to get him talking rather than touching.

"I do remember you, when you visited the cabin that summer," she said, keeping her voice soft and calm. "I thought you were the cutest, coolest guy I'd ever met."

"I know you did." Lang propped on his left elbow and ran his right index finger along the line of her jaw. Between the cuts on her face from the broken SUV window and his repeated blows, even the light pressure of his finger stung her skin and sent shards of pain racing down her neck and up to her temple.

"Why didn't you ever come back? I'd look for you every time I came out that summer."

"Did you now? I wanted to go back, but, well, you know."

Ceelie frowned. She didn't know. "What? Why didn't you come back?"

Lang pinched her cheek, and she felt the sharp sting as a cut reopened. A wet trail streaked down the side of her face toward her hairline. "Because of LeRoy, bitch. Don't play dumb."

Unfortunately, she didn't have to play. She had no idea what he meant. "Lang, I was eight years old. All I knew was that Nonc LeRoy left Tante Eva, and I think it happened that summer but I'm not sure. I don't know why he left, or where he went."

Lang turned her face toward his and studied her, then grinned. God, he had deep dimples like Gentry, but instead of an even row of white teeth, his were yellowed and two were broken. What a laugh God must have had in making these two men so similar up to a point, and then taking them in polar-opposite directions.

He released her chin. "You really don't know, do you? I keep for-gettin' how little you were. Nonc LeRoy, as you call him, didn't leave, sweet Celestine, at least not how you think. You tell me what you think happened to him."

To do that, Ceelie had to put herself in Lang's shoes, then in LeRoy's, and finally in Tante Eva's. "Eva killed him," she whispered.

"She bashed his face in with the business end of an ax." Lang's thin face, with his curly dark hair so like Gentry's but his eyes filled with hatred, grew somber.

"That's horrible." It was Ceelie's turn to stare. Was her Tante Eva capable of murder to protect those coins? And was the ax Ceelie had slept with that night in the cabin the thing that had killed LeRoy?

"Ain't it?" Lang reached in his pocket and brought out a knife with a wicked serrated blade and black handle—a tactical knife similar to the one in her purse, which was either still sitting in the blood-spattered truck or was wherever the sheriff put stuff like the personal effects of kidnapping victims.

He flicked it open and popped off a button of her blouse by shred-ding the thread holding it on. The once-white blouse was covered in blood and dirt, but at least it kept her covered.

"I think I'll ask the questions for a while. If I don't like the answers you give"—he popped another button—"then we'll see what I need to do to make you more cooperative."

Ceelie swallowed hard, hoping he couldn't hear her heart pounding. "What do you want to know?"

"You tell me, Celestine. Why would that old witch Eva kill LeRoy Breaux, the man who'd been living with her for years?"

Ceelie didn't know about any killing, but she had thought about those coins and LeRoy's anticipated windfall. "He wanted the coins, and she wouldn't give them to him."

Lang tapped her on the nose with the side of the knife blade. "Good girl. Why wouldn't she share with her loving husband?"

Biting back the point that Eva and LeRoy weren't married, which Lang might not even know, Ceelie tried again to put herself in Lang's head, in LeRoy's head. Especially in Eva's head. "She thought the coins were a curse handed down from her grandfather Julien."

That rang true to her. If Julien had found some of South Louisiana's fabled treasure when he first moved to Whiskey Bayou from Isle de Jean Charles, rousing the ill will of his Chitimacha peers, he might have considered it more curse than blessing. "She thought that it was bad luck to use them."

"Ding ding ding—give the girl a circus monkey." Lang leaned over and kissed her. It took every bit of Ceelie's resolve not to bite the son of a bitch, or at least spit in his face when he removed his lips from hers. "It wasn't the coins that was bad luck, though. It was how they got 'em. Eva and LeRoy had some pillow talk, like couples do."

Lang traced his knife edge along the shoulder of her blouse. "Eva told him her granddaddy done killed a man for those gold coins after they found them down in Isle de Jean Charles. The other guy wanted to turn 'em in to the property owner, and Julien, he figured he could take it all for himself. He took 'em and hid them at Whiskey Bayou, using one or two to live off all these years, and the family's been cursed ever since."

He popped off another button while Ceelie absorbed that information. *Sin always has to be paid for,* Eva would tell her. Julien's sin, or her own?

"So guess what Eva did?" Lang's voice was soft.

"You said she killed LeRoy, I guess with an ax." She saw the truth on his face, or at least what he thought was the truth. "I honestly didn't have any idea."

He nodded. "Yeah, you were just a kid, so I'll give you that. Let me ask you this. How do I know Eva killed LeRoy if I never went back to the cabin after that summer?"

Ceelie thought a moment, but there were only two possible answers. She whispered, "Either your friend Tommy told you, or Tante Eva told you that morning?" The morning he murdered her.

"That *bitch*." He rolled off the bed and began pacing. "She said"— he broke into a parody of a singsong Cajun French accent—"'I done kep' that no-good LeRoy from finding that money and tellin' everybody about it. Instead, I done took his head. You can see it right over dere, and you think after keepin' that secret all dese years I'm gonna tell you?"

Ceelie watched him pace and struggled to understand. "His head?"

Lang stopped and grinned. "Remember that skull hanging on the porch? My little gift to you? Well, that was LeRoy, comin' back home to Whiskey Bayou. Where his fucking *skull* had been all this time."

An unbidden memory came to Ceelie's mind. She'd been a little older, maybe twelve or thirteen, and had spotted a skull in the bottom of Tante Eva's pie safe, tucked amid her collection of candles. "Who is this?" she had asked, and Tante Eva, with a little smile, said, "Child, that is something to keep us safe."

It had been LeRoy's skull.

Ceelie's expression must have been horrified enough to appease Lang, because he began pacing again. "Well, I had to keep trying to make her tell me where the coins were and, well, the bitch died on me."

"But why? There are other ways to get money." Ways that didn't involve murdering elderly women for some coins he didn't know for sure existed.

"We all haven't had a fairy-tale life, little Celestine. My holier-than-thou father sure as hell didn't give me that fairy tale, with all the rules he tried to make when he wasn't even home most of the time. My whore of a mother who barely let the bed grow cold after dear old dad died before she replaced him—she didn't give a shit. And then there was my . . ."

He looked down at her and smiled with a look that sent chills down her spine. He stretched out on the bed beside her again. "Sure wasn't my baby brother, Gentleman Gentry, the golden boy who followed the rules and played nice and did just as he was told."

Lang squeezed her breast and ran his hand lightly down her belly. He dug his fingers into her crotch hard enough to make her flinch. "Yeah, Gentry's getting some of that; you been at that glorified trailer he calls a house for days. I think it's time Gent and I shared something. Never had much in common with my stick-up-his-ass little brother before."

Ceelie couldn't quite keep the quiver out of her body. Maybe she'd been wrong about him being impotent.

He used the knife to pop off the remaining button on her blouse, then used the tip of the blade to push the fabric away and expose her beige bra. He traced the top of the bra with the blade, not hard, but it was sharp enough to draw a light cut that instantly beaded with blood.

He leaned closer, his breath warm in her ear. "I can't screw you the way he can, but I can make it so he don't want you anymore. I've already screwed up that pretty face, and now . . .

He leaned back and Ceelie closed her eyes to brace for a blow when she saw his hand snake toward her. But instead, he grabbed her ponytail and jerked it out from beneath her head. "I bet Gentry loves running his hands through this, don't he, sweet Celestine?"

Ceelie wriggled, her composure shattered as he got on his knees, jerked her ponytail out straight and sawed across her hair next to the elastic band.

She couldn't stop the tears when he held up the ponytail, a thick, long snake of jet-black dangling from his fingers. She closed her eyes and gulped down a sob. *It's just hair. It will grow back. You will not let him break you. You can cry later. Not now.*

She opened her eyes and sucked down the rage and sorrow. "Don't you want to ask me another question?"

Lang had been stroking her inner thigh and examining her body like a starving man at a buffet, but he stopped. "What's that?"

"You want to know where the coins are, don't you? The rest of them?"

She didn't see his hand coming until it hit the side of her face hard enough to knock her head against the wall. The room spun for a moment, but her vision cleared. An open-handed slap instead of his fist for a change.

This time, Lang held the knife against her throat. "You do know. I knew it. You're just like her, with your witchy ways and your chicken bones."

If Lang thought she was a voodoo queen or a witch, well, better for her. He hadn't touched Tante Eva's throwing table, after all. "I threw the bones yesterday mornin'." She used her own version of Eva's accent. "I knew you was comin', and I knew you was determined to get it."

"Give me a break, little Celestine. Taking you was as easy as shooting that red-headed bodyguard of yours."

Not a bodyguard, but a friend who was probably dead.

Ceelie spoke softly, keeping her voice low and musical.

"Tu ne me connais pas." You do not know me.

"Je passe la malédiction à vous, Langston Broussard." I pass the curse to you, Langston Broussard.

"Tu ne me fais pas peur." You do not scare me.

For a fraction of a second, Ceelie saw a flash of doubt—maybe even fear—cross Lang's face before it settled back into a sneer. She had rattled him with a few words pulled from long-ago memories.

The momentum might have swung her way, at least for a moment.

CHAPTER 26

There were no trolling motors on today's version of the manhunt. The search was taking on a life of its own, and Roscoe Knight had told all the gathered law-enforcement officers at daybreak that he wanted Langston Broussard to hear them coming, and hear them coming hard.

Only he hadn't used such nice words.

If Gentry hadn't been so taut-nerved and restless, he'd have gotten downright teary-eyed at the dozens of officers, male and female, who'd gathered to cover every inch of the central parish east and south of Montegut. Sheriff's deputies, state police, LDWF agents he'd seen only at regional events, even some officers wearing the dark-blue uniforms of the Houma PD. He'd never seen so many patrol boats in one spot.

He prayed it would be enough, and that it would be in time. And that the media wouldn't pick up on where they'd set up base camp and put a lot of civilians in harm's way—or muck up their chance of finding Lang and Ceelie. Bad enough that it was gator season and hunters all over the bayous were on the prowl for gators, raccoons, nutria, and feral hogs.

"Ready?" Paul Billiot strapped on his duty belt and checked the ammunition in his service pistol. The LDWF boat they'd come in on last night had been refueled out here in the middle of nowhere, thanks to some miraculous display of power pulled off by the sheriff.

"Let's go. What's our area?" Gentry followed Paul through the sawgrass that seemed a much easier walk in daylight than it had last night with only a flashlight. It was a wonder they hadn't sunk through a patch of floating grass and broken a leg.

"We got the area just north of here, almost to the outskirts of Montegut." Paul attached the boat's kill switch to a lanyard and stuck the key in the ignition. They both had donned their life jackets and uniform-collar radios, and had rifles and shotguns in addition to their service pistols. Bulletproof vests added an extra layer of bulk under the life jackets. Gentry felt like a paramilitary Michelin Man. Probably a paramilitary Michelin Man who'd be on the verge of heatstroke before midday.

He didn't care, as long as they found Ceelie and his dirtbag of a brother.

For the next two hours, they cut in and out of bayous and drainage canals and cutoffs. They stopped at every house and fishing camp, occupied or abandoned. Warren had Stella deliver their supply of business cards, so they left them whenever they found people, asking questions and leaving descriptions. They carefully searched every outbuilding and storage shed.

Finally, they found signs of recent occupation in one of the abandoned houses and spent a half hour combing through it, reporting back to a deputy at the staging area every few minutes.

They found piles of beer cans, pizza boxes, wine bottles, and other trash, but after a thorough search, Gentry shook his head. "I don't think it was them."

"I reached the same conclusion." Paul kicked a pizza box out of the doorway. "This was some teenagers finding a private place to party. And it's been here long enough for animals to get in it."

They'd just gotten back to the boat when the dash radios—they had one for the sheriff's office as well as LDWF—began a cacophony of chatter. Gentry's cell phone rang, and he heard Paul's follow right behind it. He walked to the rear of the aft deck.

It was Warren. "We found a new hideout, north and east of your current location. We're still verifying but you might want to come this way." He read out the GPS coordinates and Gentry handed them to Paul, who was ending a phone call with Mac.

The ride to the new location took about fifteen minutes, and Gentry's body was pumped on adrenaline when the cabin finally came into sight. He jumped out of the boat onto the wooden pier. Sheriff Knight and Warren were standing in the front door just ahead of him. This was another fish camp, but it was a little bigger than Lang's last spot, and its condition told Gentry it had been abandoned for at least a year or two—probably since the last tropical storm had come through and flooded the whole parish.

The bottom half of the structure's outer walls were in midstage rot. The whole thing would fall in the bayou within another six months, faster if the parish drew the unlucky card and got another storm.

The area around them, a narrow waterway between Madison Bay and Bayou Terrebonne, was typical South Louisiana marsh, bits of solid ground interspersed among the flotons; floating bits of marsh that looked like land but couldn't carry the weight of an adult. Occasional trees broke the landscape, as well as fish camps like this one where people would come out on weekends for the bounty of the fish-rich waters and waterfowl hunting.

Today, it was an anthill of outboard motors on patrol boats and law-enforcement officers as news spread that another hideout had been found. Next, the sheriff would set up a new base camp here and they'd all fan out again until they found either Lang or his next stopping place.

Gentry's gut told him they were getting close.

The part of Ceelie's situation that scared Gentry the most was her lack of knowledge about the gold coins, unless Lang had talked enough for her to figure out what he was after. When Lang got desperate enough and realized she couldn't help him, would he decide she was too much trouble?

Two things worked in Ceelie's favor. One, she was smart. If she could figure out a way to mentally stay ahead of Lang and his games, she could survive long enough to outmaneuver him—if she was physically able. Two, which tied back into one, Lang was smart, but he was impulsive. He'd never been one to think situations through to their logical conclusion. In junior high, he'd decided he wanted to play football because the uniforms were cool and the players always got the pretty girls; he'd made it through two practices before realizing that he actually had to earn the uniform.

Gentry could come up with a dozen examples of Lang's lack of foresight, but this crime spree—killing Eva Savoie and Tommy Mason, shooting Jena Sinclair, kidnapping Ceelie—it all had the marks of a man growing desperate and spiraling out of control without the vaguest idea of where it would end.

Once he'd killed Eva Savoie and had the misfortune to be spotted by the one person in parish law enforcement who would recognize him, he kept digging himself deeper. He wouldn't abandon the gold mine; he'd keep digging, trying to get the coins.

Gentry finally made his way down the pier and through the clump of officers gathered around the front porch of the cabin.

"Clear out of here!" Sheriff Roscoe Knight could bellow like nobody's business. "Everybody out but Lieutenant Doucet and Agents Broussard and Billiot." He glared at a deputy who couldn't be older than twenty-two or -three. "Now!"

Everybody scattered, which made room for Gentry and Paul to go inside. The place stank of molding wood and sheetrock and animal shit. It sickened him to think of Ceelie here.

Gentry nodded at Warren and Knight, waiting to hear the details. "Looks like your brother and Ms. Savoie were here," the sheriff said. "Since you know both parties, take a look around at what they left and see what you can tell us that we don't already know. This room and the bedroom through that door." He pointed over his shoulder. "Those are the only spots here we see any signs of them. You"—he pointed at Paul—"are supposed to be some hotshot tracker. Tell us what you can see inside, then look around outside."

They nodded and took a slow walk around the front room first. A rifle lay on a side table, absent its magazine. Gentry glanced at Warren. "This Sinclair's weapon?"

"Yep—we checked the serial number. We have to assume he still has the shotgun, Sinclair's SIG Sauer, and the pistol he used to shoot her," Warren said. "He either left in a hurry, or he didn't know how to get a clip for it. Sinclair must have detached the magazine before she lost consciousness."

Smart. The shotgun and the two handguns were bad enough, but Gentry was relieved that Lang didn't have a loaded tactical rifle at his disposal.

Paul squatted and studied the floor. "Have these footprints been disturbed?"

"No, we've been walking around them." Knight crossed his arms over his chest. "Warren says you state guys have to know about tracking and you're the best he's seen. Figured you'd want to check them out."

During their training, LDWF agents learned to track wildlife and the hunters who weren't supposed to be killing them. Gentry studied the patterns over Paul's shoulder. "Definitely two sets of recent prints, although there's a lot of trash in here too," Paul said. "One larger set, one smaller."

Gentry let out a relieved breath. A smaller shoeprint meant Ceelie was ambulatory. That was a good sign.

He edged around the shoeprints and stepped into the bedroom, where an old rusted double bed had been pushed against a decaying wall. A cloth lay across the back of a wooden chair, and Gentry lifted it with one finger—a man's plain navy T-shirt.

Lang's, maybe? He examined the sleeves and found heavy bloodstains on the left side. Maybe Lang's. He threw it back across the chair.

An old dresser in the corner didn't appear to have been disturbed, but he saw something lying on the mattress and walked over to investigate. Blood—still fresh, judging by its color—spattered the mattress near the head of the bed, although there wasn't enough of it to indicate a heavy cut.

He leaned over to see what had caught his attention from across the room. Small, round, white discs. A button. No—he counted them—four buttons. Like one might find on a blouse. Small bits of white thread were scattered around them. Gentry remembered Ceelie had been wearing a white blouse this morning—one with buttons that might've looked a lot like these.

The thought that Lang would touch Ceelie—maybe cut off her clothing—sent a rage through Gentry that he hadn't felt in a long time. Not since New Orleans, when he'd called Lang's bluff and shot him. He thought all this time that he'd been angry at himself, but this anger was too familiar. All along, he'd been angry at Lang for forcing his hand. And now, for shooting Jena. For taking Ceelie.

Three years ago, they'd been in a random situation Lang had tried to play to his advantage. This time, it was very, very personal, and Gentry's anger burned hot.

He walked away from the bed, but turned to look at it again from halfway across the room. From this vantage point, he could see more scuff marks on the floor. Big boot prints. As if Lang had been pacing.

Something caught his attention from under the bed—a snake. He pulled out his pistol, ready to shoot it. When it made no movement he stepped closer, squinting in the dim light coming through the empty window casings. Not a snake . . .

He squatted and looked a few seconds longer before he recognized what were dark, soft strands of black hair.

All the adrenaline that had propelled Gentry through the past twenty-four hours drained from his body. He slumped to a seat on the floor, holding the long, thick strands of hair in his hands, stroking them as he'd done so often the last few days. Ceelie had never said so, but she was proud of her hair. It helped her define who she was, her heritage, her traditions. Lang would only do this out of meanness, to hurt her in an emotional way. Maybe trying to break her spirit.

"You okay, Broussard?" Paul walked in and studied the bed, bent over the buttons, and then looked at what Gentry held in his hands. His jaw clenched, and his dark eyes appeared jet-black in the dusky room. "That son of a bitch cut off her hair?"

Gentry nodded.

"That crazy fuck. This shit has to end." Paul Billiot, who in the three years Gentry had known him had never uttered a curse word or raised his voice, stomped out of the room. Gentry almost laughed, probably out of hysteria, because his first thought was that he couldn't wait to tell Jena that Paul had said not one, but three profanities.

Paul must have gone straight to their lieutenant with the news, because by the time Gentry had climbed to his feet, still clutching the hair, Warren was headed for him with a *don't-screw-with-me* look on his face.

"Broussard, you're off duty as of now. Go home. Feed that goofy-looking dog of yours. Get some sleep. Call me in eight hours and maybe we'll talk about bringing you back on. Hopefully, we'll have brought this to a close by then."

"No. Warren, don't ask me to do that." Gentry held up Ceelie's hair. "Do you see what he did to her? Do you realize this could be the least of it?"

The buttons. The blood.

"I'm not asking you. I'm ordering you." Warren settled a strong hand on Gentry's shoulder. "This is getting too personal for you, you're emotionally spent, and I want you off duty for a few hours."

"But—"

"No arguments, Broussard. Look, we just got word that Jena Sinclair made it through her surgery. She's got a long recovery but the doctors say she's gonna make it. If you don't want to go home, go to the hospital in Houma. The doctors are waiting for her to wake up; let her see a familiar face when she does. If she's able to talk and remembers, find out what else she knows."

"But—"

"Broussard!" Warren raised his voice, then pulled it back. "Gentry, you can walk out of here and go off duty to serve a later shift; Mac Griffin's running shuttle back and forth to the boat launch and the vehicles. Or I can fire you, in which case I'll have Sheriff Knight throw you in a cell for being an unemployed civilian interfering in an active investigation. I am not joking. Your choice."

Gentry stared at him a minute. He considered punching the man in the face, but that would be Lang's way out. He was better than that, even though Warren was wrong. He needed to be here.

But if he couldn't, at least he could talk to his partner.

CHAPTER 27

They had heard the far-off sound of outboard motors a half hour after Ceelie had finally gotten Lang to shut up. Maybe he was trying to translate the Cajun French she'd spit at him, because that had done the trick. His incessant chatter had driven her crazy, although she'd learned a lot that might help her.

After her transfer of the curse, he'd taken another pill, finished off the last of the water, and eaten the last pack of crackers in front of her, giving her the evil eye as he chewed.

The impact of two days with little food or water, and a lot of blows to her face and head, had begun to wear on her. The room tilted more often, her vision grayed, and nausea rolled through her in waves. She stayed conscious by her sheer refusal to give in to it. If she survived, she'd have time later to moan about her physical condition. When you were trying to figure out how to stay alive, little things like how your face must look, what hair you had left, or which body parts hurt the most? They didn't matter.

They heard the motors at about the same time, a drone of engines—no, multiple drones—coming through the window. Lang ran into the front room and came back with the duct tape. He tore off a length and roughly slapped it over Ceelie's mouth. As if she had enough strength left to yell.

"C'mon, bitch, time to move." He jerked her up by her bound wrists and pulled her into the front room. The rifle and shotgun, his pistol, and Jena's SIG Sauer lay on the counter of the kitchenette, along with a cell phone he'd told her belonged to the late Tommy Mason.

Lang looked at the assault rifle a moment, picked it up, turned it to Ceelie, and made a *rat-a-tat-a-tat* sound as he pretended to shoot her. Then he set it on the counter and left it. Ceelie knew nothing about semiautomatic rifles, but she thought its ammunition clip thing was missing.

He dragged her out the door and shoved her into the boat, her right shoulder taking the brunt of her fall.

Then he stopped to listen. Ceelie struggled to sit up, straining to hear the direction that the motor sounds were coming from. She'd swear she heard them on all sides, which sent a current of hope through her. Law enforcement was closing in.

Lang must have decided the same thing. He started the boat and moved slowly, his gaze in a constant loop around the horizon. He avoided open water and kept the boat as near the bank and overhangs as he could.

He was paying no attention to Ceelie and she gave serious thought to rolling herself off the boat and into the water. She imagined how it might work. Her wrists were taped together in front now, and her legs were free. She couldn't swim with her arms bound; did she have enough leg strength left to hold her breath and try to push herself to shallow water? Was the water already shallow enough? If she jumped, would Lang shoot her as soon as she surfaced?

She didn't know the man well, but she knew the type. He was unhinged. On the verge of panic. In over his head and aware of it.

He was also fixated on those coins, however. Until she'd unsettled him with her Cajun curse, he'd talked nonstop, and Ceelie knew his plans, such as they were. He'd found out about the coins when he'd gone to a Houma pawnshop a few weeks ago and recognized Tante Eva coming out. He'd talked to the pawnshop manager and learned about the Confederate gold, which reminded him of the story LeRoy Breaux had told him.

Lang considered the coins his way out. Out of poverty, and out of living in hiding with Tommy Mason's charity his only means of support other than the odd day jobs he could pick up as he moved around Houma, where he wouldn't be recognized. With the coins, he could disappear, free of law enforcement and the drug dealers to whom he owed money. A lot of money.

Maybe he'd fake his own death again. Last time, he'd been picked up by a small fishing boat owned by the cartel of drug dealers. It had been following the larger boat just in case someone needed an escape hatch. This time, he'd travel to Texas and kill some nobody who fit his description, plant Tommy Mason's cell phone in the poor dirtbag's pocket, and spend the rest of his life drinking margaritas and snorting cheap Mexican cocaine.

Langston Broussard was deeply delusional.

Ceelie had spent a lot of time making her own plans, and drowning or having her head blown off by an enraged kidnapper while she floundered in a muddy swamp didn't figure into it. She decided not to jump.

So she sat in the boat like a good abductee and waited until Lang either got his ass caught or found another spot to hide. Then she'd have to do some fast talking—assuming she could get him to untape her mouth.

Lang turned the boat a hard right into a narrow bayou overhung with trees, and came to a stop about twenty yards after making the cut.

Swiveling to look at the bank, Ceelie glimpsed a glint of sunlight on metal deep within the trees. Lang ran the boat as far up the muddy bank as he could, jumped out, and jerked her to her feet. She tried to stay upright when he slung her toward the woods, but slipped in the mud and only managed to keep her head from hitting a protruding stump by catching herself on her elbows.

God, she was tired. The mud covering her chest between the flaps of her open shirt felt so cool she was tempted to wallow in it. But Lang pulled her up by what was left of her hair and shoved her ahead of him. "In that shed. Now." He spoke in an exaggerated whisper.

The door to a rust-tinged tin shed stood ajar. A few yards beyond the structure lay what was left of a wooden house, long abandoned and on the edge of collapse. She tried to point toward the house, which wouldn't feel as much like baking inside a tin can as the shed, but Lang shoved her inside. "Get in there. We'll only be here until dark."

Ceelie had long lost track of the time, but judging by the angle of the sun, she'd guess it was about midday. She gestured toward her mouth. Unless he removed the tape, she had no hope of talking Lang into her plan and making him think it was his idea.

"Forget it. I don't want to hear your yapping." He pushed her into the back corner, and she sat, grateful for the dirt floor but keeping an eye out for snakes. With her luck, she'd talk Lang into taking her home and then get killed by a cottonmouth in this godforsaken shed.

He ignored her for a while, but after pacing every inch of the shed about a thousand times, he finally leaned over and none too gently ripped the tape off her mouth, taking a chunk of skin with it. Like that mattered at this point. Still, it hurt, and the tape-ripping had opened some wounds on her face, not to mention removing the top layer of her lower lip. Rivulets of blood tickled her chin as they ran down and ended in red droplets splattered onto her exposed, muddy chest.

Her mouth was so dry that she had trouble getting the words to start. "Lang, they're getting close. If you want those coins, now is the time."

He'd been pacing again, tapping his fists against his thighs in time to his steps. Now he stopped. "Where are they?"

Ceelie said a quick prayer that he didn't kill her. "They're at the cabin on Whiskey Bayou. I won't tell you exactly where because I'm not stupid. Once you have the location, you have no reason to keep me alive. And without me, you'll never find them."

He grinned, a macabre scarecrow with a shaggy growth of beard and sweat beading on his thin chest, which sported several bug bites since he'd left his T-shirt behind at the last cabin. "What's the difference if I kill you now or kill you at the cabin as soon as I have the coins? You know damned well I'm not leaving you to my goody-two-shoes brother."

It mattered because, at the cabin, she'd have a fighting chance. She knew where to find the ax, the kitchen knives. She knew a box of wooden matches lay inside the throwing-table drawer, so she could set the damned cabin on fire for a diversion if she had to.

That, Lang didn't need to know. "Let's just say I want to stretch out my time with you as much as I can."

The toe of his heavy boot connected hard with the muscle of her left hip, and she couldn't help but cry out. She chastised herself; that had been her fault. If she'd learned anything in the past twenty-four hours, it was that sarcasm led to pain. "That was out of line." She tried to put some humility in her voice. "I'm sorry."

"You should be." Lang took a bottle of pills out of his jeans pocket and tapped one into his palm, then dry-swallowed it. Ceelie assumed the pills were amphetamines, judging by his lack of need for sleep and jittery energy. How many could he take before he crashed or his heart stopped? It probably wouldn't happen fast enough to save her.

"There's one big problem, little Celestine, my voodoo queen." Lang resumed his pacing. "Cops will be all over that cabin." He stopped. "Can you make us invisible with your voodoo hoodoo? No, didn't think so. Useless bitch."

"Look, I want to get this done once and if I'm not going to have those damned coins, they might as well be yours. You have Tommy

Mason's cell phone, right?" She'd planned this part; she just had to sell it. "If the phone isn't dead, call the sheriff's office and tell them you want to talk. Give them a location far away from the cabin, down in South Terrebonne. They don't know where we went after that last hideout, assuming they even found that. For all they know, we went south."

"That might work." Lang kept pacing. He was making her dizzy. "I could tell 'em we're in Cocodrie."

"They wouldn't expect you to hide somewhere a lot of people lived in, like Cocodrie. Maybe say you're east of Cocodrie toward East Bayou, a mile or so behind that little church on Little Caillou Road. I was there once, so I know it's isolated out there except for a few fishing camps. A lot of places they'd have to search."

She paused to let some of that sink it. Judging by the frown on his face, he was listening. "Why the hell would I do anything you come up with, Celestine? Ain't like you've got anything to gain by helping me."

No, but she had so much to lose. She hadn't realized how much this new life back in the parish had come to mean to her, even given the circumstances. "You're right. I've got nothing to gain, so you might as well consider it. Think about it. The sheriff will send everybody he has to keep you from running that boat out to the Gulf and getting in international waters."

She got ready to deliver the coup de grâce. "Those deputies would never think you'd have the balls to show up again at Whiskey Bayou. They wouldn't think you were smart enough. They might not even be watching it—then they'll really feel stupid when you slip in and out right under their noses."

Ceelie was betting they wouldn't leave the cabin unguarded, even if they did send a lot of their resources south toward Cocodrie. And maybe, just maybe, Gentry would recognize the location as being where she and Jena had been heading to see Tomas Assaud. That, and the ax, and the matches, constituted her big plans.

Because she had no clue where those coins were, if they even existed.

CHAPTER 28

Gentry slumped in a chair in the corner of an empty room in Terrebonne General Medical Center, waiting for his partner to be brought in. She had awakened briefly before he arrived, and the medical staff was moving her to a private room—a sign of how quickly she was rebounding. She'd been lucky; the bullets hadn't gotten any vital organs.

Gentry had spent an uncomfortable half hour with Jena's parents and younger brother, who had asked him a lot of hard questions about her shooting. He knew Warren had called them, but he wasn't sure how much detail the lieutenant had provided. Probably not much, since no one except Ceelie had been present when she'd been injured. They knew their daughter had been shot by her partner's brother, though, and Gentry didn't know if their accusatory glares were real or a projection of his own guilt.

Jena's mom was as his partner had described her—tall, regal, with a darker version of Jena's red hair and a haughty attitude. Her father wore a dark suit and tie with an immaculate white shirt. Jena had described them as stuffy uptown New Orleanians, and they looked the part. They had disapproved of her degree in forensics, had fought her choice to join

NOPD, and had practically disowned her when she took the LDWF job in Terrebonne.

Her brother, on the other hand, sported shoulder-length brown hair and full-sleeve tattoos. He didn't sit next to his parents, but had moved into one of the generic blue chairs next to Gentry after the initial inquisition.

"You look burned-out, man." Jackson Sinclair was in his midtwenties; Jena had characterized him as a free-spirited computer genius. "You've been trying to find the guy who shot my sister?"

Gentry knew the elder Sinclairs were listening, so he made no attempt to keep his voice low. "My lieutenant made me take a few hours off. I'd been on duty twenty-four hours straight, since Jena was injured. I wanted to check on her, and I'll go back on duty as soon as they'll let me."

When a nurse came in to tell them Jena would be moved to a private room and it would be a while before anyone could see her, Mrs. Sinclair and Jackson went to the cafeteria while Mr. Sinclair marched off to the administrative offices, where he intended to order that his daughter be moved to a "real hospital," preferably in New Orleans. Gentry doubted his attitude would get him far, plus he knew Jena: if given a choice, she wouldn't go.

Which left him alone in the small room, waiting for the hospital staff to bring her over from the critical-care unit. The white blinds of the room's one large window looked out on the roof of the hospital entrance, with the sprawl of downtown Houma beyond. Well, as sprawling as a town of thirty-five thousand could get. Still, it was the only real city in the parish and the largest in the region.

He'd been furious when he left the operations base, snapping at Mac Griffin's chatter until the gregarious young officer had stopped talking. He'd slung gravel like a teenager when he left the staging area and headed his truck north toward Houma. The longer he drove, though, the more fatigue had set in and he realized Warren had been right. He was too emotional to be on the water, too likely to make a mistake that could hurt Ceelie rather than save her.

Yeah, he wanted to be the one to save her. That was macho bullshit pride talking, and when he stopped by his house in Montegut to shower and change, he gave himself a lecture about it. It didn't matter who saved Ceelie as long as she was saved.

By the time he ate a sandwich, endured some ankle biting from Hoss, and then loved on his little dog until even Hoss had had enough, he felt human. After three hours of sleep, calm had settled on him like a cloak. He wasn't less angry at Lang or less worried about Ceelie, but he felt centered. He'd cleaned up Ceelie's guitar, and on the way to the hospital, he'd stopped at a little music shop in Houma and left the Gibson to be repaired. His version of optimism.

At a loud bump and commotion in the doorway, Gentry turned to see a woman being wheeled into the room. It wasn't Sinclair, though. He was on the verge of telling the staff they'd made a mistake until he got a closer look at the woman in the bed. He'd been prepared for pale, but not the swollen mass of cuts and bruises covering Jena Sinclair's face and hands. Stupid on his part. She'd been hit at close range by an exploding truck window, in addition to the bullets.

By the time the hospital staff got her IV and bed adjusted and raised the head slightly, the previously silent, antiseptic-scented room was filled with the noise of machines that beeped and whirred as they constantly checked her blood pressure and heart rate.

"Gentry?"

He startled, unaware that she was awake, and walked to her bedside. "Hey, Red. How you feeling?"

He pulled a chair over and, after a moment's hesitation, took one of her hands gently in his.

"What happened? The doctor told me I was in Houma, in the hospital." Her voice was weak and Gentry leaned forward over the bedrail to hear her.

How much should he tell her? She might be strong enough to be in a private room, but she wasn't out of the woods.

"You got injured on duty," he said. "You were shot." Twice, by his murderous SOB brother.

"Shot?" She frowned and stared at the ceiling. With alarm, Gentry saw the pulse rate on the bedside monitor rise into the eighties, then the nineties.

"Shhh. Calm down. You're going to be fine. Look at you, already rockin' a private room and everything. Your family will be back in a few minutes."

Jena swallowed with some difficulty, and Gentry reached for the plastic cup of ice chips the nurse had left. "Open your mouth a little," he said, and slipped one on her tongue. She nodded and tried to smile. Hard to do with her face so bashed up.

"I remember being with Ceelie, driving down past Chauvin." Jena's voice had already grown stronger. "She was playing her guitar. This car was following us and . . . Oh my God."

Gentry kept hold of her right hand, but Jena held up her left, looking at the defensive injuries. "I held him off for a long time, but he shot out the window next to Ceelie and turned the gun on me when I stood up to check on her. I got off some shots but don't know if I hit him. Did I hit him?"

Gentry gave her hand a light squeeze. "You did, and you at least injured him. You also popped the magazine out of the rifle so he couldn't fire it." He wasn't sure he'd have had the presence of mind to do that, not with a torn-up face and two gunshot wounds.

She raised her left hand to her face and lightly touched the bruised, butchered skin. "Guess that's the end of my modeling career."

"You're too good an agent to worry about that shit. Anyway, it's only been a day—it'll get better." What kind of scars it would leave behind, he didn't know.

"Is Ceelie okay?" Jena closed her eyes, and Gentry could practically see the brain circuits firing as she tried to remember. "I had her crawl into the backseat as soon as we realized it was Lang in that car, but . . . is she okay? Did he shoot her?"

"I don't think . . ." No, more than he wanted to say. "No, he didn't shoot her."

Jena wasn't as out of it as she'd been a few minutes earlier. She turned her head to frown at him. "You don't think what? What are you not telling me, Gentry Broussard?"

Aw, hell. "Lang took Ceelie with him. But we're closing in on them, and as far as we can tell, she's still okay." Well, ambulatory didn't quite mean okay, but he wasn't about to burden his injured partner with tales of blood, and buttons, and long locks of hair.

"Oh no." Jena shut her eyes, and a tear escaped down her cheek. "I should've tried to outrun that car instead of stopping. I was—"

"Don't." Gentry's voice came out sharper than he'd intended, so he softened it. "Don't second-guess. We didn't know Lang even had access to a car, much less that he'd be hanging around near my house. I'm pretty sure he followed you all the way. At least you noticed him before you got all the way down near Cocodrie."

"Why are you here? Why aren't you out there looking?" Jena frowned at him again. "What are you not telling me this time?"

Gentry smiled. "I'd been on duty a long time and wanted to get some sleep and check in on my partner."

Jena shook her head, but winced at the pain even that movement caused. "I'm calling bullshit on that one. Try again."

They hadn't been partners long, but Jena read him very well. "Okay, if you have to know, Warren said if I didn't get out of his way for at least eight hours, he'd fire me and have Sheriff Knight throw me in a cell for interfering with an investigation."

Jena tried to laugh, but it set off a cough and a groan. "God, it feels like my whole chest is on fire."

"Then shut up for a while, and I'll fill you in on the case." He embarked on an account of the past twenty-four hours, leaving out the most disturbing details and playing up the more lighthearted ones. "Oh, and you won't believe this."

"What?" Jena had grown more alert the longer he talked; she seemed to be calm after the initial memory had hit her.

"My fill-in partner has been Paul Billiot. And he cursed. Twice. In two consecutive sentences. One was the f-bomb."

Jena gave a bruised, misshapen version of a grin. "Wish I could've heard that. What set him off?"

For a moment, Gentry saw Paul's face when he realized Lang had chopped off Ceelie's hair. "I think it was something the sheriff said."

"Good to know there's a human underneath the robo-agent." Jena closed her eyes, but popped them open again when Gentry's cell phone rang. He pulled it out of his pocket and almost choked. The screen read: *TOMMY MASON*.

It had to be Lang. Mason's phone had never been recovered. They'd even tried calling it a couple of times but it had been turned off or was out of area.

"Broussard."

"My brother Gentry. Long time, no talk." Lang sounded like the sociopath he was. Charm fueled by drugs.

"Where are you? Where is Celestine Savoie?" Gentry was aware of Jena struggling to raise the head of her hospital bed to a more upright position. "You son of a bitch. If you've hurt her—"

"Oh, relax, Gent. Your little bitch is doing just fine, although if she comes at me with that voodoo shit again, I can't be held responsible. You know how that is."

Good for Ceelie. She'd turned on her inner Eva, because she knew that on some level, Lang was afraid of it.

"So here's the deal, bro. I've gotten in a little deeper in this shit than I'd planned for, you know? I ain't got the money to make a run to

Mexico and this shitheap of a boat is about out of fuel. So I'm willing to talk to the sheriff if he'll make me a sweet deal. I can give him enough names to wipe out half the crime in Terrebonne Parish. But I ain't gonna spend the rest of my life in jail, so he's gotta cut a real deal. Otherwise, you know, I ain't got no reason to keep this witch alive, and once they find me I got a lot of firepower."

"You want the sheriff to call this number?" Because as soon as he hung up, every law-enforcement officer in the parish would have it.

"No, I want to see his face when he makes the deal. See if he's lyin' to me. If he's lyin' I ain't buyin', and you can tell him that."

Gentry paused, torn between getting Lang's rendezvous point himself or giving him the sheriff's cell number and staying out of it. But there was no guarantee Lang would follow through and, for now, Gentry had him on the line.

"Where do you want to meet him?"

Lang gave a loud, dramatic sigh. "I don't know exactly where I am, but some little shithole north of Cocodrie, behind a church on Little Caillou Road, maybe a quarter mile east of Bayou Terrebonne."

"When?" Gentry had pulled out his pad and written down the info.

"Tell him I'm waitin' but I won't wait forever."

"But—"

But, too late. Lang was gone. When Gentry tried to call the number back, he'd turned the phone off again and the call went to a voice-mail box. Lang was either conserving battery life or playing games. Or both.

Jena raised her hand to get his attention, her voice little more than a whisper now. She didn't need to be talking this much.

"That was Lang. What did he say?"

"Red, you need to get some rest and let me—"

"Damn it, what did he say?"

Gentry gave in and described the place. "Probably another half-rotted fish camp like the last hideout."

Jena's heart rate sped up enough to cause the machine to beep. She glanced at it and forced herself to breathe. "It's a ruse."

Gentry had pulled out his phone to call Warren and the sheriff but paused with his finger poised over the keypad. "What do you mean?"

"That place. It's where I was taking Ceelie—where Tomas Assaud lives. I bet Ceelie gave him that location as a sign."

Gentry stared at her, thinking. "Why?"

"I don't know, but it's too much coincidence. Ceelie would never tell him that location if there was any chance he'd go there. She wouldn't put Tomas in danger."

Understanding dawned, and Gentry's heart sped up more than Jena's. "No, but she might have convinced Lang that sending the manhunt south would open the door for him to move north."

Jena nodded with some effort. "To Whiskey Bayou."

CHAPTER 29

Before he'd made his call, Lang had taped up her mouth again, so Ceelie kicked over a bucket in the corner of the tin shed, hoping to make enough noise that Gentry would hear it. Why the hell had Lang called Gentry instead of the sheriff's department?

Dumb question, Celestine. Because he could. Because it would hurt his brother. Because it would make sure Gentry was stuck right in the middle.

Once she'd had a moment to think, however, she realized it was better this way. Gentry would hear the directions firsthand. Would have more time to think about them. Would, she hoped, recognize them as a sign.

She just had to pray Gentry was as smart as she thought he was. Otherwise, it would be either Plan B—the ax or knife—or Plan Last-Resort: matches.

"Time to go, sugar-puss." Lang hefted her up by one arm and shoved her toward the door of the shed. She gauged it was late afternoon, the sky a clear blue and the air thick as molasses from the humidity. The ability to see the setting sun helped her gauge direction; nothing in this landscape looked familiar, however, even as it all looked familiar. It was South Louisiana and that's as near as she could pinpoint.

Still, even the hot day with its hot wind felt good against her over-exposed skin, after the furnace of the tin shed.

Once he'd gotten her wedged into the bow of the boat, Lang pulled a worn map out of a small wooden storage area under his seat and studied it, tracing over it with a long, dirty finger. At the sound of an approaching motor, he froze, and Ceelie's heart sped up. They were deep against the bank, hidden behind the overhanging limbs of a tree, and the boat that passed them was moving fast. No way they'd been seen.

Lang turned to look at her, and she didn't like the calculating expression. "An ugly beat-up hag in the boat might draw attention this time of day, so . . ." He opened the bin under his seat again and dragged out a worn blue tarp. "I think you need a blanket."

Ceelie squirmed and kicked at him when he walked toward her, almost sending him over the side of the boat. She did not want to be wrapped in a blue plastic shroud.

"You want me to tape your ankles together? You want me to tape you to the fuckin' *boat*?"

He'd do it, too, Ceelie had no doubt. She willed her limbs to go still as he flapped the folds out of the blue tarp and let it settle over her, cutting off her view. As he tucked it around her body, she kept her head raised so that when he finished, she'd have fresh air and some space in front of her face. Otherwise, claustrophobia would be paying her a quick visit.

Once her initial panic subsided, Ceelie realized there were a lot of small holes in the tarp, which had definitely seen better days. Not big enough for her to see anything, but at least enough to breathe.

Once again, she considered flipping herself out of the boat, but again, she decided against it. Lang still might shoot her, and this time he was using his motor rather than trying to move silently. Everyone would think Lang was gator-hunting—the blue tarps were ubiquitous among the hunters, who used ice or cold water and tarps to keep the skin and meat of their big reptilian victims cool until they could reach the buyer.

Unless a boat got close enough for her to risk exposing her feet and legs. It would be risky, though, because unless they were caught, Lang would follow through on his threat to tape her ankles together. She didn't want that.

Having her out of sight and himself on high alert, Lang no longer talked. He navigated the boat at a slow, steady pace, not drawing attention.

At some point, Ceelie drifted off to sleep and then startled awake, disoriented at the darkness around her, thinking Lang had covered her with something heavier, or buried her.

The boat still rocked gently, though, so he hadn't moved her. The motor was no longer running, and she could hear splashes around her, and the swirl of water around an oar or pole. Night must have fallen, which increased Lang's chances of getting into the cabin unseen. It all depended on what the response had been to the phone call. She hoped Gentry would ride in like a knight on a white horse—or a black oversized pickup—and save her.

Until now, she'd never seen herself as a damsel in distress, however, and she didn't plan to start. The only thing she could rely on for certain was her belief that she was smarter than Langston Broussard and that, in the end, she'd find a time to make her move. She'd either succeed, or she would fail. If she failed, she would die. She was at peace with that.

She hadn't been a successful person by any measure the world would take. Not by a long shot. But she had carried herself with dignity. She'd stayed true to herself, for the most part. And although her Tante Eva would never know, in her death she'd helped Ceelie learn what was important in life: not record deals, but home. A sense of place. A sense of history and where you came from. Maybe even a chance to love someone and be loved in return.

A thump and splash jerked her out of her reverie, which had started to sound way too defeated. She hadn't lost yet. And her unexpected nap had sharpened her mind.

The air that hit her face when Lang yanked off the tarp sent a wash of cool relief over her skin, even though it was probably at least eighty.

He pulled her from the boat, waiting until she got her land legs underneath her, then prodded her up a bank and into the dark woods. Roots and branches grabbed at her ankles and caught on her boots, almost sending her sprawling.

Lang wrapped a hand around her throat and jerked her toward him. "You make a sound, even a stick breaking under your feet, and you're dead, coins or no coins." Lang's soft whisper hit her ear from less than an inch away. "You understand?"

Ceelie gave him a sharp nod and squinted in the dim light to see where she was going. The day had been clear and so was the night, dark enough for there to be a full canopy of stars and moonlight to give some visibility.

Lang, walking close behind her with the shotgun in the crook of his arm and both pistols stuck in the waistband of his jeans, put a hand on her shoulder and pulled her to a stop. Ceelie looked up and around, a wash of excitement rising in her chest as she recognized the wooded area north of the cabin on Whiskey Bayou, opposite the clearing where Gentry had spent the night in his truck.

She squinted through the trees, hoping to see a light or an outline of a patrol boat. No way to see the back of the cabin from here to determine if there was a sheriff's vehicle there.

Lang propped the shotgun against a tree trunk and turned her to face him, hands on her shoulders. "Not that I don't trust you, bitch, but I don't trust you. I can't have you making noise. So time for you to take a nap; I'll see you later."

Ceelie was still struggling to understand when she saw the fist coming toward her face again. Exploding pain. Black.

****

Rain splashed on her face. When did it start raining, and why was she outside?

Ceelie struggled to open her eyes. Her head had been stuffed full of cotton. Cotton filled with nails projecting outward.

"About damned time, sweetheart. We have business to tend to."

Ceelie rolled to her side and gagged. Would've thrown up if there'd been anything in her system to lose. She lay back and fought the nausea. He'd really hurt her this time.

Lang was still running his mouth, but she couldn't absorb his chatter because something else finally registered. She was inside the cabin. *Her* cabin. She was lying on her own bed. Still bound, but the tape had been pulled off her mouth, and—she wiggled a foot—her ankles remained free.

"C'mon, sit up. Drink something." Lang grasped her by the shoulders and helped her to a seated position. He had a bottle of water—Walmart brand, from her own fridge—and placed it against her raw lips. She took a couple of quick gulps, then promptly threw it up.

She steeled herself for another blow, but he simply helped her sit upright again. "Drink one sip and see if you can keep it down. When you can, I'll give you the rest."

"Okay." She took the water into her mouth, swallowed it, waited for the nausea to pass. After some rolls and growls, her stomach settled. "More?"

"Can you hold the bottle?"

"Think . . . so." Talking was hard. Thinking was hard. She just wanted to sleep, but didn't have time to baby a concussion.

Lang fitted the small water bottle between her hands, and she was able to drink by lifting both arms.

She looked around the cabin and saw nothing out of place . . . "Oh my God, who is that?" A man wearing the light-blue shirt and navy pants of a sheriff's deputy lay on the floor in front of the dining table, his ankles taped and his arms pulled behind him. A length of duct tape had been slapped over his mouth. He lay on his side, eyes closed. His right leg was soaked in blood; his pistol was still in his holster.

"That is Deputy G. Baker, according to his shirt. He had the shit luck to be guarding the cabin."

"You shot him?" Ceelie wanted to go to the deputy and see if he was alive, but wasn't sure she could stand. Not yet anyway. When she stood up, she'd have to make it count.

"Of course not, stupid. Guns are too noisy. I stabbed him."

Of course he did, because Lang Broussard was an amoral, out-of-control junkie who thought himself the cleverest man on earth. What a lethal combination of traits.

Ceelie breathed a quiet sigh of relief when Deputy Baker opened his eyes and looked straight at her. They were bright-blue eyes. Kind eyes. His gaze shifted to Lang and he shook his head slightly. She answered with a hint of a nod. Playing possum.

"Okay, sweet Celestine. It's time." Lang hovered over her. "You either tell me where the coins are, or make plans to join your Tante Eva in the great hereafter of hell."

Ceelie took a deep breath, trying to lessen the pounding headache that had set up a steady rhythm in her right temple. It would serve the stupid son of a bitch right if she stroked out and left him here with an injured deputy, a dead hostage, and no coins.

"They're somewhere on the underside of the subflooring. I don't know exactly where, but there's a loose floorboard in front of the table by the front window. That's where I'd start if I were looking."

"If you're lying to me, you know what's coming, bitch. Are you sure?"

"I'm sure." Ceelie had had time to think, over the past day and a half. If she'd lived her whole life in this place, didn't have a bank account, didn't trust outsiders in general, and considered this treasure a three-generation family curse—but not enough of a curse to get rid of it—where would she hide it?

Her memories of Tante Eva were wrapped in childhood and teen drama, but she remembered enough to know that the woman was practical about keeping things repaired, about being ready for emergencies. So if Eva had recognized the value of these coins, and Ceelie thought she had, she'd put them somewhere she could easily reach in an emergency but also a place that would be hard for a stranger to find.

There was nowhere else for the coins to be hidden—if they existed at all. It was a big *if.* Since the deputy was here, the matches had to come off her list of options. But she'd spotted the rusty old ax that had killed LeRoy Breaux, and it was singing to her.

CHAPTER 30

Gentry sat in his truck in the hospital parking lot, listening to the radio chatter from his own agency, the sheriff's office, and the state police. He'd passed on his bombshell from Lang, first to Warren, and then directly to Sheriff Knight.

"You think he's serious?" Knight had asked. "And does he think I'm a fucking miracle worker with that 'sweet deal' crap?"

Gentry had no idea, and told the sheriff so. "Sir, he's so far gone from when we were actually brothers, it's like I don't know him anymore. I don't know what he's capable of."

After leaving Jena looking like a miserable, beaten Irish setter in the bosom of her dysfunctional family, Gentry had returned to his truck, unsettled. The more he thought about the rendezvous point Lang had suggested, the more he agreed with Jena.

He passed his theory on to the sheriff and to Warren.

They were hesitant. "You really think Lang would accept a meeting spot Ms. Savoie suggested?" the sheriff asked. "It doesn't seem likely."

Finally, they agreed to split the manhunt between the area near Tomas Assaud's house and the stretch from their current location to the Savoie cabin.

"And you're still off duty," Warren reminded him before hanging up.

Gentry huffed in frustration as he punched in Paul Billiot's number. "Where are you?"

"At home," he said. "Lieutenant made me take a few hours off just after he kicked you out. Been following on the radio."

Gentry shared his and Jena's theory. "I'd bet anything they're either already at Whiskey Bayou or on their way."

Paul hesitated a moment. "You at home? Let's talk."

They agreed to meet at the Jiffy Stop in twenty minutes.

When Gentry pulled into the lot fifteen minutes later, Paul's truck already sat in the shadows nearest the road, backed in and pointed toward the highway.

Not only did Paul have seniority but Gentry respected the man, so he climbed out and went to the other agent's turf. Gentry's dark-green uniform shirt and pants, which he'd pulled out of the dryer, were rumpled and looked as if Hoss had been napping on them; Paul could've just walked out of a dry-cleaning store. His truck was a lot neater than Gentry's too. Instead of a rat's nest of cords and cables, everything was organized and excess cordage bound with twist ties; the cables to his radios and equipment were all the same color. OCD much?

"Does Ceelie know where the coins are?" Paul wasn't one for small talk, which was fine. Time was running out; Gentry could feel it. "What can she tell Lang?"

"I don't think she even knew the coins existed, but Lang never has known when to shut up. He might very well have talked enough for her to bluff him and get him back to the cabin." She might think being in her own house would shift some advantage her way.

If Gentry was reading things right.

Paul gave a curt nod and looked at his radio transmitter. Setting it back in its cradle, he pulled out his cell phone instead. "Don't want everybody hearing this." He punched a speed-dial number and put the phone on speaker just as Warren Doucet answered.

"Gentry's been sharing his theory with me, and I think he's right," Paul said. "We want to stake out the cabin."

Warren cursed under his breath, and the next voice they heard was the sheriff's.

"How sure are you about this, Broussard? Billiot?" Knight sounded like he'd been sucking on lemons again.

"I've gotta be honest—I'm not sure," Gentry said. "It's a hunch, but it's a strong hunch."

"Hold on a minute."

They sat in silence while, in the background, radios and motors and voices echoed the organized chaos of a remobilizing manhunt. Around the Jiffy Stop, business was light, and no one seemed to find it interesting that two LDWF vehicles sat at the edge of the parking lot. Most people thought of the department's enforcement agents in terms of writing citations for hunting, fishing, and water-safety violations, and that did make up the bulk of their jobs. But working in the rural corners of the parish, they were often the ones who walked into one situation only to blow open something much bigger.

There were lots of places out here for criminals to hide, and those were the places wildlife agents patrolled.

Warren came back on the line. "The sheriff has been unable to reach his man who was in charge of watching the cabin, a Sergeant Baker. Where are you guys?"

After a couple more minutes of talk, they agreed that Gentry and Paul would proceed to the cabin since they were less than five minutes away. They'd report if there was anything suspicious. Meanwhile, the sheriff would get a couple of units on their way from Houma. They'd go ahead and fan out the units in Cocodrie as planned, in case Gentry was wrong.

"Let's take both trucks," Paul told him after they ended the call. "We don't know what we'll be facing and it gives us more options."

Gentry nodded and moved back to his own vehicle. He checked his sidearm, his shotgun, and his rifle, making sure all were loaded and on the seat beside him. Who knew what they'd be walking into?

Paul followed him to the cabin turnoff, and Gentry flicked off his lights just before making the turn. Behind him, Paul did the same. It had gone without saying that they'd drive in black. Because agents worked so many night shifts out in the marshes trying to catch illegal hunters and fishermen, most had become adept at navigating in the dark. Good night vision was a job requirement.

As soon as Gentry cleared the trees overhanging the drive, he spotted a white TPSO patrol car parked far to the left. They'd figured if Lang came back here, he'd come by boat, but parking in the open had been risky. It proved no one really expected Lang to come back to the scene of his original crime.

Gentry stopped behind the patrol car, and Paul stopped beside it and exited his vehicle, holding his shotgun. He closed his truck door, but not enough to make a noise, and walked to the open door of Gentry's truck. "I'm going to take a quiet look-see. Call the lieutenant and tell him the deputy's car is here."

Paul was not as heavy-footed as Gentry, so he could move more quietly. Otherwise, Gentry would've insisted on going first. This was *his* brother, *his* woman . . . Not that he'd ever tell Ceelie he'd begun to think of her that way. Hell, he hoped he'd get the *chance* to tell her, and she could call him all the sexist-pig names she wanted.

He phoned Warren with the information on the deputy's car and got out. Something felt wrong, and it took a moment for him to realize what it was. There were lights on in the cabin—not the overhead lights, but a candle or maybe a lantern, barely visible from the outside through the curtains. Had Paul noticed?

As he approached the back side of the porch, a sound came to him from inside, some kind of rhythmic tapping.

"State officers! Open the door!" Upon hearing Paul's shout, Gentry took off at a run, gun drawn. From inside the cabin, he heard the distinctive click of a shotgun being racked. He rounded the corner to the front porch just as a shot rang out and Paul flew backward, landing in the bayou with a splash. Gentry halted at the corner. Light poured out as the cabin door opened, but the only sound came from the water. Gentry gave the bayou a quick glance, and saw Paul swimming his way to the shore farther down the bank. He moved awkwardly, which told Gentry he'd been hit, but not a serious-enough shot to immobilize him. He'd been lucky; Lang had shot through the door, and solid cypress would slow down even a shotgun slug.

Gentry flattened himself against the front wall of the cabin, hidden in the shadows, and waited. He didn't want to slip up and shoot inside the structure without knowing where people were. He might hit Ceelie or the sergeant; he had to assume they were in there and incapacitated.

Lang was not a patient man. Eventually, his brother wouldn't be able to stop himself from coming outside to see if he'd hit his target.

It took less than thirty seconds for Gentry to be proven right. Lang stuck his head out, looked left and right, and then walked onto the porch holding the shotgun. He hadn't seen his brother.

Lang's condition shocked Gentry. The brief span of time he'd seen him outside Eva Savoie's cabin, on the day of the murder, Lang had been wearing an oversized hoodie. Shirtless, every rib protruded from his shrunken chest. Mosquito bites had brought out pink splotches on his pale arms and chest. Unshaven and jittery, he looked every bit the junkie he was. Even given the circumstances, a degree of pity broke through Gentry's rage. What a damn mess he'd made of his life.

"Hey, Lang." With his gun drawn and steady, he stepped out of the shadows. "You've gotten in way over your head this time."

Lang swerved and raised his shotgun—or Jena's, in this case. As soon as he moved, Gentry took a quick sidestep in case he fired on instinct. Gentry's .45 was a solid weapon and he was a good shot, but a shotgun had more power.

"I thought you'd be halfway to Cocodrie by now." Lang's voice shook, then he seemed to gather himself. Instead of running back inside the cabin and slamming the door, which is what Gentry would've done, he began to back up, toward the far end of the porch.

"Where you going, Lang?" Gentry took another step toward him, and another. "We need to end this. Nobody has to get hurt." Except so many already had.

"Back off, Gentry."

"You know I can't do that." They continued to talk softly, moving in tandem until the open door to the cabin lay just to Gentry's left. He didn't dare take his eyes off Lang to look inside, which would give his brother a moment's advantage. He refused to step inside and lock Lang out, hoping Paul would catch him. He didn't know Paul's condition or if he even still had his weapons.

This had to end. Here. Now. However it ended.

Lang dropped his right hand to his side with the shotgun pointed toward the ground. "I'm going to back out of here before all your buddies arrive—I think I hear them. They're your brothers now, right? Not me. Not me for a long time."

Damn it, the deputies were coming in with sirens.

"You'll always be my brother, Lang. It's too late to run, and it'll be easier on you if you put down the gun and let me take you in."

Lang laughed, high and frantic. The hand he used to brush the hair away from his face shook badly, and his eyes had a crazy gleam in them. "That's not happenin', little brother. I got my boat right here. I'm gonna jump in it, and then I'm gonna be gone. Your little bitch is inside; you'll get to be her hero, although you probably won't want her now. I gave her one of those makeovers, like on TV, and it didn't turn out too good."

Gentry felt the dead calm of his training sink into his bones like a douse of cold water. "Don't think I won't shoot you, Lang. Don't think I won't shoot you *again*."

"You won't do it." Lang turned and tossed the shotgun off the porch, and it clattered into what Gentry had to assume was his boat. Lang held up his arms. "I'm not armed. It wouldn't be a case of self-defense this time, bro. Just you, being a murderer."

He took another step back and was a foot from the edge of the porch. Gentry didn't want to shoot him, but one more step and he would. He adjusted his pistol for a kill shot, trying to remember not his brother but Eva Savoie. Tommy Mason's wife and son. Jena. Ceelie. Especially Ceelie. "Damn it, Lang, last chance to walk away from this. Don't make me shoot you."

"Nobody's makin' you do nothing, Brother." Lang took another step back, but before Gentry could squeeze the trigger, a blast from behind him sent Gentry rolling to the porch in a defensive move.

Lang disappeared with a midair pinwheel, a spray of blood from the center of his chest, and a splash.

"Law enforcement! Drop your weapon!" Gentry quickly pivoted and aimed. In the center of the porch, illuminated by the light coming from the cabin door, stood a woman with short, uneven hair, half a muddy, bloody blouse, and wild blue eyes. Silver duct tape covered her mouth; the face behind the tape was barely recognizable. But Gentry knew her. God, how well he knew her.

In her hands, despite wrists bound with more tape, she held out a .45, still ready to fire, on the edge of breaking. She didn't seem to see Gentry, or anything else. What had that SOB done to her?

"Ceelie." Gentry kept his voice even, but only because he'd been trained to do so. He wanted to cry. Hell, he *was* crying, unless hot rain had started falling just on his face. "Baby, it's me. It's Gentry. You can drop the gun now. It's over. You're safe." He laid his weapon on the porch and got up slowly, with his hands at his sides and open so she could see them.

For a second she stared at him without a spark of recognition, the gun pointed at him. Then her arms began to shake, and she dropped the pistol. It landed on the wooden porch with a solid thud.

Gentry closed the space between them in two long strides, scooping Ceelie up and taking her back inside the cabin. She shook violently. He laid her on the bed, pulled out his knife, and cut the tape on her wrists. "I'm going to the kitchen to get something to take the tape off your face, okay?"

She blinked at him and turned her head. He followed her gaze to a deputy lying on the floor. He blinked a couple of times, so he was conscious, but he'd lost a lot of blood. Gentry went over and freed the man's arms and legs. "Are you Sergeant Baker?" The officer nodded.

"Gentry Broussard, LDWF. Your guys are already on the way. I'll call an ambulance." For both of them.

Paul, with a shoulder wound, arrived just ahead of three teams of TPSO deputies—probably the first three of many. Gentry filled him in quickly and let Paul do the rest of the communicating. Gentry rummaged in the kitchen until he found a bottle of olive oil and took it to the back corner, where Paul had been keeping everyone away from Ceelie while they awaited the EMTs.

Gentry sat on the bed next to her; she flinched and turned her head away slightly, as if steeling herself to be hit. She'd been hit a lot, and by closed fists. There were a few glass cuts on her face similar to Jena's, but the worst of Ceelie's injuries had come at the fists of his brother. He hoped the SOB drowned, and that Ceelie didn't ever feel a moment of guilt for shooting him. He'd make sure of it.

"It's okay, baby. I'm going to get the tape off your face, okay? It's over, Ceelie. Lang's gone. You outsmarted him."

She turned back to him with the first sign of tears in her beautiful eyes. She was finally starting to understand, although she was still shaking. The work to remove the tape was slow; he soothed her skin with the oil and eased it off a fraction at a time. He was afraid she'd go into shock before the EMTs arrived. From the rawness of her lips, it looked like Lang had been engaging in a lot of the *rip-off-the-duct-tape-fast* method. The pain she must have endured was beyond his imagination.

By the time he gently tugged off the last of the tape, she was crying and whispering his name, over and over, like a mantra.

"I'm here, Ceelie." He picked her up and sat back on the bed with both arms wrapped around her, rubbing her back until the shakes grew less violent, the tears more sniffles than sobs.

Outside, he heard motors and the sound of drag chains being dropped from boats. Most of the LDWF vessels were equipped with them—long chains with sharp treble hooks on the ends—used to drag the waterways in search-and-rescue missions.

Only in this case, it was search and recovery for his brother, he guessed. It had happened so fast that he'd registered Lang falling with a chest wound, but not whether it looked like a kill shot.

The EMTs arrived, but Ceelie clung to Gentry when he tried to let her go. Finally, one EMT agreed to examine her while she sat in his lap; the other medic attended to Sergeant Baker.

"We need to take her in." The EMT, a young woman with a head of long, beautiful braids that reminded Gentry of yet another thing Ceelie had lost, sat on the bed next to them. "Ms. Savoie is suffering from dehydration and exposure. She has a lot of bruising on her face and body, but nothing seems to be broken."

The EMT, whose name tag read "S. THOMPSON," looked across the room, where her partner was moving Sergeant Baker to a stretcher with the help of a couple of the deputies. "We have room for two patients in the ambulance, so—"

"You have three patients." Paul had removed his shirt and bandaged his own shoulder with one of Ceelie's towels, from the look of it. He still looked neat and competent. "Langston Broussard is seriously injured, but when the deputies found him, he'd managed to pull himself to the bank."

"Il est le diable." Ceelie whispered against Gentry's chest. *He is the devil.*

"I will take Ms. Savoie to the hospital myself." Gentry spoke forcefully. He would not let Ceelie within sight of Lang again. If his brother survived, she might have to meet up with him in court, but that was way in the future. She did not have to see him tonight. She sure as hell didn't have to share an ambulance with him. "Otherwise, you'll have to call another ambulance."

Ms. Thompson consulted with her partner and returned quickly. "Since you're with the state, if you'll sign a release, you can take her to the ER at Terrebonne General."

"The sooner the better." He'd spotted Warren and Sheriff Knight at the cabin door, and he wanted to get her out before she had to face a barrage of questions she wasn't capable of answering yet.

As soon as the papers were signed, he got Paul to retrieve his pistol from the porch and let the agent—and now his friend—clear a path to the door so he could get Ceelie out of the chaos.

"Can it wait?" he asked Warren before the man could open his mouth. The lieutenant looked at Ceelie, who'd closed her eyes but kept her arms in a chokehold around Gentry's neck.

He nodded. "Yeah, we'll get both of your statements later. Get her out of here. Good work tonight."

Ceelie was the one they needed to thank. She'd been incredible, and now that it was over, everything was catching up with her.

Paul followed them to the truck, which was going to take some maneuvering to back out. At least a dozen law enforcement vehicles and the ambulance, with blue and red lights flashing, were parked haphazardly all the way along the drive.

When Paul opened the passenger's door and put Gentry's guns in the back, Gentry carefully lifted Ceelie into the seat. She let go of him and let him strap her in, but didn't take her eyes off him. She still had a wild look, and he wasn't sure her safety had fully sunk in.

"Listen." Paul followed Gentry around the truck and put a hand on his arm before he climbed in. He kept his voice low. "When the guys had the drag chains out, they pulled up the ribcage of a human skeleton. There's something else big down there, but they say the divers will have to recover it."

Jesus, what now? Gentry shook his head. "Heard there's a tropical system moving in within the next couple of days. It's going to be a while before a dive team will be able to see shit in that bayou after it stirs up the mud."

"Yeah, just letting you know." Paul stuck his head in the cab of the truck. "I'm glad you're okay, Ms. Savoie. You showed a lot of courage and quick wit out there. You made your ancestors proud—Cajun, Creole, Chitimacha."

For the first time, Ceelie took her eyes off Gentry and looked at Paul with a faint smile. And for the first time, Gentry knew she was going to be okay. It might take a while, physically and emotionally, but she'd come back to him. The Ceelie he'd come to know was inside that shocked, battered body.

"Okay, let's take a ride and get you all well again, okay?" Gentry cranked the truck, but leaned over and kissed Ceelie on the cheek. Those lips had to heal before anyone came near them. He whispered, "I was so afraid I'd lose you, and I couldn't have stood that."

Then he backed out of the drive before he could cry again.

CHAPTER 31

"Need anything else?" Gentry set a glass of iced tea on the portable wooden table he'd picked up at Walmart and set up on Ceelie's porch.

From her Tante Eva's rocking chair, she'd been watching the goings-on in the water in front of the cabin. Now she looked up at Gentry and smiled. Physically, it still hurt to smile. Emotionally, after six days of being free, it felt damned good.

"You make a pretty good butler, Broussard. I might have to keep you around."

He leaned over and kissed her forehead before flopping on the porch. With his LDWF T-shirt, jeans, and bare feet, he looked younger. Of course, he was also better rested for a change. "Just try getting rid of me. I'm unemployed for the next thirty days."

He'd been hovering for the past forty-eight hours, since she'd been released from the hospital, the same day Jena had been dragged back to New Orleans by her family to finish her recovery. Jena was on medical leave but swore she'd be back.

In other words, Gentry had nothing but Ceelie to keep him busy while he underwent mandatory counseling and testing to determine when he was emotionally ready to return to the field. He thought he was ready; Ceelie knew otherwise.

His nightmares had been bad, and Ceelie knew she played into those things that haunted him in the dark. He blamed himself for everything. That was his nature, she'd learned, and if they were going to have a shot at a relationship, she'd have to accept that and help him work around it.

She'd also have to work on his tendency to be overprotective—understandable given what they'd been through, but she'd had a lot of time in the hospital to talk with Jena. Male law-enforcement officers, Jena had told her, were alpha males by nature. They had a wide dominant streak that made them good at their jobs but hard on relationships. They kept things to themselves. Once they'd accepted you into their circle of protection, often unconsciously, they would hover. They would be overprotective.

"You won't be able to break him of that," Jena had told her. "Don't think the wildlife agents are any better than regular city cops—they aren't. It's in the genes. They're good men; you just have to learn how to work around those tendencies."

Ceelie didn't know if she and Gentry would make it as a couple, but she wanted it—desperately. When they'd finally made love last night for the first time since Lang had taken her, they'd both ended up laughing and crying at the same time. It was the most intimate, beautiful experience she'd ever had, both bitter and sweet.

She could no longer imagine her life without Gentry Broussard in it. And to give him credit, while he'd been hovering this week, he'd also let her be silent and spend some quality time in her own head. She had learned a lot about herself in the past month.

She was stronger than she thought. Smarter than she thought. And this was home. If she were meant to have a career in music, she'd have one. This wasn't the Stone Age. She could be at a recording studio in under an hour, at a club within twenty minutes, at an airport in thirty.

Thanks, ironically, to Lang, she could live here quite a while, even repair the cabin, without worrying about income. She'd been more surprised than anyone when one of the deputies, collecting evidence in the cabin while she was still in the hospital, had examined parts of Lang's excavation of the cabin floor and found, just beyond where he'd reached, a small plastic bag holding a dozen gold coins—rare Confederate coins, according to Gentry, that could be worth as much as half a million dollars. Once the case was closed, they'd be hers to sell at auction. If her great-great-grandfather Julien Savoie had committed murder in order to get them, there was no proof.

She'd use the money for good things, if she got it. If she didn't, that was okay too. She wanted those coins gone—either sold, or returned to someone else if they rightfully belonged elsewhere. It was time the Savoie curse was put to rest.

A big splash jolted her out of her ruminations.

"Looks like they got something," Gentry said. They watched as a sheriff's-office dive team brought up handfuls of something and turned it all over to the officers waiting in their patrol boat. Then the two divers upended and went back under.

Gentry walked to the edge of the porch nearest the boat. "What is it?"

"They found the rest of the human skeleton." Adam Meizel held up a long thighbone, from the looks of it. "It's tied with chains onto an old fishing boat anchored to the bottom of the bayou. Looks like the boat was sunk on purpose—big holes in it."

Ceelie had no doubts as to who the boat and the bones belonged to. "It's LeRoy Breaux. Or at least that's what Lang told me."

She ran her fingers through the short haircut she was still trying to get used to. It was so much easier to take care of, she wasn't sure she'd grow it long again. Gentry claimed to like it, but then he would, regardless.

"You think Eva chained him to the boat and sank it?" Gentry came back to sit beside her.

"Absolutely. She had his freaking skull in the pie safe when I was a teenager. That much of Lang's wild tales, I believed." If Lang Broussard hadn't spotted Eva at the Houma pawnshop, her great-aunt would've gotten away with murder and the coins might or might not have ever been found. The only mystery left was where in Isle de Jean Charles Ceelie's great-great-grandfather Julien Savoie had found the coins in the first place, and who he supposedly murdered. Of course, she only had Lang's word for that story too.

After talking to a coin expert, Gentry had learned that most of the coins from the last Confederate minting were believed to have been buried by plantation owners or other wealthy Southerners to keep them out of Yankee hands.

Terrebonne had been a land of sugarcane plantations, and, as soon as she was able, Ceelie would research the history of who'd owned the land around the isolated Chitimacha community. Maybe she'd find those answers; maybe she wouldn't.

It took several hours for the divers to find all the bones they could and examine the boat for any other evidence or clues. They didn't expect much after almost twenty years of the things being submerged in the brackish water of Whiskey Bayou.

Ceelie leaned back in the rocker and stroked her fingers through Gentry's thick, curly hair, which had started getting long. She began to hum an old song from her childhood, and he turned to grin up at her.

"I've been waiting for that." He got to his feet.

"Waiting for what?" Ceelie started to get up, but he motioned for her to stay. Which was good. The bruises on her face were fading, but her body was still sore.

He walked toward the far end of the porch. "Hang on. I'll be right back."

She traced the sound of his footfalls around the house and off the porch, then heard his truck door open and close.

He rounded the corner with both hands behind his back, and Ceelie had to suppress a shudder at the image it conjured of herself, bound. She still had some work to do on her mental state.

"I found this thing on the side of the road and thought you might like it." He smiled like a kid at Christmas.

"What? You're trash-diving now?"

What he pulled from behind his back took her breath away. A Gibson. No, *her* Gibson, back in pristine condition. Just before Lang had taken her, she'd seen it, partially crushed and covered in blood and glass.

She got up and pulled him into a long hug, crying again. She'd sworn she wouldn't shed another tear, but this was different. These came from a good place, not a bad one.

"Hey, you okay?" Gentry's eyebrows were bunched in worry as he pulled back and wiped her tears away with gentle fingers.

"I need some more tea, butler." She laughed for the first time in what felt like a lifetime. "I have a song to finish writing now that I have my guitar."

A song about Whiskey Bayou.

A song about home.

ACKNOWLEDGMENTS

Thanks, as always, to my fabulous agent, Marlene Stringer; editors Chris Werner and Melody Guy, who made my story so much better, and editor JoVon Sotak, who shared my initial vision; my alpha reader Dianne Ludlam, who always spots the plot holes; longtime law-enforcement officer, author, and consultant Wesley Harris at Write Crime Right, for steering me through the world of law-enforcement procedure, weapons, and terminology (any errors are purely the result of my willful nature); and my Auburn Writing Circle compatriots Larry Williamson, Shawn Jacobsen, Robin Governo, Matt Kearley, Julia Thompson, and, in absentia, Peter Wolf and Mike Wines. You guys are all awesome!

ABOUT THE AUTHOR

Photo © 2013 Studio 16

Susannah Sandlin is the author of the award-winning Penton Legacy paranormal romance series and The Collectors romantic suspense series. Writing as Suzanne Johnson, she is the author of the Sentinels of New Orleans urban fantasy series and several urban fantasy novellas. Susannah was a finalist for the *RT Book Reviews* Reviewers' Choice Awards in both 2014 and 2015, and she is the 2015 winner of the Holt Medallion for romantic suspense, the 2015 Booksellers' Best Award for romantic suspense, and the 2013 winner of the Holt Medallion for paranormal romance. A longtime New Orleanian, she currently lives in Auburn, Alabama, which explains her penchant for SEC football, gators, and cheap Mardi Gras trinkets.

To learn more, visit www.suzannejohnsonauthor.com and subscribe to her monthly newsletter, or follow her on Facebook at www.facebook.com/AuthorSuzanneJohnson.